Titles by Amanda Lee

BETTER OFF THREAD

AN EMBROIDERY MYSTERY

AMANDA LEE

BERKLEY PRIME CRIME
New York

BERKLEY PRIME CRIME
Published by Berkley
An imprint of Penguin Random House LLC
375 Hudson Street, New York, New York 10014

Copyright © 2016 by Penguin Random House LLC
Excerpt from *The Calamity Café* by Gayle Leeson copyright © 2016 by Gayle Trent
Penguin Random House supports copyright. Copyright fuels creativity, encourages
diverse voices, promotes free speech, and creates a vibrant culture. Thank you for buying
an authorized edition of this book and for complying with copyright laws by not
reproducing, scanning, or distributing any part of it in any form without permission.
You are supporting writers and allowing Penguin Random House to continue to
publish books for every reader.

BERKLEY is a registered trademark and BERKLEY PRIME CRIME and the B colophon
are trademarks of Penguin Random House LLC.

ISBN: 9780451473851

First Edition: December 2016

Printed in the United States of America
1 3 5 7 9 10 8 6 4 2

To Tim, Lianna, and Nicholas

Chapter One

I locked the door to the Seven-Year Stitch, my embroidery specialty shop, walked over to the sit-and-stitch square, and slumped onto the sofa facing away from the window. My gray Irish wolfhound, Angus, flopped onto the floor beside me and heaved a sigh.

"What a day, huh, Angus?" I looked over at our mannequin, Jill—who normally resembles Marilyn Monroe—and noticed that her wig was now sideways and covering her entire face. I laughed. "I think Jill has had an even rougher day than we have."

Black Friday. Although the other merchants in Tallulah Falls and I couldn't offer the deep discounts provided by the large chain stores, we'd all done something to try to sway customers to shop with us today. My friends Blake and Sadie MacKenzie of MacKenzies' Mochas had offered customers free coffee with the purchase of a pastry. Todd Calloway of the Brew Crew had forgone giving out free beer and had instead provided shoppers with bottles of water and a place to leave their bags so they wouldn't have too much to carry as they wandered from shop to shop.

I'd brought in a toaster oven this morning and had provided patrons with freshly baked cookies and a twenty-five percent discount off their total purchases. I'd expected an upsurge in traffic, but I hadn't been prepared for the amount of business I'd received today. I'd been open last year on Black Friday, but the Seven-Year Stitch had been in business but a few weeks then, and although business had been good, I don't think people were as aware of the shop as they were now. Plus, I was getting better at the promotional side of things. I'd been closed for the past few days, but for two weeks prior to that, I'd been putting flyers in everyone's bags advertising the Thanksgiving celebration.

I pushed myself off the sofa and went over to adjust Jill's wig. I smoothed it down and then straightened her apron. I typically dressed Jill to coincide with the season. With the Thanksgiving holiday upon us, I'd dressed her in a 1950s-style A-line dress—complete with crinoline—and a ruffled apron. She looked darling . . . or, well, she did after I fixed her wig.

I looked around the rest of the shop. Beyond Jill and the checkout counter to the left were bins of floss and yarn. Maple racks containing pattern books, needles, hoops, crochet hooks, and other needlecraft supplies filled the rest of the left side of the shop. To the right of the counter was the sit-and-stitch square. Two navy sofas faced each other and were separated by an oval maple coffee table atop a red-and-blue braided rug. Red club chairs and matching ottomans rounded out the seating area, where patrons were invited to—you guessed it—sit and stitch.

On the walls and atop the maple racks were embroidery projects I'd completed, as well as dolls whose outfits I'd made or embellished with embroidery. Candlewicked pillows usually adorned the sofas in the sit-and-stitch square, but I'd placed them in the office today. I'd been afraid that children with chocolaty fingers and faces would latch onto the white pillows. That was something I hadn't originally considered when I'd decided to offer cookies to the Stitch patrons.

Deciding that putting the pillows back in place was the next-easiest thing to do—after making Jill presentable again—I retrieved the pillows, fluffed them, and placed them on the sofa. With my hands on my hips, I surveyed the rest of the shop. I needed to straighten the floss bins, restock the yarn, vacuum, dust the shelves, clean the glass. . . . But I was so tired.

"We'll get here early and tidy up in the morning, Angus," I said. "Let's go home, buddy."

He leapt to his feet, apparently as delighted by the prospect of going home as I was.

When we got to our white, two-story home and saw Ted's car in the driveway, my heart lifted even more. I'm pretty sure Angus felt the same way. Ted was the most wonderful man in the whole wide world, and he was mine. Well, Angus would say he was *ours*.

Ted opened the door as Angus and I got to the porch. He was wearing a black apron emblazoned with Kɪss ᴛʜᴇ Cook. Being a stickler for following rules, I did as instructed . . . several times, in fact.

The house smelled wonderful. I closed my eyes and took in the blend of scents: oregano, beef, sausage, basil, tomato sauce, garlic.

"Did you make lasagna?" I asked.

He smiled. "I did. I'm tired of turkey, and I guessed you and Angus are, too."

"You're absolutely right."

We'd had a whirlwind week. Last Saturday after work, I'd closed up the Stitch and Ted, Angus, and I had flown to San Francisco. Mom had insisted on our bringing Angus, and she'd even made the necessary travel arrangements. I was glad. I hadn't wanted to spend four days away from him.

Ted and I had stayed with Mom. On Sunday, she'd had a delicious Thanksgiving meal catered for us. Alfred Benton, Mom's longtime lawyer and recent boyfriend, joined us. He always joined us for holiday celebrations—he'd been a surrogate dad to me ever since my own father had died when I was a toddler—but this time it was more special. It was apparent that he and Mom were in love. And since I'd left San Francisco last year to open my shop in Tallulah Falls, it was great to see her with someone—especially someone she loved and who obviously made her feel so loved. I just couldn't figure out what had taken them so long.

We'd flown back from San Fran on Wednesday morning, and we'd had dinner with Ted's mom yesterday. I'd been nervous about spending Thanksgiving Day with Ted's family. Not only was his mom there, but his sister and her family were there as well. Tiffany was married and had a two-year-old son.

Ted's sister was two years younger than he. Like Ted and his mother, she had those striking blue eyes. But there the resemblance ended. I imagined Tiffany must've taken after her father. She had chestnut brown hair with honey highlights, and she was only about three inches taller than me. Ted was around six-feet-one or two, and I was five-foot-nothing if I stretched out my spine and held my head high. And Ted's hair was black with flecks of premature gray.

I ran my hands through his hair as I stood there looking up at him. "I'm so glad to finally have you to myself. Not that I haven't enjoyed spending time with Mom and Alfred and your mom and meeting Tiffany and her family, it's just . . ."

"I know, Marcy." He lowered his mouth to mine. "I've missed being alone with you, too."

After dinner, we went into my all-white living room. Some people probably thought I was crazy for having a white sofa and chair *and* a huge, wiry gray dog that shed pretty regularly. But I found the color peaceful, and regular vacuuming and lint brushing took care of any wayward hair.

After dinner, Angus went out to the backyard to play. Ted and I cuddled up on the large overstuffed sofa. He kissed the top of my head.

"Thank you for making dinner," I said.

"You're welcome. I knew you'd be exhausted when you got here. How'd the cookies go over?"

"Really well. People were delighted with them."

"I was half-afraid you'd get busy and burn a batch and the whole shop would smell like smoke for a week."

I gaped at him. "Gee, thanks!"

He chuckled. "I didn't mean it that way. I just thought about you being there by yourself, trying to manage all the customers and bake cookies at the same time. Since I had to work only half a day, I started to come by. But I figured you probably had things under control and that you'd rather have dinner waiting for you than a guy who knows very little about embroidery helping out at the Stitch."

I smiled. "Well, you were right." I snuggled against him, wrapping one arm around his waist. "Although I wouldn't have minded your stopping by."

"I know. How *did* you manage, anyway?"

"I had most of the cookies baked by the time people started coming in. Then as I started to run out, I'd put in a batch, set the timer, and then run to get them when the timer went off," I said. "People were good about my having to stop now and then to get the cookies. They understood that I was the only person working. Well, that is, except for one dotty little lady who thought Jill was rude for not helping out."

"Well, Jill is a fairly realistic-looking mannequin."

"Ha! You should've seen her by the end of the day when her wig was on crooked!"

We were laughing about that when the doorbell rang.

I froze. "Did you invite anyone over?"

"Not me."

"We could pretend we aren't here." I was sitting up even as I spoke.

"With both our cars in the driveway? Not likely." Ted stood. "I'll go to the door. Maybe it's just an early caroler or something."

"It's still November."

"And Christmas merchandise has been in the store since September," he pointed out.

Ted went to the door. When I heard Captain Moe's voice, I joined them in the foyer. Captain Moe was a large, beefy man with white hair and a full white beard. I often compared him in my mind to Alan Hale, who'd played the Skipper on the classic television show *Gilligan's Island*.

Captain Moe swept me off my feet in a hug. "I'm sorry to barge in on you fine folks."

"You're always welcome," I said. "Would you like something to drink? Are you hungry?"

"No, Tinkerbell. After the past few days, I shouldn't need anything to eat or drink for a week." Captain Moe had called me Tinkerbell since the first time we'd met. I didn't know if that was due to my size or my hair color, but, either way, I took it as the endearment that Captain Moe intended it to be.

"Come on into the living room," Ted said.

He and I sat on the sofa, and Captain Moe filled the matching armchair across from us.

"I'm here with my proverbial hat in my hands," said the captain.

"What's wrong?" Ted asked.

"You know we'll do whatever we can to help you," I said.

Captain Moe held up an index finger. "You'd best hear me out before you say that, Tink. You see, I agreed to play Santa Claus for the Tallulah County General Hospital. I was there today, and I'll be there tomorrow evening and Sunday evening."

"That's wonderful." I smiled. Captain Moe would be the perfect Santa. He already looked the part, and he certainly had the heart of the jolly old elf.

"It is nice," he said. "I'm meeting primarily with children, but I'll also be seeing a few of the elderly patients and anyone else who'd like to join in the fun."

"I'm surprised the hospital is having you come in so early," Ted said.

"I was, too. But the administrator explained to me that it's difficult for these patients and their loved ones not to be able to have their traditional Thanksgiving Day meals and visits with extended family members, and she hopes having me there will brighten their weekend. I'm to go back the weekend before Christmas and on Christmas Eve."

"It's awfully thoughtful of you to volunteer so much of your time," I told him.

He winced slightly when I said that.

"What?" I asked.

"I have absolutely no right to ask you, and you can most certainly say no and I will understand completely, but you're the first person who came to mind," he babbled.

Captain Moe was not a babbler. This was really

important to him. "Please, just ask whatever it is you want to ask."

"I need an elf," he said.

Ted covered his mouth with his hand and his shoulders started to shake.

"Um, excuse me?" I asked.

"You see, I had an elf. The hospital had one lined up. She was there half the day today, and she was a tremendous help. In fact, I didn't realize how helpful she was until she'd left."

"She left?" I asked. "You mean, she quit?"

"Well, she didn't simply up and quit. Her babysitter called, and one of her children has a stomach bug," he said. "She won't be coming back tomorrow."

"And you'd like me to take her place?" Me? An elf? Okay, I could understand why Captain Moe would think of me for the job: I'm short. But the Stitch was open tomorrow. And I didn't have anyone lined up to run the shop in my absence. On the other hand, this was Captain Moe. How many times had he been there for me?

He seemed to have read my mind. "I know you have to work, but we don't have to be there tomorrow evening until six o'clock. You can even bring Angus. We can put some antlers on him and he can be our reindeer."

Ted laughed out loud at that. "That's fantastic!"

"Isn't it, though?" Captain Moe agreed. "The children would adore him."

"But I don't have a costume," I said.

"The hospital will provide one for you. We just need to let them know your size."

"What would I have to do?"

"You pretty much keep the children corralled and happy until it's their turn to talk with me. Hand out coloring books and peppermint sticks—that sort of thing." He held up his hands. "Again, don't feel obligated. If you can do it, I'd greatly appreciate it. But if you can't, I'll try to find someone else."

"And this is just for tomorrow night?" I asked.

"And Sunday," he said. "If you can."

"I can." I smiled a little uncertainly. "You can count on Angus and me."

"Thank you so much. You don't know how much I appreciate this."

After Captain Moe had left and we'd nestled back onto the sofa, Ted turned to me with a mischievous grin. "He doesn't know how much *I* appreciate this! I can hardly wait to see you in your elf costume."

"Ted . . ."

"He said it was for anyone who wanted to join in the fun. I want to join in the fun."

I whacked him with a throw pillow.

"You know what we should do? We should watch some Christmas movies so you can pick up some pointers."

I hit him again. He was laughing so hard, I don't even think he noticed.

Chapter Two

I did manage to get to work early on Saturday morning. I tidied up the bins of floss and yarn, dusted all the shelves, and cleaned the windows. I vacuumed while Angus hid in his bed under the counter, and then I took the trash out to the Dumpster.

"Good morning!"

I turned to see Blake coming out of MacKenzies' Mochas with a large black garbage bag.

"Hi, there! Did you guys have a good turnout yesterday?" I asked.

"We did. We were busier than cats covered in tartar sauce all day long." He tossed the bag into the Dumpster. "How about you?"

"I was busy—a lot busier than I'd expected to be. Angus and I were totally wiped out when we got home." I smiled. "Thank goodness Ted was there and had dinner ready."

"He's a good guy. Then again, I'm a pretty good guy, too. I let Sadie sleep in this morning."

"You *are* a good guy."

"Why don't we get together for dinner this evening?" he asked. "I'm sure Sadie would love it."

"I can't. I have a . . . thing."

He raised his brows. "You have a *thing*? You're ditching Sadie and me for a *thing*?"

I sighed. "It's a prior commitment. To Captain Moe."

"Does Ted know about this commitment to Captain Moe?"

"I'm afraid so," I said.

"Well, you've got to spill it now." Blake put his hands on his hips and waited.

"Just suffice it to say I can't do dinner tonight. We'll do it one night next week, okay?" I started to go back inside, but Blake blocked my path.

"I'm not going to let this go. You should know me that well by now."

He was right. I'd known him since I was Sadie's college roommate. He was like a bloodhound with a scent to follow. He wouldn't give up until he'd found what he was after.

"Fine. Captain Moe is being Santa at the Tallulah County General Hospital this evening, and he needs my help."

"Doing what?" he asked. "Being an elf?"

I didn't answer.

His eyes widened. "You're being an elf? For real?" He laughed and slapped the side of his leg. "Oh, my gosh. This I've gotta see."

"No, you do not. I'm doing a favor for a friend. I'll make a great elf."

"Oh, I know you will. You'll be adorable. Wait until I tell Sadie." He took his phone out of his pocket. "See you later, Marce! Really, we will."

I went back into the Stitch, where Angus was waiting for me. He was prancing around in a circle. He'd heard me talking with Blake and had wanted to be in the alley with us.

"Don't worry, Angus," I said. "I've got a feeling you'll be seeing Blake later. And I didn't even tell him you're going to be a reindeer."

Satisfied that the Seven-Year Stitch was tidy and ready for customers, I unlocked the front door. Then I retrieved my tote bag from behind the counter and took it over to the sit-and-stitch square. I was making small cross-stitch Christmas ornaments to give to friends. I could make one in approximately two hours and then put it in a hoop frame and embellish it with ribbon or lace. I'd made five so far: a drum, holly, bells, a Christmas tree, and a nutcracker. The one I was currently stitching was a snowman.

Vera, a sophisticated widow who'd become one of my dearest friends in Tallulah Falls, breezed into the shop. "Good morning!" She hugged Angus before coming to sit beside me on the sofa facing the window.

"Good morning. How are you?"

"I'm great," she said, looking at my snowman. "He's going to be adorable."

"Thank you. I have a piece of snowflake-patterned blue ribbon I'm going to use to make his scarf."

"That'll be precious. So, did you have a lot of customers yesterday?"

"I did," I said. "I could hardly believe how busy we were."

Before we could discuss it further, Sadie came in. I knew from the expression on her face what she was about to say. I cut my eyes to Vera and gave my head a little shake, but either Sadie didn't notice or she chose to ignore my silent plea.

"So, tell me all about this elf gig," she said with a wide grin.

"I'm going to kill your husband," I said.

"Elf gig?" Vera leaned forward. "What elf gig?"

"Captain Moe came by my house last night and asked me to play an elf tonight and tomorrow at a hospital event he's doing as Santa Claus. Plus, he said we could put antlers on Angus and have him be a reindeer. He said the children would love it."

"Of course, they will." Vera clapped her hands together. "How wonderful this is! I must let Paul know so he can be sure and get you in tomorrow's newspaper. We'll come by tonight, and he can take photographs and interview Captain Moe and you and maybe some of the hospital staff. Where did you say it's going to be?"

"Tallulah County General," I said. I was beginning to think it was my lot in life that my fifteen minutes of fame would be as an elf. I hoped that at least the costume would be cute.

"I'll go talk with Paul now." She stood and smoothed out her beige slacks. "See you tonight."

Vera's boyfriend Paul Samms was a reporter for the *Tallulah Falls Examiner*.

After Vera left, I gave Sadie *the look*.

"Sorry," she said, although she didn't sound contrite to me. "I guess I wasn't thinking. But come on. The story *will* make a nice personal-interest piece for the newspaper. It'll be especially good for Captain Moe."

"I know."

Sadie was right. I'd agreed to be an elf; now I simply had to have fun with it. Captain Moe loved playing Santa. I should love being an elf. After all, it was for children . . . and for Captain Moe.

I'd first met Captain Moe soon after Angus and I had moved to Tallulah Falls. We'd gone to the beach in Depoe Bay and then had stopped by Captain Moe's diner for something to eat. I'd left Angus in the Jeep and was planning to run into the diner and get some food to take home. Captain Moe always closed the diner on Sunday, but that day he was there taking inventory and had left the door unlocked. Despite being closed, he invited both me and Angus inside and made us cheeseburgers. We'd been friends ever since.

Ted brought grilled-chicken sandwiches and kettle-cooked chips for lunch. I put the cardboard clock on the door indicating that I'd be back in twenty minutes, and then we went into my office to eat.

"Have you been busy today?" he asked, as I handed him a bottle of water from the mini fridge.

"Moderately. Nothing like yesterday." I nodded toward the toaster oven that was taking up entirely too much room in my small office. "I need to remember to take that back home this afternoon."

"I'll take it," Ted said. "I know you'll be rushed this afternoon."

"Thank you." I told him about spilling the beans to Blake and then Sadie mentioning my being an elf in front of Vera.

He smiled. "Oh, well. You know you'll be the most beautiful elf in the world."

"Hmmm. Flattering me *and* offering to take the toaster oven back home. What's up?"

"I'd like to bring Jackson to see Captain Moe at the hospital this evening."

Jackson was Ted's sister Tiffany's little boy.

"Captain Moe is the most realistic Santa I've ever seen," Ted continued. "And I think Jackson would love him."

"I'm sure he would. Who wouldn't love Captain Moe?" I smiled.

"And who wouldn't love Marcy the Elf?"

"And Angus the reindeer?" I added.

Angus wagged his tail, thinking we'd mentioned him because he was going to get a chip or a bite of chicken. I pinched off a piece of my sandwich for him.

"I'm sorry I laughed last night," he said. "But, honestly, I'm looking forward to seeing you in that costume."

"You and Vera and Blake and Sadie."

He looked down to try to hide his grin.

"It's okay," I told him. "I agreed to be Captain Moe's elf, and I'm gonna be the best darn elf you've ever seen."

*   *   *

Angus and I got our fair share of double takes when we walked into the hospital. Of course, we generally did whenever we went somewhere—the petite woman with her enormous dog. And this was without our Christmas costumes. Wait until they got a load of us all decked out in elfin regalia and antlers.

I smiled to myself as I led Angus down the corridor toward the conference room. As we approached, we heard a heated discussion. One of the people speaking was Captain Moe. I realized I'd never heard Captain Moe raise his voice before.

"I won't do it, and that's final," he said. "If that's what you want, you can get yourself another Santa."

"You know good and well it's too late for me to do that now," a woman said. "And this is not an unreasonable request. I'm only asking that you show some extra attention to Dr. Carstairs's son."

"And I'm telling *you* that I will treat all the children the same."

The woman—a middle-aged woman in a red silk suit—noticed Angus and me standing in the hall. "May I help you?"

"Yes, I'm Marcy Singer. I—"

"The elf," she said. "Of course."

Captain Moe, already in his Santa Claus suit, managed a tight smile in my direction. "Thank you again for doing this."

"You're welcome."

The woman thrust a bag into my hand. "You need to change into this. Moe, can you watch the dog?"

"Of course."

I handed Captain Moe the leash. "Is everything all right?"

"Everything's fine, Tink. You go ahead and get changed. Angus and I will be okay without you for a few minutes."

I hesitated. Angus didn't seem comfortable given the tension in the room, and neither did I.

"Very well. I'll leave you to it." The woman left the room and strode down the hall.

"Who's she?" I asked.

"She's the hospital administrator, Sandra Vincent. She wants me to show preferential treatment to one of the board member's children, and I refused. She even wants me to give this child a present when all the other children will be getting the standard coloring books and candy canes. All the children deserve to be treated the same."

"I agree." I looked around the room. "Where can I get changed?"

"There's a ladies' room down the hall about eight feet and to your left."

I nodded. "Be back in a jiffy."

I went into the bathroom and changed my clothes in the handicapped stall. My elf costume was a green velvet dress with white plush trim, a wide red belt, green-and-red striped tights, green shoes turned up at the toes and adorned with jingle bells, and a green hat trimmed with white faux fur.

By the time I got back to the conference room, Captain Moe had the antler headband on Angus. Angus didn't like it. As I walked into the room, Angus shook the antlers off his head.

"I don't think this is going to work," Captain Moe said. "We might have to settle for a North Pole puppy rather than a reindeer." He turned, looked at me, and gave a resounding *"Ho, ho, ho.* You look fantastic!"

I held out my skirt and curtsied. "Thank you, kind sir."

Captain Moe looked at his watch. "They should be here by now."

"The children?" I asked.

He shook his head. "The maintenance men. They have just over half an hour to turn this room into a Christmas setting."

I glanced around at the conference table, chairs, and oak-paneled walls. The men had their work cut out for them. And they'd better get here soon.

I'd no more than finished the thought than a group of men entered the conference room. Captain Moe and I stood out of the way as they began stacking the chairs and moving them out into the hallway. They pushed the table into a far corner.

One of the men called, "You can bring it in now!"

Two men in coveralls brought in a red sleigh with a long, wide bench seat.

"The seat is sturdy," one of the men told Captain Moe. "You can easily sit there with a child or two on your lap." He nodded toward me. "And even her and maybe the dog. But the rest of the sleigh is just plywood. Be careful that none of the kids fall into it or anything. It might break and hurt someone."

"All right. I know the drill from yesterday."

"So, they take this down and set it back up for every appearance?" I asked.

Captain Moe nodded. "Pretty impressive, huh?"

The men continued working, and before the half hour was up, they'd transformed the room into a winter wonderland. On the back wall, they'd put up a large poster of a snowy meadow with trees, a small cabin with smoke rising from its chimney, and a plump, happy snowman. White felt batting had been spread onto the floor to simulate snow, and round mosaic stepping stones led up to the sleigh.

Ms. Vincent returned with a large basket of peppermint sticks and a stack of coloring books. She placed them on the conference room table that had been pushed into the corner of the room.

"If you're ready, I'll let the children start coming in," she said.

It was showtime.

Chapter Three

I wasn't prepared for the first group of children who came into the room. Of course I'd realized we were doing this primarily for the kids admitted here at the hospital, but it was heartbreaking to see them so frail and weak. Some were in wheelchairs, a couple of them wheeled oxygen tanks beside them, and a few had limbs in casts. And yet, when they saw the room and Captain Moe and Angus—and even me—their faces brightened. Their eyes filled with wonder, and they smiled and laughed.

Marcy the Elf came to life. I looked over at Captain Moe, and he grinned and gave me an exaggerated wink. I laughed.

"Welcome!" I said to the group. "Thank you for stopping in to see Santa!"

"Is he the *real* Santa?" asked a little boy with his arm in a cast.

"Yes. He really is." The boy was first in line, so I asked him if he'd like to go on over and say hello to Santa.

The child stepped forward shyly, almost reverently.

"Hello!" Captain Moe's voice boomed out cheerily. "What's your name, young man?"

"I'm Jeffrey."

Captain Moe nodded. "Jeffrey! Of course! You've grown so much this past year that I didn't recognize you at first."

"I'm getting big," Jeffrey said. "Mommy says I'll be even taller than my dad."

"Oh, I think you will. You dad wasn't as tall as you when he was your age."

Jeffrey's eyes widened. "Really? You knew my dad?"

"Of course. And your mom, too."

I had Angus by my side. I was concerned at first about how he'd react to so many children at once—and how they'd feel about him—but they all seemed fine. In fact, Angus pulled me over to a tiny girl of about six years old who was in a wheelchair.

The nurse who was pushing the wheelchair raised her eyebrows at me when Angus approached, but I nodded slightly to let her know I thought everything would be okay.

Angus walked up to the child, sat down, and placed one huge paw on the arm of her chair.

She giggled and patted his paw. "He's funny! Is he a dog?"

"He is," I said.

"Like Clifford."

I knew she was talking about the big red dog from the children's book series. "That's right. Only his name is Angus."

"Are *all* dogs this big at the North Pole?"

I considered her question. "A lot of them are."

She leaned over and kissed Angus on the nose. "I love you."

"He loves you, too," I said.

"Is he a therapy dog?" the child's nurse asked.

"Only to me," I said.

"Well, he's wonderful with the children," she said. "You should consider training him for therapy."

After the children from the hospital visited Santa, the general public was allowed to come in. That's when Ted, Tiffany, and Jackson—Tiffany's two-year-old son—arrived. Jackson recognized me from the day before and ran to me with open arms. Ted smiled and took Angus's leash.

I scooped the boy up. "Hi, Jackson! How are you?"

"Santa?"

"You're here to see Santa?"

He nodded, blue eyes enormous as he peered past me to Captain Moe.

"Hello, Jackson," Captain Moe called. "Ho, ho, ho!"

Jackson looked back at me, his mouth forming an O.

"Would you like for me to take you to see Santa?" I asked.

He nodded.

I walked over to the sleigh where Captain Moe sat.

Captain Moe patted the seat beside him. "How'd you like to help me drive this sleigh, Jackson?"

Jackson nodded. I eased him down onto the seat beside Captain Moe.

Angus went over and climbed into the sleigh beside Jackson. As he sat down, the photographer snapped a photograph.

"I'd like a copy of that one for tomorrow's paper," Paul said to the photographer. "I'll give you credit, of course."

I smiled and waved at Paul and Vera. I hadn't noticed them come in. They made a striking couple, though. They were about the same height, since Vera was wearing three-inch wedge heels. Paul was a slender man with dark brown hair—not a speck of gray, due, I suspected, to a professional colorist—and a wardrobe that Tim Gunn would've been proud of. This evening, he wore navy slacks, a light blue dress shirt, and a pin-striped blazer. Vera was dressed to coordinate in a sky blue wrap dress.

She hurried over to me. "You look adorable."

"Thanks."

"By the way, I wanted to warn you that the gang's all here."

"The gang?" I asked.

She nodded. "Todd, Audrey, Blake, and Sadie."

"Oh, well, the more, the merrier. Maybe the photographer can gather us all around the sleigh and snap a picture before we leave."

"Wouldn't that be fantastic? I'll offer to pay him, of course." She hurried off to discuss the matter with Paul and the photographer.

By this time, Jackson was finished with Santa and was calling for Mommy to come and get him.

Tiffany joined us and lifted Jackson out of the sleigh. "Cute costume."

"Thank you." I had no idea what to think about Ted's sister. I'd been intimidated when I'd first met his mother, Veronica, but the situation with his sister was entirely different. Tiffany was polite but distant, as if she were watching me and sizing me up.

Ted had been married briefly to a woman named Jennifer. She'd decided she couldn't handle being a police officer's wife and had run out on him, so I understood Ted's family withholding judgment until getting to know me better. I felt like I'd won over his mom, but Tiffany was proving to be tougher.

"Marcy!" Jackson said.

Apparently, I'd won him over, too.

"Did you have fun with Santa?" I asked.

He nodded. "Twain. He bwing twain."

"He's bringing you a train for Christmas?" I asked. Jackson nodded again.

I asked Tiffany if Jackson could have a coloring book. She said yes, and I got him one. She thanked me and went back to stand near the wall with Ted and Angus.

"Look, puppy! Book!"

I smiled as Jackson showed Angus the coloring book.

Finally, all the visits were done. Blake, Sadie, Todd, and Audrey—Todd's girlfriend, who was also a deputy—came into the conference room. Sadie was snapping photos using her phone's camera as she came through the door.

"Oh, my gosh! Look at you!" Sadie laughed. "Strike a pose."

I held out my arms, put one leg out to the side, and lifted the curly toe of my shoe.

"Ted, you and Angus get over there with her. Then I want one of you with Captain Moe."

Ted led Angus over beside me. He wrapped one arm around me and pulled me against his side. I put both arms around his waist. We smiled as Sadie took her photo.

"Me, Marcy! Me!"

"Let's get Jackson in here," Ted said.

Tiffany sat Jackson down, and he toddled over to us.

"Jackson, meet Sadie," I said, as I swept him up into my arms.

"Say?" he asked.

"Sadie," I repeated. "Sadie, Jackson is Ted's nephew."

"Hey, Jackson," Sadie said.

"Hi, Say."

I introduced Sadie, Blake, Todd, and Audrey to Tiffany, but she was reserved with them, too. I imagine she saw them as my friends rather than Ted's, and she wanted to see if they measured up before getting friendly.

Paul interviewed both Captain Moe and me for the article he was writing. And, at Vera's urging—and payment, I was sure—the photographer managed to squeeze everyone around the sleigh for a group shot. Tiffany was reluctant to join us, but Ted coaxed her into it.

Not long after that, everyone left and Captain Moe,

Angus, and I were in the conference room alone. Captain Moe dropped the Santa facade for the first time in hours and smiled at me.

"Thank you for doing this, Tink."

"Thank *you*. I thought I was doing you a favor when I agreed to this, but you were the one doing the favor for me. All those children are precious."

"Aren't they, though? And, you know, your Mr. Nash looked very comfortable with little Jackson."

I laughed. "Don't go there. Not yet, anyway."

He held up his hands. "I'm not going anywhere. Not speculating; merely observing."

Being an elf *had* made me feel maternal, and Captain Moe was right: Ted was sweet and attentive toward Jackson. But Ted and I weren't even engaged. How could I possibly consider a future and children at this point? So, I changed the subject.

"You know, I was surprised to find you arguing with Ms. Vincent when I arrived."

His smiling face morphed into a grimace. "I'm sorry you had to be a witness to that. As I told you, she'd asked me to give preferential treatment to one of the children. I wouldn't do that to the others—not in this setting, in front of the children. I might visit his room again tomorrow, but I won't single him out and pretend he's Santa's favorite or some nonsense. I don't give a fig who his father is."

"I understand that. Who *is* his father?"

"Dr. Bellamy Carstairs. He's on the board of directors of the hospital—semi-retired, I think, in order to handle his administrative duties." Captain Moe shook his head. "I'm sorry that his son is sick. I'm sorry that all these children are sick. But they should all be treated the same, especially when they're all gathered in this room together."

"I agree wholeheartedly. You're the most wonderful Santa I've ever seen."

He leaned back and placed a hand on his chest. "I'm not the only one?"

On Sunday I was looking forward to my last stint as elf. In fact, I was considering buying a costume of my own in case Captain Moe needed me again in the future. I mean, surely he'd be doing some Santa work closer to Christmas and would need an elf, wouldn't he? I knew he'd said the hospital wanted him to come back the weekend before Christmas and on Christmas Eve. He'd certainly need my help then.

I hummed "Jingle Bells" as Angus and I strode down the corridor toward the conference room. As I approached, I noticed there was a brawny security guard standing outside the room. Before I could wonder why a security guard was needed, I saw the yellow crime-scene tape across the door.

Gasping, I ran forward. "What's happened?"

"I'm sorry, ma'am." The guard was bald and nearly as broad as he was tall, but all muscle. In his uniform, he resembled a brown and tan brick wall. Dark, thick eyebrows and a goatee rounded out his intimidating appearance. "You can't go in there."

"Captain Moe—Santa—is he all right?"

"I'm not at liberty to comment on this situation."

I took the man's forearm. "Please. I'm his friend. Tell me whether or not he's okay."

He glanced from side to side. "He's fine. But some-one else isn't." He nodded at my costume. "There's no need for that today. The event has been canceled."

"But—"

"You need to go."

Angus uttered a low growl.

"Come on, baby," I told him, and led him back down the hall. I took out my cell phone and called Riley Kendall, Captain Moe's niece, who also happens to be an attorney.

"Hey, Marce," she answered. "I can't talk right now. I'm on my way to the jail."

"To the jail? What's going on?"

"Uncle Moe is being questioned about the death of Sandra Vincent. When he got to the hospital today, he found her in the sleigh with a knife in her chest."

Chapter Four

I left the hospital, drove home, and changed out of the elf costume. I hadn't called Ted yet. I wanted to talk with him in person, and I knew he'd gone to his mother's condo to have lunch with her and Tiffany and her family today. They should be finished by now, so I wouldn't be interrupting.

Leaving Angus at home with the promise that I'd be back soon, I went over to Veronica's place. The building actually looked more like a resort hotel than a group of condominiums, and there was even a sweet doorman there named Bill. It was designed to be self-sufficient for residents who were reluctant or unable to go out much. Manicurists, hairstylists, chefs, and even nurses were all on staff.

I parked the Jeep and approached the door.

Bill opened it for me. "Good day, Ms. Singer. It's a pleasure to see you again."

"It's good to see you too, Bill. Did you and your family have a nice Thanksgiving?"

"We did, and I hope you did, as well."

"Yeah. It was great."

My expression must've betrayed me, because Bill asked me if everything was all right.

"I'm fine," I said. "Just a little on edge, I suppose." I didn't want to go into the specifics.

He stepped closer and lowered his voice. "Don't overly concern yourself about meeting the future family members. We've all been through it. And if we don't like one of them, we don't have to see them except for holidays, now, do we?"

I forced a smile. "Right. Thanks again, Bill."

I went on inside. I supposed it was nice for people to care about Ted and me, but I'd rather they didn't speculate about our lives so much. We'd been dating for only a few months. Did everyone in Tallulah Falls already have us married with two children and another on the way?

There was a phone in the lobby. I called Veronica to let her know I was downstairs.

"I don't want to interrupt lunch," I said. "I just have something to talk with Ted about, and it can't wait. It's about Captain Moe."

"By all means, come on up."

Ted met me outside his Mom's door. "What's up, babe?"

I explained how I'd gone to the hospital and had been informed by the security guard that the event had been canceled. "Then I called Riley to see what was going on, and she told me that Captain Moe is being questioned in the murder of the hospital administrator, Sandra Vincent."

He drew his brows together. "The hospital is in Tallulah County's jurisdiction, but I'll make a few calls and see what I can find out."

"Thank you."

He pulled me into his arms and kissed the top of my head. "Everything will be all right."

"I know. I just hate for Captain Moe to be in hot water. Plus all those kids are going to be so disappointed."

"Let's go inside and get you something to drink," said Ted. "Are you hungry?"

I shook my head.

He opened the door. "Hey, guys, look who's here."

Jackson sat in the middle of the living-room floor on a play mat spread out over the thick taupe carpet. He looked up from the blocks he was playing with and gave me a wide grin. "Marcy!"

I smiled at Ted. "He knows my name."

He nodded. "Said it all the way home last night."

"That's so precious." I spoke with everyone else, and then went to sit on the floor with Jackson.

"I'm going into the den to make those calls, and I'll be right back," Ted said.

"What's going on with Captain Moe?" Veronica asked quietly as she came over and sat on the blue floral ottoman near me. Her silvery bob brushed against her chin as she leaned forward to talk with me.

"He's being questioned about the death of the hospital administrator," I whispered. "He found her body."

"Oh, that's terrible. It must've been such a shock."

"I didn't even realize what was going on until I

arrived at the hospital and was turned away by the security guard. I called Riley Kendall, and she told me what had happened."

Jackson handed me a block, and I placed it on top of the other two he'd stacked together. He slapped the tower down and chortled.

Veronica and I both laughed.

"Scamp," said Veronica.

"Where's Clover?" I asked. Clover was Veronica's large brown and white rabbit.

"Clover isn't terribly comfortable with Jackson yet, so she's keeping pretty much to the bedroom during his visit."

Tiffany, in a pink angora sweater, walked over and placed her hand on her mother's shoulder. "What are you two being so hush-hush about, and what's got Ted making what appears to be business calls on his day off?"

"He's trying to find out what's going on with a friend of theirs who's had a traumatic experience today." Veronica looked up at her daughter. "Marcy needs our support right now, as well."

Tiffany merely looked at me. I didn't know what to say. Fortunately, I was saved by Jackson giving me another block to stack on the tower he'd decided to rebuild.

"Thank you, Jackson." I smiled at Tiffany. "I think it's sweet that he's already learned how to say my name."

"Marcy, would you like something to drink?" asked Tiffany's husband, Mark, as he got off the sofa and headed toward the kitchen.

"No, thank you. I'm fine."

"You sure? We've got raspberry iced tea that Veronica actually made herself, believe it or not."

Veronica scoffed at Mark. "Just because I don't often choose to show how handy I am in the kitchen doesn't mean I'm not."

"Whatever you say." He rolled his eyes. "But seriously, it's good. You should try it."

"All right," I said.

"He teases me mercilessly," said Veronica. "He thinks I won't beat him in front of my grandson."

I laughed. "I once saw you put a federal marshal in time-out. Mark had better not push you too far."

Veronica joined in my laughter. Tiffany did not.

"I need to put Jackson down for his nap," Tiffany said, scooping up the child and inciting a screaming fit. She took him down the hall.

I neatly stacked the blocks and rolled up the play mat before moving from the floor to the armchair next to where Veronica sat. Mark returned with my tea.

"Thank you." I took a sip. "This is really good."

"Must you sound so surprised?" Veronica winked.

Elsewhere in the condo, Tiffany had managed to quiet Jackson. I was glad. I'd hoped I hadn't been the reason for the abrupt naptime.

"How does Tiffany manage to keep Jackson on schedule so well?" I asked.

"She doesn't always," Mark said. He was a bear of a man, with an easy smile. "But right now it's important that we don't give in to his tantrums. He's testing his limits . . . and our patience, more often than not."

"The terrible twos, huh?"

"It's not that bad. He's a good kid. Takes after his dad."

Veronica gave a snort of derision.

"You know it's true, Mother Nash," Mark teased. "And, Marcy, pay no attention to my wife. You'll grow on her. When I first met Ted, I thought he was the spawn of Satan."

"I just wish I could make her like me," I said.

"She was good friends with Jennifer," Veronica said. "And then Jennifer burned Ted so badly—burned us all, in fact. Tiff just needs to see that you're nothing like that shrew."

"Well, I hope I'm not."

"You aren't, darling." Veronica smiled. "If you were, I'd have already done my best to have gotten rid of you."

My eyes widened.

Mark hooted with laughter. "Gee, Veronica, don't be so subtle."

Ted returned from the den, sat down on the edge of my chair, and draped an arm around my shoulders. "Hey, are you two ganging up on my girl?"

"Hey, not me, man. It's your mother."

"They're being wonderful," I said to Ted. "What'd you find out?"

"Well, our old pals Bailey and Ray are in charge of the investigation."

I remembered detectives Bailey and Ray from two previous investigations that had been outside of the Tallulah Falls Police Department's jurisdiction. And I was fairly certain they'd remember me, too.

"They've released Captain Moe," Ted continued.

"He hasn't been charged with Ms. Vincent's murder, but he is a suspect. That's only natural, given that he found the body. I'd imagine that when you arrived at the hospital earlier today, the crime-scene techs were still working the room."

"Well, they've got to find something to exonerate him, Ted. I know Captain Moe didn't do this."

"So do I," he said. "But witnesses saw him arguing with Ms. Vincent yesterday."

"Heck, *I* saw them arguing," I said. "Captain Moe refused to give one of the children preferential treatment over the others. But that's no reason to kill her. We've got to find out who did this, Ted."

"No, *we* don't. That's up to the Tallulah County PD. We just need to be supportive of Captain Moe."

"But they're not as good as you—not as thorough." I placed both hands on Ted's knee. "Plus, you know Captain Moe. They'll look at him as an honest-to-goodness suspect."

"Sweetheart, if he were under investigation in my department, I'd look at him as a valid suspect myself."

"But you'd find the *real* killer," I said. "I'm not so sure we can count on Bailey and Ray to do that."

Veronica turned to Mark. "I adore her spunk. She once was willing to fight an armed assailant for Ted."

"Do not encourage her, Mom."

"It turned out he wasn't really armed," I said.

Veronica raised an index finger. "Ah, but you didn't know that at the time you went running at him."

"That's true."

"I said, don't encourage her!" Ted repeated.

"Oh, hush," Veronica chided. "You love her spunk, too."

Ted ran a hand over his face.

"Need a beer, buddy?" Mark asked.

"Not right now. I'm driving. But I might be back later for something even stronger," Ted said.

"You've got it."

Ted squeezed my shoulder. "Captain Moe's at Riley's house right now. I asked if we could come over, and she said it was fine."

I leapt up from the chair. "Then let's go." I took another drink of my tea. "Veronica, this really is delicious, and I'd love to finish it, but—"

"Go." She took the glass from my hand. "You two need to be with Captain Moe right now."

I hugged her before Ted and I hurried out the door.

When we arrived at Riley's house, her husband, Keith, ushered us into the living room. Their baby, Laura, was asleep—it must be a common naptime for little ones—so he raised his finger to his lips and asked us to keep our voices down.

Captain Moe was sitting on Riley's burgundy leather sofa, looking tired and defeated. I went over and gave him a hug.

"How are you?" I asked.

"I've been better a time or two, Tink."

"I can imagine. Detectives Bailey and Ray aren't my favorite people, either."

"Really? Because they asked me to give you their best," he said.

I gaped. "They did?"

"No," he said with a chuckle. "I just wanted to see your reaction. They asked me over and over again all about Sandra Vincent."

Riley came in with a mug of coffee. Her long black hair was swept up into a bun, she wore a navy silk blouse and black dress slacks, and she was barefoot. "Thank goodness he had the good sense not to talk with them before calling me first. Would you guys like some coffee?"

Ted and I both declined.

"Obviously you're a suspect because you found the body," Ted said. "But what other reasons are they giving you?"

"They're saying that someone saw me arguing with Ms. Vincent more than once over the course of the event," said Captain Moe. "Granted, she and I didn't see eye to eye on some things. We argued Friday and then again yesterday. Tink was there for that round."

"I was. But there was nothing threatening or intimidating said. I can vouch for that."

"I might ask you to," Riley said.

"Who are their other suspects?" Ted asked.

"They aren't saying—at least not to me."

"They certainly didn't clue me in," Captain Moe added.

"I'll see what I can find out," Ted said. "I have a couple of connections with the Tallulah County PD, and Manu has even more."

Chief Manu Singh . . . If Ted couldn't find out who the suspects were, maybe Manu could.

Chapter Five

On the way back from Riley's house, Ted and I stopped at a newspaper box and bought a few copies of the *Tallulah Falls Examiner*. There we were—Captain Moe and me—smiling from the front page. Who could've guessed that less than a day later, things would be such a mess?

When we got to my place, we fed Angus and then cuddled up on the sofa to read Paul's article. It was a feel-good piece, to be sure. Paul had written about the magical way Captain Moe had with the children.

"And everyone was beguiled by his charming elf," Ted read aloud.

"Oh, I'm sure."

"Well, you beguiled me. You captivate and charm and enchant and mesmerize me every day." He punctuated the verbs with kisses.

"Wow. You can almost make me forget that our friend's fate rests in hands of detectives Heckle and Jeckle."

"Detectives Ray and Bailey aren't incompetent, you

know. They're simply doing their jobs. And they'll do a good job."

"But not as good as you and Manu would do. I so wish this case was in your jurisdiction."

"So do I, sweetheart. But it isn't. And there's nothing I can do about that."

"I know."

"And if you go poking your nose into Tallulah County Police business, you're going to get into trouble," he said.

"I know that, too."

He sighed. "But that doesn't mean you won't."

"If I do any snooping at all, I'll be extra careful about it. And I'll keep you looped in every step of the way." At the dubious look he gave me, I decided to change the subject. "Do you know what we should do? Put up our Christmas trees. We can do mine first and then go over to your house and decorate yours."

"I don't have a Christmas tree."

My eyes widened. "Why not? I know you celebrate Christmas."

"Yeah, but I don't need a tree in an apartment by myself."

"Of course you do!" I hopped up off the sofa. "Let's go."

"Where?"

"To get you a tree and some fabulous ornaments!"

Three hours later, we were back at my house with a pizza and a movie. We'd bought Ted a seven-foot-tall artificial tree and assembled it in front of his living

room window. Then we'd decorated it with the ornaments we'd acquired. We'd gotten some things—
lights, red satin balls, and garlands—at the nearest
department store, but then I'd remembered seeing a
Christmas specialty shop between Tallulah Falls and
Depoe Bay.

At the specialty shop, we were able to find a
snowman–police officer ornament, a tiny pair of hand-
cuffs with a key, and an Irish wolfhound. We had to
get two of those; they were so adorable, I wanted one
for my tree as well. And Ted found a miniature blond
fairy ornament. He got two of those, one for himself
and one for Captain Moe.

By the time we got back to Ted's apartment and
finished his tree, we were both happily exhausted.
We'd decided that decorating one tree was enough for
today and that we'd do mine tomorrow evening.

Angus was thrilled that we'd brought home pizza.
Feeling happy and generous, I cut a slice of the thin-
crust cheese pizza into bite-size pieces and put them in
Angus's dish. He was in the living room, wanting more
before we could get the movie put into the DVD player.

"You had yours, Mr. Pig," I told him.

He sat by the sofa and waited expectantly, knowing one of us would cave sooner or later. And, of
course, he was right.

On Monday morning, Angus and I got to work just in
time to tidy up a little and put on a pot of coffee before
unlocking the doors to the Stitch. I retrieved my laptop from my office and looked up more Christmas-

ornament patterns. Of course, I still had plenty to make, but now I wanted to make a couple of special ones for Ted's tree.

The bells over the door alerted me to Vera's arrival. Angus got up from his spot by the window to greet her.

"Good morning," I said. "Would you like some coffee? It should be finished brewing by now."

"No, thanks." She sat on a red club chair. "I can't stay long. I just came by so we could brainstorm about Captain Moe. What're we going to do?"

"Well, Ted told me yesterday that detectives Ray and Bailey are very good at their jobs and that we can trust them to find Sandra Vincent's killer."

She inclined her head. "We're just supposed to trust those two yahoos with Captain Moe's life?"

"I don't like it any better than you do." I bit my lower lip. "I read in Paul's article that he'd spoken with Ms. Vincent. Is it possible that he picked up any clues as to who might have wanted to harm her?"

"No. I've asked him already. And he's no more thrilled about our investigating than Ted is. But we *have* to do something."

"Agreed." I thought a second. "You know, for November and December, I've cut my classes back to one night a week—Wednesday—so that gives me some extra time. I *could* offer to volunteer at the hospital."

"I'm way ahead of you on that one. I called the hospital this morning and said I'd like to come around today with some magazines and stuff. I even have a little collapsible cart in the trunk of my car to carry the magazines, books, newspapers, and snacks."

"That's a great idea," I said.

"I know. I'll nose around and see what I can find out." She stood. "I guess I'd better be on my way."

"Just don't get yourself thrown out."

She smiled. "I'll try."

"And keep me posted," I called as she left.

I was working on a Christmas ornament—not for Ted; just one I'd started and needed to finish before beginning a new one—when a young mom walked in with a toddler in a stroller. I put my work aside and hurried to help her.

"Hi," I said. "Welcome to the Seven-Year Stitch. I'm Marcy."

"Hi, Marcy. I'm Dani and this is Nicole." She looked at me closely and then spotted Angus ambling in from my office, where he'd been getting a drink from his water bowl. "Wait, I know you. You're the elf! From Saturday night."

"I am. Are you all right with Angus around Nicole, or would you rather I put him up?"

"He's fine," said Dani. "She loved him the other night."

As if on cue, Nicole stretched out her hand toward Angus. "Doggie!"

He walked over to the stroller and sat down. Nicole patted his fur.

Nicole appeared to be the picture of health. I hoped she was one of the children who'd simply come to visit after the patients had seen Santa, like Jackson had been. "Do you work at the hospital, Dani?"

"No. We were actually visiting my mom when we

heard about Santa visiting on the third floor. I thought it was really nice of the hospital to allow nonpatients to participate. And that guy was the best Santa I'd ever seen."

"Isn't he though? His name is Maurice Patrick, and he owns Captain Moe's diner in Lincoln City."

"Well, how about that? We'll have to go have lunch with Santa sometime, Nicole."

Nicole was paying too much attention to Angus to listen to what her mother was saying.

"I'm sorry about your mother," I said. "Is her condition serious?"

Dani nodded. "She's waiting on a liver transplant. We thought we had a donor last week, but somehow it fell through at the last minute. I even went to the hospital administrator about it."

"What did she say?" I asked.

"Ms. Vincent said there was a mix-up and that someone was higher up on the list than she'd originally thought—someone even sicker than Mom." She sighed. "Mom has been on that list for so long. I even offered to be a living donor, but my tissue was incompatible with hers."

"I'm very sorry. I hope she gets a donor soon."

"So do I. I just want her to see Nicole grow up. . . . At least be around long enough for Nicole to be able to remember her."

"Of course," I said. "May I get you some coffee or water?"

"No, thank you. I'm fine. I'm actually here looking

for some Swedish weaving or huck-embroidery patterns," Dani said. "Mom used to love to stitch, and although she's too weak to do it herself now, I thought she might enjoy it if I stitch while I'm sitting with her at the hospital."

I had some huck-embroidery snowflake ornament kits and a couple of tea towel kits. Dani took both the tea towel kits and one of the snowflakes.

"I enjoyed seeing you again," I told Dani. "And I hope we can meet again under happier circumstances."

"Me, too. I just pray that Mom gets a liver before . . . well, soon."

"So do I."

"Tell the doggie bye, Nicole."

"Bye, doggie!"

I opened the door for them. "Thank you for stopping in."

"We'll probably be back," Dani said before heading off down the street.

I went back to the sit-and-stitch square and resumed work on the cross-stitch teddy bear holding a red-and-white gift box. I felt terrible for Dani and her mom and for the rest of their family, as well. To be that close to a cure and then have it fall through at the last minute. How sad.

It wasn't long before Todd came striding into the Stitch, sporting a smile a mile wide.

Angus trotted over to him happily, but I narrowed my eyes suspiciously.

"What're you up to?" I asked.

"Nothing. Can't a guy just come over and visit his best gal pal without raising suspicion?"

"Not with a smile like that on your face."

When I'd first moved to Tallulah Falls, it had been Sadie's hope that Todd and I would make a love connection. We had hit it off, but as friends. He was tall, athletic, and had wavy brown hair and chocolate eyes, and he seesawed back and forth between being a terrific friend and an obnoxious big brother.

He plopped onto the sofa beside me and pulled out his phone. "Take a look."

I'd forgotten how ridiculous I'd felt when I'd first put on the elf costume. Not anymore. Todd scrolled through photo after photo of me making one goofy expression after another.

"Thank you so much for taking these. Now delete them."

"No way! I'm thinking of making this one"—he pointed out a particularly crazy photo where a child appeared to be trying to look up my nose—"my Christmas card."

"I will kill you."

He laughed. "Help me come up with a clever caption. *You can pick your friends, and you can pick your nose, but you can't pick your friend's nose.* Or what about *Have your elf a boogie little Christmas*?"

"I do not have a booger in that photograph!"

"That kid will see about that, Missy."

"Todd!" I wailed.

Angus didn't know what game we were playing,

but he was in. He barked, ran, and got a Kodiak-bear squeeze toy, threw it into the air, and barked some more.

Amid the cacophony, my cell phone rang. Todd and I were able to persuade Angus to hush so I could answer the phone. I didn't recognize the number.

"Hello and thank you for calling the Seven-Year Stitch. This is Marcy. How may I help you?"

"Hi, Marcy, it's Veronica."

Of course it was. I'd recognize that cultured voice anywhere.

"I was wondering if you'd have lunch with Tiffany and me today," she continued. "Could you maybe close up shop for a few minutes and meet us at that coffee shop down the street from you at around one?"

"Sure. Will Ted be there?"

"No, I called and asked him to make other plans."

"Um . . . all right."

Todd caught my eye and mouthed, *Is everything okay?* I shrugged.

"I thought it would be nice to visit—you know, just us girls."

"Okay," I said. "I'll see you at one."

As I ended the call, Todd said, "You look pale."

"That was Ted's mom. She wants me to have lunch with her and Tiffany, Ted's sister, today."

"And I take it that Marshall Dillon won't be in Dodge City at the time?"

"No. Veronica said she called and asked him to make other plans. She said she wanted *just us girls* to visit."

"Why does that have you freaked out?" he asked. "I thought you liked Ted's mom."

"I do. And though I've tried my best to be friendly toward Tiffany, she shuts me out."

"Then maybe this is Veronica's way of allowing the two of you to get to know each other better."

"Maybe," I agreed.

My phone buzzed. I'd received a text from Ted.

Hey, babe. Mom wants you to herself today, so I'm heading to Tallulah County for lunch.

And he'd told *me* not to poke my nose into the investigation. I smiled.

"Good news?" Todd asked.

"Yeah. Ted's going to Tallulah County for lunch. I take it that means he's going to be seeing what, if anything, he can learn about Captain Moe's case."

"Captain Moe's case? What're you talking about?"

I explained how the Santa Claus event was canceled yesterday after Captain Moe had found the hospital administrator dead in his sleigh.

"That's terrible. Who'd want to kill a hospital administrator?"

"That's what we need to find out."

"You mean, that's what the *police* need to find out," Todd said.

"Of course that's what I meant."

"*You* need to stay over here in your oak tree and make cookies."

"I know," I said.

"And I know you won't." He looked at Angus. "You know as well as I do that she never listens to anyone."

Angus woofed.

"Does Audrey have any friends at the Tallulah County Police Department?" I asked sweetly—very sweetly, with a smile and batting lashes and everything.

He groaned. "I'll ask."

Chapter Six

I looked down at what I'd decided to wear today—dark jeans, a black-and-white striped sweater, and black espadrilles. Darn! I probably looked like either a criminal or a referee . . . or a criminal referee. Normally, I loved this outfit—the sweater was roomy and had a cowl neck, and the shoes were comfortable but still gave me some extra height—but I hadn't realized I'd be meeting Ted's mom and sister for lunch today!

I wished I could hurry home and change into something elegant and classy. I couldn't very well close the shop to do that, though. Besides, I knew there was nothing I could put on that would make Tiffany say, "Oh, that's a great outfit. I like you now."

At a little before one, I put the cardboard clock on the door saying I'd be back in half an hour, locked up, and then headed down the street toward MacKenzies' Mochas. Angus ran back and forth in front of the window as if to say, "Hey, aren't you forgetting somebody?" I silently promised him a peanut butter cookie for his trouble . . . again. I'd vocalized the promise before locking him up in the Seven-Year Stitch with only Jill and his Kodiak bear for company. Trust me, I wasn't any happier about the arrangement than he was.

I walked into MacKenzies' Mochas, where Veronica and Tiffany were already waiting for me. As always, Veronica looked as if she'd just stepped out of a fashion magazine. She wore pink slacks, a cropped pink-and-white tweed jacket, and taupe heels. I was relieved to see that, like me, Tiffany was wearing jeans. However, she also wore an emerald jersey wrap blouse, a strand of pearls, and silver ballet flats.

Sadie, for whom I'd been an open book since college, read my expression effortlessly. She came out from behind the counter, hugged me, and said, "Marcy, how beautiful you look! May I show you ladies to a table?"

I love you. I hoped she could read that on my face as easily as she'd seen my discomfort in comparing myself to the glamazons.

She winked. *Message received.* She showed us to a table and said she'd send our waitress right over.

"I'm so glad you could join us," Veronica said.

"Me, too," I said. "Where are Jackson and Mark today?"

"They're having guy time." Veronica smiled. "I imagine that means they're lying on the floor, playing with Jackson's toy cars, and that we'll find them asleep there when we return. How's your friend the captain? Have you spoken with him today?"

"Not today." I opened my mouth to say something more, but then I closed it.

"Let me guess," said Veronica. "Everyone, including

my precious firstborn, is telling you not to meddle and to allow the police to do their jobs."

I nodded. "That would be easier to do if Ted was on Captain Moe's case. He's the best detective there is."

Our waitress arrived, took our orders, and then scurried away.

"And yet you still felt the need to defend Ted when you thought he was in danger?" Tiffany asked.

That got my hackles up. "Yes, I did. At that time, I thought the man was drawing a gun, and I didn't think Ted had backup."

"You could've been shot," Tiffany said.

"That thought never even crossed my mind. All I could think of was protecting Ted." I looked at Veronica. "He was so angry with me."

"Because all he could think of was protecting you." She chuckled.

"Jennifer would've hidden and let the chips fall wherever," said Tiffany.

"What was she like?" I asked.

"She was a total b—"

"Ah-ah." Veronica interrupted her daughter. "We don't speak ill of the dead."

I gasped. "Jennifer is *dead*?"

"She is to us," said Veronica. "And she isn't worth talking about and ruining our lunch. Let's talk about Captain Moe and how we can help him."

I smiled slightly. "I think you've done a lot already. By asking Ted if we could have lunch alone today, you gave him the green light to go to Tallulah County to look into the case himself."

"Good. But what can *we* do?"

Before Veronica could speculate further, our waitress brought our drinks. "Your food will be out in just a few minutes."

We thanked her, and Veronica continued.

"The big question here is, Who would want this Sandra Vincent dead? And, of course, we need to determine whether his or her motivation was business or personal."

"Or a bit of both," I said. "In Ms. Vincent's position, one bad business decision could cost several patients their lives, right? I mean, fire a competent doctor and many patients suffer."

"Or keep an incompetent doctor and patients die, too," said Tiffany.

"How dreadful." Veronica took a sip of her tea.

"You know Vera Langhorne," I said to Veronica, and she nodded slightly. "She's gone to volunteer at Tallulah County General today to see what she can learn about Ms. Vincent."

"Keep us updated on her findings," Veronica said.

As I promised to do so, our food arrived. We spent the rest of the meal in companionable chitchat about the weather and other trivial subjects. But I knew it had to be in the backs of all our minds that there was a killer on the loose and that none of us wanted Captain Moe blamed for a murder he didn't commit.

Angus forgave me for my absence once I'd given him his peanut butter cookie. I hadn't been back at the Stitch long when Sadie arrived.

"What was *that* all about?" she asked.

I explained how Veronica had called and had wanted to have lunch, just us girls. "I was so nervous. I met Tiffany and her family on Thanksgiving, but I can't get her to warm up to me at all. She did seem a bit friendlier today, though."

"What does she do for a living?"

"She's an elementary-school teacher. She and her husband, Mark—who is an industrial engineer—have a gorgeous son named Jackson. He's two years old."

"That's right. I saw them at the event at the hospital the other night. Do they live here in Tallulah Falls?" Sadie asked.

"No, they live in Washington, not far from Seattle, if I'm not mistaken."

"I didn't think I'd seen her in MacKenzies' Mochas before. How long will they be in town?"

"They're staying with Veronica until this coming Sunday," I said.

"So just a few more days." She patted Angus's head. "How'd you like your cookie, Angus? Blake made sure you got the biggest one in the case."

"He inhaled it. Thanks . . . for everything."

"You're welcome. I could tell you were on edge. You can't let people make you feel inferior, Marce."

"I know. It's just that she's Ted's sister, and I want her to like me."

"Whether she does or not, Ted loves you."

"I know. But I want her to know I'm not like Ted's ex-wife, Jennifer."

"I never knew Jennifer, but I would almost bet

you're absolutely nothing like her. Be yourself. If Tiffany doesn't like you, you've always got me. And Angus. And Jill." She grinned. "Gotta get back. I'll talk with you later."

I was still smiling at Sadie's parting comments when Ted called.

"Hey, babe. How was lunch?"

"It was good. How was your lunch?"

"Fine. I met with a friend who's with the Tallulah County Police Department. I'm afraid that, so far, they don't have many suspects in Sandra Vincent's death."

I let out a breath. "Oh no."

"But they're actively investigating. It's only been a day. They're literally at the beginning of the investigation, and they have a lot of ground to cover. I merely wanted to see if there was some glaring suspect that would almost immediately exonerate Captain Moe."

"And there's not," I said.

"No. But, again, they're still looking. And they'll find whoever killed this woman."

"I so wish you and Manu were on this case," I said. "I don't trust Captain Moe's fate to detectives Ray and Bailey."

"I know you don't. But they're good at their jobs. Have a little faith, all right?"

I mumbled that I'd try.

"About Tiffany," he said softly. "She's younger than me, but she's always been part mother hen and part guard dog where I'm concerned. She'll warm up to you."

"I know."

"Hey, you won Mom over. That was no small feat."

I laughed. "I know that, too. Don't forget we're decorating my tree this evening."

"I haven't forgotten. Mine looks beautiful. Thank you for that."

"You're welcome."

A customer came in, so I ended the call and introduced myself. "Welcome to the Seven-Year Stitch."

The woman was in her late thirties, and she loved Angus on sight. "What a cool dog! What kind is he?"

I told her Angus was an Irish wolfhound and gave her a bit of background about how I'd rescued him from a puppy mill.

"The reason I stopped in," she said at last, "is to ask you about something called stump work. Do you know what I'm talking about?"

"I do. Stump work is a form of raised embroidery. It has something of a three-dimensional effect."

"Well, my grandmother loves embroidery—this stump work, in particular—and I wanted to make her a little something for Christmas. I know that might not be possible, with it being so close to December."

"If you do something small like a Christmas ornament, I think you'll have plenty of time," I said.

"Is it hard to do?" she asked.

"Not really." I got her the necessary supplies and invited her to sit with me on the sofa. After an hour and a half, she was well on her way to creating an adorable ornament for her grandmother, despite my having to stop and wait on customers throughout the time we were working.

In fact, we were still working when Vera came in, sat on one of the red club chairs, and put her feet up on the ottoman.

"I'm pooped," she said.

I introduced Vera to my customer, who I now knew as Jane. "Vera has been volunteering at Tallulah County General Hospital today," I said.

"I hate that place." Jane looked at Vera. "No offense."

"None taken, dear. After today, I feel much the same way. Did you ever work there?"

"No, but my husband is a contractor. He had the absolute lowest bid for their cancer ward, and his company was shot down. He was told that the job was given to a more experienced company." She shook her head. "But when Aaron did some digging, he learned that the other company *wasn't* more experienced than his. He made a stink about it and wound up getting blackballed. He couldn't get work anywhere in Tallulah County, and we wound up having to move closer to Lincoln City for him to be able to get back on track."

"What a shame." I exchanged glances with Vera. "That's so unfair."

"Unfair and, I'd venture to say, unethical," said Jane. "I can't help but wonder what other shady practices were going on at that hospital." She glanced at her watch. "Oh, goodness. I'd better run. I have to pick up my daughter from school."

Jane gathered up her materials and I went over to the counter and got a periwinkle bag to put them in. After ringing up Jane's purchases, we all said our good-byes. I told Jane to come back if she needed any further assistance.

Once she'd left, I went back and sat down across from Vera. "That was interesting."

"Wasn't it? I wish we knew the name of the company that got the contract Jane's husband was bidding on," she said.

"I imagine that's a matter of public record."

"I'll put Paul to work on it." Vera gave me a sage nod. "If anyone can find out, he can."

"Great. What did you find out at the hospital today?"

"I found out that being a volunteer is hard work, that patients are demanding, and that some of the staff can be downright picky about handouts." She affected a whiny voice. "Well, I *like* that magazine, but don't you have *this* one or *that* one?" She rolled her eyes before resuming her normal tone. "I also learned that Sandra Vincent was something of a chameleon and that people either loved her or hated her—there wasn't much ambivalence. I gathered that information by offering freebies to the whiny staff members."

"Good thinking. Give me some examples about Ms. Vincent. Which people hated her, and which people loved her?"

"Well, that's just it," said Vera. "I can't narrow it down to groups, like all the doctors I spoke with hated her but the nurses loved her. Each individual— no matter what purpose they serve at the hospital— either hated Sandra and, although not happy that she's dead, weren't shedding any tears over her, or loved her and couldn't believe she was gone."

"So, you didn't really come up with any suspects, either?"

"No." She frowned. "Wait. What do you mean, *either*?"

I told her about Ted having lunch with a friend who worked with the TCPD. "Their only real suspect right now is Captain Moe."

Chapter Seven

After Vera left, I called Tallulah County General Hospital and asked the nurse in charge of the pediatric ward if I could come in tomorrow after work and read to the children. I even volunteered to wear the elf costume.

"I have to return the costume, anyway, and I thought I might make use of it one more time before saying good-bye to it."

"I think that's a charming idea, Ms. Singer, and the children would love it. Could you be here at six thirty tomorrow evening?"

"I certainly can. I'll look forward to it."

I had a customer come in immediately after speaking with the nurse. Once she'd finished browsing and had made her purchase, I called Riley.

"Hi, Marcy." She sounded tired. I wondered if she'd been up with the baby the night before or if it was worry about Captain Moe that was draining her. I debated asking, but then decided it was better if I didn't.

"How are you?" I asked.

"I'm okay."

"I know you're busy, and I won't keep you but a minute, but I wanted you to know that everyone is rooting for Captain Moe. Vera even went to the hospital today to do some recon."

Riley laughed. "That's sweet. Did it do any good?"

"Not really. She said that everyone either hated or loved Sandra Vincent. Apparently, there was no middle ground where this woman was concerned."

"Still, the only suspect the Tallulah County Police Department has in their crosshairs seems to be my uncle."

"I know. But Ted says the investigation is in its infancy. I'm sure the real suspect will turn up soon."

She sighed. "I hope you're right, but the longer the police go without a more viable suspect, the guiltier Uncle Moe looks. I'm just grateful he hasn't been charged yet. All the evidence they have against him is circumstantial at this point—anyone could have walked into that room and discovered Sandra Vincent's body."

"Exactly."

"And yet I'm concerned that the hospital is pressuring the police to make an arrest."

"Have you talked with your dad?" I asked.

Riley's dad, Norman Patrick, was also an attorney. Unfortunately, he was currently incarcerated in a minimum-security prison for fraud. He was halfway through his three-year sentence.

"I spoke with him last night," she answered. "He's

upset, of course. He wishes he could be here to help. I promised to consult him every step of the way. I did assure him that Uncle Moe hasn't been arrested and that all this worry might be for nothing, but he knows me better than that. Had I not been worried, I wouldn't have called him."

"I've volunteered to read to the children as Marcy the Elf tomorrow evening. I'll see what I can find out about Sandra Vincent while I'm there. We'll get Captain Moe out of this. I know we will."

"I wish I had your optimism. I just get the feeling there's something Uncle Moe isn't telling me— something that's going to come back and bite us all. I *know* him, and he's hiding something."

When I got home, Ted was already there. He'd gone up to the attic, brought down my Christmas tree, and had it ready for us to decorate.

"I wasn't sure where you wanted it," he said. "That's why it's here in the foyer."

I smiled. "Let's take it to the living room and put it in the corner next to the fireplace."

"Sounds good to me."

"Have you had a good day?" I asked.

"I've missed you. Other than that, it was all right, I guess. What about you?"

"It was okay." As I followed Ted and the tree into the living room, I went on to tell him about talking with Vera and Riley about Captain Moe's case. "Neither of them is hopeful about the police finding another suspect, but the only evidence against Captain Moe is circumstantial."

"It's too soon to start jumping to conclusions. I'd have thought Riley, at least, would realize that."

"I believe she does. But this is her uncle we're talking about."

"That's true. What do you say we get to decorating this tree and leave our worries behind for a little while?"

I stood on my tiptoes and kissed him. "Sounds good to me."

While we unpacked the ornaments and began putting them on the tree, I told him the significance of each one.

I held up a small porcelain angel. "This one was a gift to me from the late, great McDonald Murphy."

Ted raised his brows. "The Solitary Cowboy?"

"That's the one. Mom worked on a television show in the mid-eighties, and Mr. Murphy came on as a guest star. I was about four years old then. I don't remember it, but Mom said she took me to work one day and that Mr. Murphy thought I was the cutest thing ever." I gave Ted what I hoped was a coquettish smile. "He said I was a little angel."

"If he could see you now . . ."

I huffed. "What's that supposed to mean?"

"Well, if he could see you now, he'd realize how right he was." Ted rolled his eyes.

I laughed. "Anyway, he gave this to Mom and asked her to pass it along to me. And whenever I'm flipping through channels and see that *The Solitary Cowboy* is on the oldies station, I watch for a few minutes and remember that distinguished gentleman cowboy thought I was an angel. So there." I hung the angel on the tree.

"That's a nice story."

"Uh-huh." His tone was still a little patronizing, so I wasn't about to let him off the hook quite yet. "It's more Mom's anecdote than mine, but it's my Limoges angel." I pointed toward myself. "Because *I* was an angel in McDonald Murphy's big brown eyes, mister."

"Maybe so. But you're my Inch-High Private Eye." He swung me up into his arms and kissed me.

"Do you think I should tell Mom about Captain Moe?" I asked. "I haven't spoken with her since I called her on Thanksgiving Day."

"That's up to you. He hasn't been charged yet, and I know you wouldn't want to worry her for no reason. But, then, if he's charged—"

"Do you think he will be? Have you heard something?"

"I haven't heard anything. And I thought we were forgetting about our troubles for the time being." He picked up a cross-stitched bear in a round frame and grinned. "Who gave you this teddy bear? Was it Elvis? Did he sing that teddy-bear song while rocking you to sleep or something?"

I smiled. "No. No one gave me that bear. It was the first cross-stitch ornament I ever made."

He held it up and looked at it more closely. "You did a good job. How old were you?"

"I was eight."

Ted put the bear on the tree, and I lifted a Marilyn Monroe ornament out of the box. The porcelain piece depicted Marilyn in the subway-grate scene in *The Seven-Year Itch*.

"I just got this one last year after opening the Stitch," I said. "I thought it was a fitting memento."

"Indeed it is. We should bring Jill here on Christmas Day so she can enjoy it."

I laughed. "That would be downright creepy."

"Wouldn't it, though? We'd leave the room, and when we'd come back she'd be in a slightly different spot. We'd wonder if we imagined it or if she really had moved. It'd be like we were in the Twilight Zone."

"Will you stop it? You're gonna make me afraid to go back to the shop!"

Ted was still laughing when the doorbell rang. "I'll get that. Get your next ornament and story ready."

When Ted returned to the living room, Todd and Audrey were with him. Audrey was a tall, athletic redhead who was a deputy on the police force. She and Todd seemed to be a good match.

"Hey, we're just in time to help decorate the Christmas tree," said Todd.

"At the rate we're going, you could've come this time tomorrow and still had time to help decorate the tree." Ted winked.

I made a squeak of protest. "I thought you *wanted* to hear the stories that go along with my ornaments."

"I do, darling. I do." He began pointing out ornaments to Todd and Audrey. "This one was a gift from the pope. This one came from Queen Elizabeth . . . or was it Princess Diana?"

I playfully slapped his shoulder. "Fine. I'm not telling you another thing about my ornaments. Todd, Audrey, would you like something to drink?"

"I'd love some coffee if you have some," Audrey said. "It's getting chilly out there."

"Come with me to the kitchen and we'll make some."

"Let my boy Angus in!" Todd called. "He was looking at us over the back fence all sad and dejected because he's being left out of the merriment!"

"He can't come in until after the tree is decorated!" I called back.

Once we got to the kitchen, I asked Audrey if she wanted regular or decaffeinated coffee.

"Regular, please, if that's all right with you."

"It's fine with me."

"Do you *really* have an ornament from the pope?" she asked.

"No. Ted was just teasing. I told him about the ornament McDonald Murphy gave me, and now suddenly every ornament I have has a pedigree."

She smiled, then glanced over her shoulder to make sure the men weren't coming to join us. "Todd told me about Captain Moe, so I called my friend at the TCPD today. She doesn't really know anything that you guys don't already—at least, according to what Todd told me—but she says she'll keep me updated on any new developments."

"Thanks."

I filled the carafe with water and poured it into the

top of the coffeemaker. As the water heated and fil-
tered through the coffee, the kitchen filled with the
rich scent of the dark-roasted beans.

"Have you ever met Captain Moe?" I asked Audrey.

"Todd took me to eat at his diner once. The food
was wonderful, but I can't do that very often without
gaining a ton. Todd introduced us, and he seemed
like a really nice guy."

"He's a sweetheart." I took some cookies from the
freezer, put them on a plate, and warmed them in the
microwave. "I know he's innocent. I just wish the case
was with your department instead of theirs. I trust
Ted and Manu much more than detectives Bailey
and Ray."

"How do you know detectives Bailey and Ray?"

"I've dealt with them on a couple of·occasions—
once when an elderly woman named Louisa Ralston
died in my shop, and again when Mom was a suspect
in the murder of that movie star a few months ago."

"I remember that. The film crew was working on
the outskirts of town, weren't they?"

I nodded. "So it was their jurisdiction rather than
Ted's and Manu's."

"My friend speaks highly of those two detectives.
What did they do to destroy your faith in them?"

I thought about that for a moment. "The main
thing is that they just aren't Ted and Manu. But they
also went after me—hard—and if Ted, Manu, and I
hadn't been doing our own detective work, they'd
have arrested me instead of the real criminal in both
instances."

She smiled. "Give them a chance. They'll do right by Captain Moe."

I put the coffee, sugar, creamer, mugs, and cookies on a tray and took it into the living room. Ted and Todd had sat down and were discussing the Ducks— the college football team, not actual waterfowl.

I placed the tray on the coffee table and allowed everyone to help themselves.

"Did we miss anything?" I asked.

"Nope," said Todd, stuffing a cookie into his mouth. "We were waiting for you." He chewed and swallowed before picking up a wooden reindeer. "I want to hear about the Tibetan monks who carved this for their precious little Marcy."

I anchored my fists to my hips. "I'm going to kill you both. And then Audrey is going to have to arrest me."

"Nah, we'll take 'em out back and bury them, and then we'll come back in here and eat cookies and finish decorating this tree." She smirked at Todd.

"Gee, it's nice to be so highly thought of," he said.

"And, for your information, that particular ornament was whittled for me by Gary Cooper." I snatched the reindeer from him and hung it on the tree.

"Really?" he asked.

"No, not really. My seventh-grade boyfriend made it for me."

"Oooh, Wyatt Earp, you have some competition."

"I'm not worried," Ted said. "I could make a better reindeer than that with one hand tied behind my back."

Before I could respond, Audrey's phone rang. She took it from her pocket, glanced at the screen, and said she needed to take the call.

As she stepped out to the foyer, we all got serious. When police officers get calls that they have to take, it's rarely good news.

I tried to make light conversation while Audrey was speaking in hushed tones ten feet away. "Todd, do you have your tree up yet?"

"The one in the pub is up, but not the one at home. My mom always comes over and, um, helps me with that."

"You mean, you watch her put your tree up?" Ted teased.

"Pretty much," said Todd.

Audrey came back into the living room, her face grim. "That was my friend with the TCPD. The warrant just went out for Maurice Patrick's arrest."

It took me a millisecond to register the fact that Audrey was talking about Captain Moe. "What? That can't be!"

Ted got up and put his arm around my shoulders. "What new evidence did they uncover?"

"The victim had DNA beneath her fingernails," said Audrey. "When Captain Moe was questioned the other day, he agreed to allow the police to take a DNA sample. It was a match."

Chapter Eight

After Audrey gave us the news, Ted made a few phone calls.

"The Tallulah County Police Department called Riley, and she was able to accompany Captain Moe to the police station, where he turned himself in. He was processed and is being held until his arraignment tomorrow morning at nine."

"Processed?" I asked. "What does that mean?"

Ted put his arms around me. "Fingerprinted, photographed." He kissed the top of my head. "He'll be all right, babe."

"How can you say it'll be all right? They've found solid evidence against Captain Moe! It has to be a mistake! I told you those detectives were incompetent!"

"They don't have evidence that he murdered Sandra Vincent," he said. "Only that . . ."

They must've been exchanging looks over my head, because Ted, Audrey, and Todd all began speaking at once.

"They made physical contact," said Ted.

"Maybe Captain Moe killed the old broad in self-defense!" This came from Todd.

Audrey said, "We all pass along DNA every day. Still circumstantial."

"But this DNA was under the victim's fingernails and it was strong enough evidence for Bailey and Ray to make an arrest," I said, feeling deflated.

"Hey, there's nothing we can do to help Captain Moe tonight," Ted said. "Why don't we finish decorating the tree?"

"We could help," Audrey said.

"At least, we can until I have to get back to the Brew Crew." Todd picked up a Santa Claus ornament that was older than I was and looking a little worse for wear. "Dang. This is the saddest Santa I've ever seen."

"I imagine you could find a sadder one at the Tallulah County jail about right now," I said.

Needless to say, the rest of our tree decorating was kind of a downer.

The next morning, Ted picked me up at eight thirty. It was drizzling rain, so I left Angus inside while Ted and I went to the Tallulah County courthouse. I promised the reproachful-looking hound that I'd be back to get him before going to work.

Ted and I sat in the back of the courtroom. I squeezed his hand when the bailiff led Captain Moe out to the table to sit beside Riley. They conferred quietly for a moment before the judge called Captain Moe's case. Riley pled not guilty on Captain Moe's behalf, explained the importance of his being able to run his business while awaiting trial, and requested bail. Bail was set and paid.

We waited for Riley and Captain Moe in the lobby of the courthouse. When they came through the double doors, it was all I could do not to launch myself right at them.

Instead, I hovered and waited for them to approach Ted and me. While we waited, I spotted detectives Bailey and Ray walking in our direction. I glanced back toward Riley and Captain Moe, wondering whether or not the Tallulah County homicide detectives would be inclined to stop and chat with Ted and me. They were.

"Well, Ms. Singer and Detective Nash," said Detective Ray, a square-bodied, white-haired detective with a gravelly voice. "Why am I not surprised to see you here?"

"You're not surprised, Ray, because anytime a denizen of Tallulah Falls is involved in any sort of trouble, you can bet that Ms. Singer's pert little nose will be right there." Detective Bailey planted his hands on his hips and rocked back on his brown leather loafers. "Right, Ms. Singer?"

Bailey was the younger of the two, was tall, and had thinning dark blond hair and a thick mustache.

"That's uncalled for, Bailey," Ted said. "Marcy and I are here as friends of Maurice Patrick. We're concerned about him—that's all."

"We can appreciate that," said Bailey. "Just make sure your concern doesn't translate into your meddling in our investigation."

I lifted my chin. "And *you* make sure you find the person truly responsible for Sandra Vincent's death. Captain Moe is innocent."

"You're sure?" Detective Ray asked. "You were with Mr. Patrick at the time of the murder?"

"No, but—"

"Stay out of our way and let us do our jobs," said Detective Bailey. "If Patrick is indeed innocent, then he and his attorney have the opportunity to present evidence to attest to that. But if he's guilty, he's going to prison for life."

Ted stepped forward. "Look, Bailey, you need to—"

"Hi, guys!" It was Riley whose appearance and bright greeting interrupted Ted.

"Hey, Riley," he said.

"If you'll excuse us, we need to get back to the precinct," said Detective Ray. "Ms. Singer, give your mother our regards."

As soon as the detectives had walked away, Riley said, "I'm sorry for interrupting like that, but it appeared your discussion was getting heated. I didn't want you guys to get into trouble." She smiled. "My caseload is kinda heavy at the moment."

Captain Moe waited for the detectives to leave to approach us.

"Are you all right?" I asked him. "Did they treat you well?"

He smiled and gave me a hug. "Yes, Tink. I'm fine."

Ted looked to make certain detectives Ray and Bailey had indeed left the courthouse before addressing Riley. "What do you think?"

"This additional evidence is circumstantial, but it's huge. I'm calling in Campbell Whitting."

Campbell Whitting was said to be the best criminal attorney on the West Coast. In fact, he'd helped Mom out with her case not too long ago. I pictured his steely glare and bushy gray hair and beard.

"What I can't understand is how Sandra Vincent got your DNA under her fingernails," I said to Captain Moe. "Did she attack you?"

He blushed and looked down at the floor. When he spoke, his voice was barely above a whisper. "Um, Tink . . . When I found Ms. Vincent in the conference room Sunday, that wasn't the first time we'd seen each other that day. We'd had brunch together."

I didn't get it. "And that's when she attacked you?"

His lips twitched. "She didn't attack me. She kissed me. And when she did, she ran her fingers through my hair. I guess that's when she got my DNA under her nails. Naturally, the police are refusing to believe that."

I was literally dumbstruck. I just stood there slack jawed and rooted to the floor, gazing up at the man.

Ted finally put a finger beneath my chin to remind me to close my mouth.

"B-but . . . but . . . But you two *hated* each other!" I sputtered.

"We disagreed on some things," said Captain Moe, "but we certainly didn't hate each other. We'd been socializing for a couple of weeks. It's how I became aware that the hospital was seeking a Santa."

"But when I arrived on Saturday, the two of you were arguing."

"As I said, Marcy, Sandy and I disagreed on some things—one of those things being that I wouldn't give preferential treatment to one child in the presence of the others. But she was an attractive woman. Intelligent, too." He shrugged. "I'm human. I like female companionship."

"Well, yeah, but . . . *her*?" I shook my head. "I just don't get it."

"Babe, we'd better get you back to town," Ted said. "Your customers are going to be wondering where you are. Riley, Moe, please let us know if there's anything you need or anything we can do."

They both said they would, and Ted got me out of there before I could say anything else derogatory.

Still, all the way home, I thought about—and talked about—how absurd the situation struck me.

"Captain Moe and *her*? I mean, yes, she was attractive, but she wanted him to kowtow to somebody named Carstairs. And Vera said the people at the hospital either hated her or loved her, but everyone loves Captain Moe. I just don't get the attraction." I turned to Ted. "Do you?"

"He said she was intelligent. Maybe she was someone with whom he could discuss the mysteries of the universe."

"You don't discuss the mysteries of the universe with somebody who has her hands buried in your hair."

Ted rubbed the bridge of his nose. "Then maybe he just thought she was hot."

I gasped. "Captain Moe is not that kind of guy."

"What kind of guy? The kind who enjoys spending time with an attractive woman?"

"Okay, so I guess he *is* that kind of guy." I slumped in my seat. "I just never thought of him in that way before. Was he ever married?"

"I have no idea, babe."

"I wonder if he has children." I slapped my hand to my forehead. "And I call this man my *friend*? I know nothing about him!"

"So, what? Now you're thinking maybe he did kill Sandra Vincent?"

"Of course not! I'm thinking I'm a lousy friend."

"You're not a lousy friend," he assured me. "You're a wonderful friend. If you handed out questionnaires to potential friends, that'd be creepy." He tried—and failed—to make his voice sound feminine. "Hi, I'm Marcy. Wanna be my friend? Then please answer the following questions: Have you ever been married? What's your favorite color? Do you have children? Have you ever been convicted of a crime? If so, felony or misdemeanor?"

"Oh, ha ha. You're hilarious."

"Sorry."

His smirk told me he was not sorry. He was amused. But I let the matter go.

Thankfully, Vera was the first person to step into the Seven-Year Stitch after Angus and I got there.

"Did you hear about Captain Moe?" she asked.

"Yes. Ted and I went to the arraignment this morning."

"Paul will have to report on it now. He doesn't want to, but now that Moe has been arrested, he has no choice."

"What's he going to say?" I asked.

She leaned forward. "What do you know?"

"Something that Paul can't put in the paper because it isn't public knowledge."

"It won't go any farther than the two of us. . . . At least, until you tell me otherwise."

"That woman got Captain Moe's DNA under her fingernails by running her fingers through his hair."

Her eyes widened. "You are kidding me!"

"I'm not. They had brunch and apparently had a make-out session, and then when he went to the hospital, he found her stabbed to death."

"What a horrible thing!" She went over to the sofa and sat down. "I mean, you leave someone after basking in her kisses and then find her dead? That's utterly tragic . . . so *Romeo and Juliet*."

"Vera, they aren't star-crossed teenage lovers. They're—" It dawned on me that Captain Moe was probably the same age as Paul and Vera.

She pursed her lips. "They're what? Old fogies?"

"No. They're *real*. And he's about to go on trial for her murder. Now it's more important than ever that we find out who killed Sandra Vincent. . . . Or at least provide Detectives Ray and Bailey with another viable suspect."

"That's true."

"I'm going there to the hospital tonight," I said. "I'll be reading to the children as Marcy the Elf, but I'll dig a little to see what I can find out."

"I hope you have more luck than I did."

"Do you think I'm a bad friend, Vera?"

"No, hon. I think you're a marvelous friend. Who told you that you aren't?"

"It just struck me today that there's so much about Captain Moe that I know nothing about and that maybe I'm insensitive."

"Oh, you're the last person I'd call insensitive. Maybe a little self-absorbed once in a while, but aren't we all?"

"I don't even know whether or not Captain Moe has any children."

"Well, for the record, he doesn't. I think that's why he's so crazy about Riley. Moe and Maggie never had any children of their own. I heard that she couldn't—some condition she was born with, I think—but they always treated Riley like she was their daughter instead of their niece."

"Tell me about Maggie," I said softly.

"She was a sweet woman. Petite and a little on the plump side." Vera's eyes wandered to the ceiling, as if she could see a scene playing out up there. "Boy, could she cook. We'd have potlucks and things like that—you know, for church or community events like the Fourth of July—and you always had to hurry if you wanted a taste of anything Maggie Patrick had brought. People loved her food."

"Did she work in the diner?"

Vera nodded. "Moe actually opened the diner for her. John gave them the loan based primarily on the popularity of Maggie's cooking, I believe."

John, Vera's late husband, had been a banker.

"So, if the diner was for Maggie, why is it named after him?" I asked.

"You know as well as I do that Moe can cook, too. But because he'd retired from the fishing-boat business to make her dream come true, she insisted on naming the diner Captain Moe's."

"That's sweet," I said. "So, where is she now?" I couldn't imagine that they'd divorced, because they seemed to have loved each other.

"She died of cancer about five years ago. Captain Moe was devastated."

"I'm so sorry." I sank down beside her on the sofa. "I should've known all this."

"Darling, how could you have possibly known?"

"I know a lot of things about your past. I know about John and how he died and—"

"That's because you were there," she interrupted. "I don't want to shout my life story from the rooftops, and most other people don't, either. It's one of the things people love about you, Marcy. You accept us as we are."

Chapter Nine

I was in the sit-and-stitch square, working on Christmas ornaments when Captain Moe came into the Seven-Year Stitch. As I greeted him, Angus snapped up his tennis ball and loped over to our guest.

He patted Angus before taking the tennis ball and lobbing it across the room. Angus scampered after it, and Captain Moe joined me on the sofa.

"How are you?" I asked.

"I've been better." He answered. "Do you think poorly of me for not telling you I was dating Ms. Vincent?"

Angus returned with the tennis ball, and Captain Moe threw it for him again.

"Of course not. I am curious as to why you didn't mention it, though."

"I didn't want you to think we were unprofessional, especially Sandra. She prided herself on maintaining her image. No one at the hospital knew that she and I had been seeing each other."

"Vera was in earlier," I said. "She was talking about your late wife."

He smiled slightly. "Margaret Ann Patrick was a wonderful woman. She hated that her initials upon marrying me became MAP, but I told her she was the map that had led me to happiness, and that made her okay with it."

Angus brought the tennis ball again. Rather than toss it, Captain Moe simply rubbed the dog's ears as if lost in thought.

"I adored that woman," he said. "She was a saint to have put up with me for as long as she did. I suppose Vera told you I lost Maggie to cancer."

"She did."

"Cancer is a cruel executioner, Tinkerbell. I hope you never cross paths with him."

Angus sensed the shift in mood and placed his head gently on Captain Moe's knee.

"I'm sorry I didn't know more about your past, about Maggie, before now," I said.

"I'd rather not dwell on losses. Life's too short to be sad all the time. Maggie and I had a wonderful life together, and I pray we'll see each other again on the other side. In the meantime, I must have something else to do with my life or else I wouldn't be here. Would I?"

"No, you wouldn't. And that something is *not* going to jail."

"Are you sure about that, Tink? Do you know something I don't?"

"I know you didn't kill Sandra Vincent, and I know the police will find her killer before it's too late."

"I hope you're right," he said.

"I know you and Riley have undoubtedly gone over all of this already, but did you see anything that gave you any indication of who might've been in that room before you got there?"

He shook his head. "Nothing appeared to be out of place—except, of course, that knife in Sandy's chest." He closed his eyes briefly. "I called for help. I hoped she was still alive. It must've happened minutes before I got there."

"Vera said it seemed to her that nobody was neutral about Ms. Vincent—that they either loved her or hated her. Was that your experience, as well?"

"I suppose so. She was an administrator, so naturally made enemies. She had to make some tough decisions sometimes, and that ruffled more than a few feathers."

"What about Carstairs—the man whose child she wanted you to be extra nice to?" I asked. "Was he friend or foe?"

"I'm not sure. I imagine Sandy would've wanted to count him among friends, since the board can limit what the administration can and can't do."

"But you aren't so sure they were friends?"

"No. I couldn't say for sure. We didn't talk too much about her work."

"Was Ms. Vincent in charge of the organ transplants?" I asked.

"I wouldn't say she was in charge," he said. "But

she did have some knowledge of it, I guess, maybe some control over it . . . I don't know."

I realized I was pretty much grilling Captain Moe about his deceased girlfriend and that I needed to be more sensitive.

"I'm really sorry for your loss," I said. "And I'm sorry I never knew Maggie."

"Thanks, Tink. I wish you could've known Maggie, too." He patted Angus's head one more time as he rose from the sofa. "I must be on my way, but I wanted you and Ted to know that I appreciated your support this morning. Riley did, too."

"We were serious. We'll do anything we can to help you."

"I know, my dear. See you soon."

He left, and Angus gave a slight sigh as he stretched out on the floor between the sofa and the coffee table.

"It'll be all right, Angus," I said. "At least, I hope it will."

I was restocking the floss bins when Veronica came by the shop. Tiffany wasn't with her this time, and I was a bit relieved. I liked Tiffany, but it was hard work watching everything I said and did in the hope that she'd like me.

"Hi, there," I said. "This is a nice surprise."

"Well, I saw Captain Moe getting indicted for murder on the noonday news. I thought I'd drop in and see what our plan might be."

I put my now-empty floss basket behind the counter and invited Veronica to join me in the sit-and-stitch square. We took the two club chairs on either end of the coffee table. Angus stayed where he was, halfway dozing beside the window. He tended to give Veronica a wide berth.

I told Veronica of my plan to go to the hospital and read to the children later that afternoon. Since I was giving classes only on Wednesdays during the months of November and December, I had more time to spare.

"And to snoop," she added.

"That, too. I thought that while I was at the hospital, I'd see what I could find out. Vera didn't have much luck turning up anything new."

"So, what do we know so far?"

Just as she said that, Ted came through the door with lunch. "I'd like to hear the answer to that myself."

"Hello, darling." Veronica turned and looked over her shoulder at her handsome son.

"I didn't know you'd be here, or I'd have brought extra. Let me run down to MacKenzies' Mochas—"

"I've already eaten. Marcy, dear, put that paperclock thing on the door, and let's get back to business."

Ted shot me a look of exasperation. I grinned and did as I was told. Angus got up and came to sit on the floor by Ted's side.

"You were getting ready to give Mom the rundown on what we know about Captain Moe's case," Ted said, as I sat beside him on the sofa.

"All right," I said. "We know that he and Sandra Vincent were dating. We know that she had wanted him to show favoritism to the son of Dr. Bellamy Carstairs—a request that Captain Moe refused."

"Wait. Carstairs." Veronica furrowed her brow. "I know that name. I think there's a couple named Carstairs who live in my complex. Maybe they're the doctor's parents. I'll look into it."

"Captain Moe came by earlier. He didn't know of anyone who might've wanted to hurt Ms. Vincent, but he did say that she likely made enemies in her business," I said. "There was a woman who stopped in yesterday whose mother was bumped down on the organ transplant list at the last minute. She said she'd spoken with Ms. Vincent about it."

"I'd certainly be upset if someone I loved was denied a needed organ," said Veronica. "Maybe even mad enough to kill."

"Mother!"

"I'm speaking hypothetically," she said. "I'm simply saying this woman might've had motive to murder Ms. Vincent."

"I don't think so," I said. "The woman was very sweet and had a toddler."

"Yes, but maybe she has a psychotic brother or something." Veronica raised an index finger. "You never know."

I looked at Ted. "She has a point."

"Don't encourage her." He opened his box of sweet and sour chicken and began eating.

"She'll encourage me, and I'll encourage her right back," she said. "Someone has to find the real killer.

Obviously, those Tallulah County detectives aren't going to do it." She brightened. "I've got it. We could be like *Charlie's Angels*, and you could be our Charlie. What do you say?"

I'd never seen Ted so completely absorbed by his food before. He ignored his mother and kept shoveling in that chicken.

Undeterred, she turned to me. "We can do this. You, me, and Vera. We'll find out who's behind this. Why, this person might even be framing Captain Moe."

I looked at Ted. He was still looking down into that box of chicken as if it contained the answers to all the questions in the universe.

She stood and got her purse. "Oh, well, I'll be off. Let me know what you find out tonight." She kissed the top of Ted's bent head before she left.

"Later, Mother." He looked up at me. "Let her know what you find out tonight?"

"Um, yeah. Didn't I tell you? I'm reading to a group of children at the hospital as Marcy the Elf this evening."

"You hadn't mentioned that."

"Well, that's because I was going to tell you after you got here." I smiled. "Want to tag along?"

"I believe I'll pass." He addressed Angus. "What do you say, pal? Want to watch some television while Inch-High Private Eye meddles at the hospital?"

The dog looked at him adoringly and panted.

"Good. It's a plan." He broke his fortune cookie in half and gave part of it to Angus.

"What does your fortune say?"

"Two beautiful women will be the death of you."

"Aw . . . you think your mom and I are beautiful."

Not long after lunch, a young woman came in. She appeared timid and unsure of herself. Sensing her general discomfort, Angus stayed where he was near the window.

"Hi, I'm Marcy. Welcome to the Seven-Year Stitch. How may I help you?"

"I'm working on a pillow for a project in my art class? I'm in college?"

I hoped that when she gained more confidence, she would outgrow the habit of making everything into a question.

"And the instructions said I need to finish the pillow using a Palestine stitch? Do you know what I mean?"

"I believe you're talking about a Palestrina stitch." I went over to the shelf, took down a book on embroidery stitches, and turned to the Palestrina-stitch illustrations. "Is this how the pillow was finished in your instructions?"

"Yes." Her face broke into a smile of relief. "Could you show me how?"

"Of course. I wish you'd brought the pillow with you. We could simply complete it here."

"Wait. I could do that? You'd help me?"

"Sure. I mean, I don't want to get you into any trouble with your instructor. . . ."

"Oh, I won't get into trouble," she said. "Let me run home and get the pillow, and I'll be back. Is that okay?"

"That's fine. I close at five."

"I only live about fifteen minutes away." She hurried out the door.

I decided I should probably take Angus up the street before the young woman returned. When she got back, we were likely to be busy working on her project until almost closing time. I put my cell phone in my pocket and snapped Angus's leash onto his collar.

He hadn't seemed particularly eager to leave his sanctuary by the window, but once I opened the door, he took off like a shot. It was all I could do to hang on to him.

I barely missed a customer coming out of Nellie Davis's aromatherapy shop, Scentsibilities. She was a woman wearing nursing scrubs.

"I'm sorry!" I called over my shoulder.

"No problem." I could hear laughter in her tone.

We got up to the town square, a grassy area flanked by wooden and wrought-iron benches. Angus made a beeline for the large clock at the top center of the square. He sniffed all around the base of the clock and then went to snuffle the benches.

My phone rang. Glad that Angus was calmly investigating the square so I could answer, I fished the phone from my purse. It was Veronica calling.

"Hi," I said. "Have you solved the case already? If so, you're really quick."

"I wish. I did confirm that the Carstairs who have a unit in my condo building have a son who is a doctor and also on the board of directors at Tallulah County General. I'm lunching with them tomorrow."

"Did they mention a grandson who's ill?"

"No, but I'll see what I can find out," she said.

Chapter Ten

After talking with Veronica, I called Rajani "Reggie" Singh, our local librarian. She is also married to Manu Singh, Chief of Police. I explained to Reggie that I needed a few Christmas books to read to the children at Tallulah General Hospital that evening.

"Would you mind pulling a few for me, and I'll leave early so I can run by the library and pick them up before you close?"

"Actually, I'm in dire need of a coffee break, so I'll bring them over in a few minutes. Will that work?"

"That would be fantastic."

When Reggie arrived, she brought not only the Christmas books, but also a dog biscuit for Angus. She and Manu had no dogs of their own, but she kept the treats on hand for her library patrons to pass along to her favorite pets.

Unlike her husband, Reggie favored her traditional Indian dress. Today, she was wearing a turquoise tunic and matching slacks embellished with white embroidery. She spread the books out on the counter. There were some familiar titles—*A Christmas Carol*, *How the Grinch Stole Christmas*—and some unfamiliar ones, like *The Christmas Puppy* and *Snowmen at Christmas*.

She held up one book titled *Junie B. Jones and the Yucky Blucky Fruitcake*, with an impish little girl on the cover. "This is Junie B. I don't know if you'll have time to read one of these books or not, but the kids love them. This one isn't Christmassy—the Christmas book is checked out, and I don't think you'd have time to read it, anyway—but there *is* a fruitcake in this one."

"A nutty person or an actual fruitcake?"

She smiled. "The cake."

Reggie left and headed toward MacKenzies' Mochas. I opened the fruitcake book and began reading it. In minutes, I was laughing aloud. Marcy the Elf was definitely reading this to the children.

When I walked up to the nurse's station on the pediatric floor of Tallulah County General Hospital, I saw the woman I'd nearly bumped into when Angus and I were walking past Scentsibilities.

After work, I went home and changed into my elf costume. Ted had called before I left work and said he'd be there soon to feed Angus, so before leaving the house, I kissed the top of the dog's furry head and told him to be good and that Ted would be there to feed him and watch TV with him. In turn, he licked my nose. I felt we'd understood each other perfectly.

When I walked up to the nurse's station on the pediatric floor of Tallulah County General Hospital, I saw the woman I'd nearly bumped into when Angus and I were walking past Scentsibilities.

"Hi," I said. "I apologize again for nearly plowing over you earlier today."

She looked confused until I mentioned the words *Irish wolfhound.*

"Oh, it's you!" She hooted with laughter. "I'm just glad to see you made it back from your walk in one piece."

"Thanks. I'm here to read to the children this evening."

"Right. I wrote myself a note about that." She looked around on the desktop until she located a sticky note. "You're Marcy?"

"That's me."

"Well, nice to meet you, Marcy. I'm Carrie Monahan."

"Good to meet you. I suppose I also need to turn in my elf costume after the reading. It *does* belong to the hospital, doesn't it?"

"Gee, I have no idea. I'll have to look into that."

"I was thinking it belonged to the hospital because Sandra Vincent gave it to me to put on when I came in to take the place of the elf whose child got sick on Friday," I said. "I was here Saturday, and then I came back on Sunday. Of course, the security guard didn't let me in. I was stunned to find out about what had happened."

"I know. It was awful. And Ms. Vincent must've been murdered not long before you'd arrived." Her lips twisted into a wry smile. "Poor Charlie. He's the security guard put in charge of guarding the door by the homicide detectives. He was only supposed to be there until the crime-scene technicians arrived, but he stayed his whole shift."

"Well, no one can accuse him of abandoning his post."

"That's for sure, even though I know the entire ordeal probably scared him half to death. He looks tough, but he's really a softie."

"I know it would've freaked me out. What was your opinion of Sandra Vincent?" I asked. "I only met her once, and though she didn't strike me as overly friendly, I wouldn't have thought she'd have an enemy who'd go so far as to kill her."

"You never do know." Carrie shook her head sadly. "I think that for the most part, Ms. Vincent was a pretty good administrator, but I don't believe she was prepared for all of the politics involved. In order to keep her job and to keep the hospital running smoothly, she had to keep the board members satisfied. And, naturally, each of them have their own agendas—construction kickbacks, favorite programs."

"I do recall her asking the man who played Santa to show favoritism to a child by the name of Carstairs," I said. "But Santa refused."

"Brendan Carstairs is a good kid," she said. "Yeah, he comes from a privileged home, but if I had a son with leukemia and I had the means, I'd give him everything he could possibly want." She glanced at the clock. "We'd better get you into the playroom. The natives will be getting restless."

She led me into the playroom, which was primarily an empty room with cushions and bean-bag chairs on the floor gathered around a large wooden rocking chair. The nurse was right. The children were already there and waiting. They cheered when she brought me into the room.

The ones who were unable to sit on the floor were in wheelchairs. I wondered if Brendan Carstairs was among those gathered to hear the story.

I sat down on the rocking chair and read to my captive audience for nearly an hour. When I got up to leave, many of them raised their arms for a hug. There were a handful of nurses standing about the room. I caught one's eyes, and she gave me a nod that it was all right for me to hug the children. I guessed they would've been quarantined or I'd have been asked to wear a surgical mask had germs been a high risk for these particular patients. I hugged each one of them at least once.

I went back out to the nurse's station. Carrie Monahan wasn't at her post, but she returned after only a few moments.

"How'd it go?" she asked. "I heard lots of laughter coming from the room."

"I wish I could stay. And the kids seemed to want that, too, but I could tell some of them were getting tired. Someone asked if I could come back, and I said I'd try. I don't think I'd be as much fun if I returned as just Marcy as opposed to Marcy the Elf."

"Everyone in the administration office has gone home tonight. Let me check with them tomorrow and see what I can find out about the costume, and I'll give you a call and let you know when and where to return it." She shrugged. "For all I know, some costume shop is wondering where its elf suit went."

I wished her a good night and headed for the elevator. The car stopped on the floor below, and a woman got in. She was sobbing.

She raised her head to make sure the car was headed for the lobby, and I could see that it was Dani, the woman who'd come into the Seven-Year Stitch, looking for the huck-embroidery patterns.

"Dani?" I put my hand on her sleeve.

She turned slowly. "D-do I know you?"

"I'm Marcy Singer from the Seven-Year Stitch."

"Of course. I d-didn't recognize you. Like that."

"I've been upstairs reading to the children," I said. "Is there anything I can do?"

She gulped. "M-mom just d-died."

"I'm so sorry."

The elevator doors opened, and we stepped out into the lobby together.

"Let me buy you a coffee," I said. "Are you alone? You can't possibly drive in this condition."

"I'll be okay."

"Please. Let's go down to the cafeteria and get a coffee. I can't leave you like this."

"O-okay."

The cafeteria was located on the basement floor, which was just below the lobby. We got back into the elevator and went down. The kitchen part of the cafeteria was closed, but there were vending machines, and the area where patients and staff could sit at the tables was still open.

Dani got a soda, and I got a hot cocoa. My cocoa tasted more like hot water than anything, but I only got it to keep Dani from feeling out of place. We sat at a table near the door.

"Is there someone I could call for you?" I asked softly.

She shook her head. "My husband is home with Nicole. She's sleeping. The only other person I have here—or *had* here—in Tallulah Falls was Mom." Fresh tears spilled onto her cheeks, and I got up and retrieved some napkins from the condiment counter.

Dani thanked me as she dabbed at her eyes and blew her nose. "This was just so unexpected. I mean, I realized there was a chance she could die, but I'd held on to the hope for so long that she'd get that liver transplant in time. I was shocked when her body just gave out."

"I'm so terribly sorry."

"You want to know the real kicker?" she asked. "The person who got put in front of Mom on the transplant list, his body rejected the liver, and he's in intensive care. If they'd just left the list as it was supposed to have been—if they hadn't bumped him up in front of Mom—then maybe they'd both have received the livers they were supposed to have received, the ones that would've been most compatible for them."

I wanted to say there was no way of knowing that for sure, but I realized that wouldn't have been of any comfort to Dani. So instead I said nothing.

"And now Nicole is going to grow up without her grandmother," she said.

"But you'll always keep her in your daughter's

heart," I said. "I know you will. You'll have photos and stories. . . ."

"Yeah, but it's not the same. It's not like they'll get to make their own memories."

"I know."

"I'm sorry," Dani said. "Here you are, trying to help, and all I can do is complain."

"I don't blame you a bit," I said. "If I were in your shoes, I'd be inconsolable. I'm here to listen whether you want to rant and rave or whether you just want to reflect. I'll help you any way I can—goofy outfit and all."

She smiled slightly. "Thank you. You're sweet to do this. You don't even know me."

"I know you're hurting, and I wish I could help."

"You have," she said. "I think I'm actually calm enough to drive home now."

"Are you sure?"

She nodded. "I really appreciate your staying with me."

"You're welcome. If there's anything else I can do to help, please let me know."

I went home to the coziest, happiest scene. It almost made me feel guilty over my good fortune.

Ted, wearing jeans and an Oregon Ducks sweatshirt, was stretched out on the sofa, watching TV with a big bowl of popcorn on his lap. Lying on the floor beside him, Angus munched his bite of popcorn. There was a fire in the fireplace, and the Christmastree lights were twinkling.

I began to cry.

Ted jumped up off the couch, upsetting the popcorn bowl, and hurried to me. "Are you all right? I didn't hear you come in. What's wrong?"

Poor Angus was torn between seeing what was wrong with me and letting Ted handle it while he gobbled up the popcorn.

Ted enfolded me in his arms.

"I'm all right. In fact, I'm fantastic. I think I must be the luckiest woman alive."

"And that makes you sad?"

"No. It makes me so happy." I explained about meeting up with Dani in the elevator. "I didn't know what to do, Ted. I couldn't just leave her there. I wish I had her number so I could call and make sure she got home all right."

"She's fine, thanks to you. It was wonderful of you to take the time to help her calm down before she got out on the road."

I snuggled against his chest. "And it wasn't just Dani. Seeing all those children there in the hospital was terrible. Children shouldn't be in a hospital. They should be running and jumping or swinging on the playground."

"And, hopefully, they will again someday soon. You're looking at all the bad and at none of the good. Did the kids enjoy having you read to them?"

I smiled. "They did. It was precious. And they all had to have a hug before I left."

"See?"

"I do see," I said. "It's just that sometimes it strikes

you how very blessed you are, and you need to take the time to cherish those blessings."

"I have to agree with you there. Be like Angus. Gobble up those blessings, even if it means having to crawl under the sofa to find them."

I laughed. Angus was doing a bang-up job of cleaning the carpet, although I'd get the vacuum cleaner and finish the job soon.

"Speaking of finding things, did you learn anything that might be helpful to Captain Moe's case?" Ted asked.

"Maybe. I spoke with one of the nurses—Carrie Monahan. She said that she thought Ms. Vincent had tried to be a good administrator but that politics had gotten in her way. She mentioned construction kickbacks, and that made me remember a customer who came in the other day," I said. "Her husband is a construction contractor. He put in the lowest bid for the hospital's cancer ward but lost out to another company. After he began looking into the matter, his company stopped getting work, and they had to move to Lincoln City."

"What was the name of the other construction company?"

"She didn't say. Vera was there at the time, and she mentioned after the woman left that she'd ask Paul to look into it. I haven't heard anything more about it, though."

"I might look into it myself."

Chapter Eleven

Wednesday morning was unseasonably sunny and warm for Tallulah Falls in December. I loved it. When I went into the Stitch in my jeans and long-sleeved T-shirt, I felt like changing Jill out of her dress and apron and putting her in a bathing suit. But, of course, I didn't. Tomorrow it would probably be cold and rainy again.

While Angus was gnawing on a granola bone by the window, I did a quick inventory to see what I needed before the holiday rush. I knew I'd need more complete kits—cross-stitch, needlepoint, hand embroidery, and crewel—for those looking for last-minute gifts. And I needed pattern books and floss for those patrons who had projects they were trying to complete.

My cell phone rang. It was Salt-N-Pepa's "Whatta Man," so I knew before I even got the phone out of my pocket that it was Ted.

"Hi, sweetheart," I answered.

"Hey, there. I found the name of that construction company that won the bid for Tallulah County General's cancer ward. It's Martin Brothers Construction. I called my friend at the TCPD and gave him the information."

"Do you think he'll pass it along to Bailey and Ray or look into it himself?"

"I'm not sure," he said. "I wish *I* could follow up and talk with the Martins myself, but, of course, I can't. It isn't our case. And I have my own cases to work."

"I know, babe. You're doing all you can. I know that and so does Captain Moe."

"I hope he does. Anyway, Doug will see to it that someone talks with the Martins if any connection can be made between them and Sandra Vincent. For example, if there was some new construction project in the works and she or the board had earmarked someone else for the job, then the Martins could be suspects in Vincent's death."

"It's worth looking into," I said.

"Doug will take care of it. I know you don't particularly trust Ray and Bailey, but they'll investigate the lead and find out whether or not there's any possibility that someone at Martin Brothers Construction is involved in this murder. Those detectives don't want an innocent man convicted, either, Inch-High."

"I know."

"Gotta run. See you at lunch."

After talking with Ted, I finished my inventory and then got the laptop from my office and brought it into the sit-and-stitch square so I could order my supplies. I'd just pressed PLACE ORDER when Reggie came into the shop.

"Hi, there," I said. "You didn't have to make a special trip. I was going to drop your books off this afternoon."

"It isn't a special trip. I was on my way to MacKenzies' Mochas. I stopped in to see if you'd like anything."

"I would." I put the laptop aside and got my purse. "Would you please bring me back a low-fat vanilla latte with cinnamon?"

"Will do." She looked at Angus, who had come to sit at her feet. "And what would you like, Mr. O'Ruff?"

He just panted.

"Bring him a peanut butter or a shortbread cookie please. Tell Blake it's for Angus and to pick out one that's smaller than the others or broken or something."

Reggie covered Angus's ears with her hands. "You want Blake to give this baby an inferior cookie?"

"Well, if there was one he was going to throw away because he can't sell it to a customer, then that would work out fine."

She shook her head. "All right. Be back in a minute."

When she returned, she had her cappuccino, my latte, and a peanut butter cookie as big as a saucer. There was a note written in Blake's block-style handwriting: *Angus doesn't get reject cookies.*

I rolled my eyes at Reggie. "Well, *I'd* settle for a reject cookie."

"He said you say that," Reggie said. "And he wanted me to tell you he doesn't *make* reject cookies."

I laughed. "And the win goes to Mr. MacKenzie."

I handed Angus his cookie and he sprinted off to

the office with it. That was probably smart, as he'd likely need a drink of water after eating it.

Reggie sat down on the sofa as I got her books from my tote behind the counter.

"You were right." I brought the books over and sat on a red club chair. "The kids loved the little girl in this book. It was great."

"I'm sure you did a fantastic job with it. Have you heard how things are going with Captain Moe's case?"

"He was arrested on Monday."

"I heard about that. He's out on bail, right?"

"Right," I said. "And hopefully another suspect will turn up soon. I know Captain Moe didn't kill that woman."

"Do the police have other suspects?"

"I have no idea. Detectives Bailey and Ray aren't very forthcoming with information, at least not to anyone I know." I told her about the customer whose husband had submitted the lowest bid for the cancer ward and had practically been run out of town by the company who was awarded the contract.

"What was the name of the other company?"

"Martin Brothers Construction."

She frowned. "I know that name. I can't remember the specifics, but they were involved in some shady business practices that had to do with a case Manu was working a few years back. I'll ask him if he remembers the case."

"Ted keeps telling me to have a little more faith in Ray and Bailey. He says they don't want an innocent man to be convicted. I'm just afraid they want a conviction so badly that they'll convince themselves of Captain Moe's guilt."

"I don't think so. I know that Manu has been pressured to make arrests before." She shook her head. "In fact, every time you have a murder, there's pressure from the public, from the owners of the place where the body was found, from the victim's family. But the point is, that doesn't force Manu to give up. He has to make sure within himself that the person is guilty."

"And you believe the other detectives hold themselves to the same standards?"

"I hope they do. Granted, they'll be looking at evidence that justifies their arresting Captain Moe at this stage, but they can't ignore something that points to another suspect."

"Okay."

"Captain Moe will be all right," she said. "Riley is a wonderful attorney."

"And, on top of that, she's calling in Cam Whitting."

"Well, there you go. Plus, all the evidence against Captain Moe is circumstantial. Everything will be fine."

I desperately hoped so.

I was waiting on a customer when my phone rang. I finished checking out my customer's purchases before calling the number back.

"Tallulah County General Hospital. Head Nurse Monahan speaking."

"Hi. This is Marcy Singer. I just got a call from your number."

"Yes, that was me—Carrie. I'm over the pediatric ward. We spoke last night?"

"Of course. How are you?"

"I'm just great. I did find out about your costume. We rented it from a local shop. They understood about the extenuating circumstances and told me we could keep it for a few more days at no extra charge."

"Oh, that's good. I'll bring it to you tomorrow, if that's okay."

"That would be fine. I was actually hoping that when you bring it, you could *wear* it and read to the children one more time. They enjoyed having you here so much."

"Um, all right. Sure." How could I say no? "What time would you like for me to be there?"

"Could you be here at six thirty tomorrow evening?"

"I can. I'll look forward to seeing you—and the kids—then."

I made a mental note to call Reggie and ask if I could borrow the Christmas books again. Maybe she had another funny book she could recommend.

I had an older customer come in looking for spiral-eye needles.

"My eyesight just isn't what it used to be," she said. "And it's so darn hard to thread a needle anymore. A friend told me to look into these spiral-eye needles."

I took her over to the needles and showed her the various sizes of spiral-eye needles I had in stock.

"If you need a different size, I'll be happy to order it for you."

"I think one of these will be good to get me started.

I want to try them out before I invest too much in them." She squinted at the needle. "I can't see how the thread keeps from coming out after you put it in there."

"It's the spiral design that keeps the thread from moving back out the side once it's in the needle. Would you like to try it out?"

"No. I'll take this one. May I return it if it doesn't work for me?"

The bells over the door heralded Vera's arrival as I assured my customer that she could return the needle if she didn't like it. She paid for her purchase and left.

I joined Vera on the sofa, where she was patting Angus's head.

"How are you today?" I asked.

"I'm doing fantastic, and I'm a virtual font of knowledge."

"Wow. Speak, oh, wise one."

She leaned toward me. "Well, I found out the name of that construction company that beat out your customer's husband and ran him out of town."

"Let me guess: Martin Brothers Construction."

She huffed. "How'd you know?"

"Ted found out. He passed the name along to his friend on the Tallulah County Police force to see what he could find out about the company and whether or not it has any ties to Sandra Vincent."

"Well, do you know the three finalists who were up for Sandra Vincent's job when she was hired this past June?"

"No."

Vera immediately brightened. "They were Sandra Vincent, of course, Carrie Monahan, and Melanie Carstairs."

"Melanie Carstairs? The doctor's wife?"

"The very same."

"If her husband is on the board, I wonder why she didn't get the job," I mused.

"Maybe he didn't want her to have it. Or maybe he was the only board member who *did* want her to have it."

"Interesting. Ted's mom is having lunch with Dr. Carstairs's parents today. I'll let her know what we've found out. Maybe she can find a way to ask them about it."

"If she does, let me know what they say," said Vera.

"I will. By the way, Carrie Monahan . . . She's a nurse, isn't she?"

"I don't know. Why?"

"There's a Carrie Monahan who is over in the pediatric ward at the hospital. She called me this morning and asked me to come read to the children again."

"Then I imagine she's the one who was a finalist for the job. I wonder if they'll give it to her now that Ms. Vincent is dead."

"I'm going there tomorrow. I'll see what I can learn." I patted Vera's shoulder. "Thanks for doing all this digging. You're a regular Nancy Drew."

"Aw, I'm a little old to be Nancy Drew. I'm more like her older, more sophisticated sister."

After Vera left, I called Veronica.

"Hi, darling," she said. "Do you have news about the case?"

"Possibly." I told her about Vera's findings.

"So, Melanie Carstairs was a finalist for the hospital administrator position but she didn't get the job. How can I finagle the reason out of Mr. and Mrs. Carstairs?"

"I have no idea how you could inconspicuously broach that subject. When is your lunch?"

"In half an hour, so I'll have to think quickly. Don't worry, though. I'll come up with something."

"I have confidence in you. If anyone can charm this information out of Mr. and Mrs. Carstairs, it's you."

"Thank you. By the way, Tiffany, Mark, and Jackson are coming to town and would like to know if you're available for lunch. Tiffany has already called and left a message on Ted's phone."

"Okay. I'm sure he'll call me when he gets the message, then."

"So you're free?" she asked.

"Yes."

"Good. Then hopefully, it's all set. Even if Ted can't make it, I'll tell Tiffany that you can. I know it's easiest for you to meet at MacKenzies' Mochas like we did the other day. And it's a charming place."

"Right."

"Don't sound so disconsolate, darling. Mark and Jackson will be there, even if Ted can't make it. They both like you very much."

"Gee, thanks."

She laughed. "And Tiffany is getting there. Just give her a little more time."

Chapter Twelve

Ted walked into the Seven-Year Stitch at one o'clock with a dental bone for Angus. He thought maybe the bone would keep the dog happy while he and I were down the street at MacKenzies' Mochas. Angus immediately took the bone over to his favorite spot in front of the window and began chewing on it.

"Thank you," I said.

"Thank *you*. I know being under Tiffany's scrutiny isn't easy for you, and I appreciate your continuing to make the effort to get to know her better."

"I just hope she'll come to realize that I'm nothing like . . . people from your past."

He pulled me to him and gave me a thorough kiss. "You aren't like anyone I've ever known."

I smiled. "Ditto."

The bells over the door jingled.

"Get a room!" yelled Mark.

Blushing, I took a step backward.

"I got woom!" Jackson laughed and ran to Ted with his arms outstretched.

Ted swooped him off the ground and spun around with him.

Angus watched disinterestedly from his spot by the window. Then he resumed gnawing on his bone.

The little boy giggled. "More!"

Ted spun him again. "We'd better stop now, pal, or we'll both be dizzy."

"Dizzy."

Tiffany wandered around the shop. "This is nice. I like that you have a conversation area set apart from the merchandise."

"Thank you," I said. "It gives people a place to hang out and work on their needlecraft projects or chat. And sometimes I help people learn particular stitches—things like that."

"Marcy also teaches classes here three evenings a week," Ted said.

"I typically have classes Tuesday, Wednesday, and Thursday evenings," I said. "But I pared down to one class for the months of November and December."

"What class are you currently teaching?" she asked.

"Crewel embroidery."

"Sounds cool," Tiffany said.

"Are any of your classes available online?" Mark asked.

"No. I actually hadn't considered that."

"You should think about it. It's a good passive-income builder." Mark smiled. "I love passive income."

"I'll look into it," I said. "Thanks."

"We'd better go on to lunch," Ted said. "I need to get back to work soon."

"Big case?" asked Mark.

Ted shrugged. "Nothing I can't handle."

I wondered what Ted *was* working on. He hadn't mentioned anything to me. But, then, all our time talking about investigations had centered on Captain Moe and his predicament.

I locked up the Stitch, and we all walked down the street to MacKenzies' Mochas. Sadie was delighted to see Jackson again, and so was Blake. They'd been trying to have a baby. I truly wished they could.

"Tell me your name again, handsome fella," Sadie said.

"Jackson," he answered her.

"Well, you certainly are precious. Isn't he, Blake?"

"I'll say. You wouldn't steal my wife away from me, would you, buddy?"

"Steal!" yelled Jackson.

We laughed.

"After lunch, come back up here to the counter, and I'll give you a cookie," said Blake. "Do you like cookies?"

Jackson nodded.

Sadie showed us to a table, and we sat down.

"They seem like a nice couple," Tiffany said.

"They are. I've known them since Sadie and I were in college together."

"This is a really nice coffee shop, too," she said.

"It was a bar until Blake and Sadie converted it," said Ted. "That's why the counter is, well, a bar."

"I like this town," Mark said. "I mean, we've visited before, but we've been able to spend more time here than usual."

"Would you think of moving here?" Ted asked, looking at his sister rather than at Mark.

"We aren't sure. It'd be great to live closer to Mom. Mark would like to switch jobs, but I love the school I'm at." She and her husband exchanged glances. "We're going to talk more about it over the Christmas holidays."

The waitress arrived and took our orders. After she left, no one was willing to pick back up the discussion of Tiffany and Mark possibly moving to Tallulah Falls.

"Mark, do you have any brothers or sisters?" I asked.

"I have an older brother. He's a dentist in San Antonio."

"Is that where you're from—Texas?"

"My family is actually from Oklahoma," he said. "Now we're scattered hither and yon. What about you, Marcy? Ted tells us you moved here from San Francisco."

"I did. I worked in an accounting office, and then Sadie urged me to come here and open the Seven-Year Stitch. It was the best decision I've ever made." I smiled at Ted. "In more ways than one."

Mark groaned. "Here we go with this again."

"Go 'gin," said Jackson.

When Ted and I got back to the shop, Angus appeared eager to go out.

"I'll take him," said Ted.

"Thanks." I handed Ted the leash, and he snapped it onto Angus's collar.

I noticed as they headed up the street that Ted had a much easier time making Angus heel than I did. I often felt that if the sidewalk was icy, Angus would have me practically skiing to the town square.

Before we'd left MacKenzies' Mochas, I'd borrowed today's *Tallulah Falls Examiner* from Sadie. I turned to the obituaries page and scanned the listings until I came to one that contained the phrases *survived by daughter Danielle* and *granddaughter Nicole*. The visitation by the family would take place on Friday evening.

When Ted and Angus returned, I asked Ted if he'd go with me to see Dani.

"I realize I don't even know the woman—I'd only met her the one time she'd come to my shop—but I was there in the elevator right after her mother died, and I just want to pay my respects."

"I know, and of course I'll go with you." He gave me a quick kiss.

Ted hadn't been gone but half an hour when his mom called.

"Let me tell you, Marcy, the Carstairs don't think highly of their daughter-in-law."

"Why not?" I asked.

"I get the feeling it's because she exists," said Veronica. "The Carstairs wanted their darling Bellamy to marry a woman with both money *and* breeding. Melanie didn't have much of either, but they made do with the fact that she was beautiful. At least, she was until caring full-time for an ill child took its toll."

"I don't think I'd like the Carstairs very much."

"I didn't. I snobbed it up with them over lunch, but I declined their invitation for bridge tomorrow. I told them I needed to spend time with my daughter and her family before they left town."

"If Melanie cares for her son full-time, then why did she even apply for the hospital administrator position?" I asked.

"The Carstairs seemed to think she was using it as an excuse to get away for at least eight hours a day. She'd planned on taking the nanny on full-time rather than part-time. She'd told Bellamy that she'd wanted to be able to make decisions that could ultimately affect the life of their child and of others."

"That seems very noble."

"Well, of course that wasn't true." Veronica affected an outraged tone. "She merely wanted to play around all day while someone else took care of their grandchild. She couldn't possibly have an altruistic motive, because the perfect Bellamy said so."

"And I wouldn't be surprised to learn that *the perfect Bellamy* kept her from getting that job."

"You'd be right on the money with that bet. The Carstairs laughed about how Bellamy had her application shot down by the board."

"But how could he do that?" I asked. "If she was qualified and wound up being one of the final candidates, how did he persuade the board to choose Sandra Vincent over her?"

"He either had enough influence or enough dirt to make a majority of the board vote against her. He did vote for her, though, to make himself look good in her eyes."

"What a jerk. If he doesn't care for her any more than that, then why doesn't he divorce her?"

"It would upset the child, darling. And Bellamy is *perfect*. He'd never do anything that would upset the child."

"How did you get Mr. and Mrs. Carstairs to open up about Bellamy and his wife?"

"I can assure you it didn't take much," said Veronica. "All I had to do was ask how their poor son was dealing with someone on his staff having been murdered."

"How *is* he dealing with it?"

"As well as can be expected. They said he didn't know Ms. Vincent terribly well but that he was saddened by her loss. And the thought of someone killing her right there in *his* hospital was abominable."

"Abominable?"

"As abominable as it gets, darling."

"Did they know of anyone who might've wanted to harm Ms. Vincent?" I asked.

"No, but I joked that perhaps it was their daughter-in-law, and said I seemed to recall that she was one of the finalists for the position of hospital administrator. We all had a hearty laugh over that, and then they told me the story of Melanie's quest for the position."

"I feel sorry for Melanie."

"So do I, Marcy. I hope she and her son can somehow find a way out of the gilded cage they're in. But enough about that for now. Tell me about how your lunch went."

I took Angus home and then I went to the library. The Tallulah Falls Public Library was located in a Victorian house with white rocking chairs on the front porch. It being December, however, the chairs were turned over and leaning against the wall. I went inside and spotted Reggie manning the front desk.

"Hi, there," I said. "The hospital called, and they'd like for me to come back and read to the children again tomorrow evening. Do you have any other funny books they'd like?"

"I'm sure I do." She led me into the large children's area off the main library. "By the way, I spoke with Manu and he remembered that construction company. With the case he was working, Martin Brothers Construction had been underbid by an independent contractor. That contractor was later mugged and beaten so badly that he wound up in the hospital."

"Oh, my gosh! Did Manu think Martin Brothers Construction had something to do with the mugging?"

"He thought they had *everything* to do with it, but there wasn't enough evidence to prove it. Manu said they're a shady crew and that he wouldn't trust them to build a shed in our backyard, much less a hospital cancer ward."

"That's scary," I said. "If the Martin brothers are that ruthless, who knows what else they might do?"

"Exactly." She spread her hands. "I wouldn't doubt they use substandard materials and cut corners every way they can."

"And they might not be above killing someone."

I didn't have time to go back home and eat dinner before class, so I ate a protein bar I had in my desk drawer. Vera arrived early for class.

"Yoo-hoo! It's Vera!"

"Hi, Vera! I'm in the office. Come on back."

She came in and sat on the chair beside my desk. "Is that your dinner?"

I nodded.

"Bleh. You should've called me. I'd have brought you something."

"I'm fine," I said.

"Did you ever find out anything about Melanie Carstairs and why she didn't get the hospital administration job?"

"I did." I told her what Veronica had told me after having lunch with Mr. and Mrs. Carstairs. "They're apparently pieces of work."

She harrumphed. "I think that's sad. Poor Melanie would've probably been good at that job. She has more motivation than most, you know?"

"That's what I thought."

My phone rang. I looked down at the screen and saw that it was Veronica. I hadn't come up with an appropriate ringtone for her yet, so it was just my default ring.

"Let me get this," I told Vera. "Hold on."

I took the call and was surprised that Veronica was inviting Ted and me to a holiday soiree at her complex Friday night.

"The Carstairs will be there," said Veronica. "*All* of them. Mrs. Carstairs just told me so in the lobby."

"I wouldn't miss it," I said.

After ending the call, I gave Vera the news.

"I'll tell Paul. Of course, he might know about it already and just assumed it was simply another boring party. No offense to Veronica."

"None taken."

"But I think it would be good for Paul and me to be there as well, don't you? That way we could all do some sleuthing."

"The more, the merrier," I said.

Chapter Thirteen

Wednesday evening's crewel class had been a nice distraction from all the craziness that had been going on for the past few days. When I got home, I'd called Ted and we worked out the details of attending the visitation for Dani's mother and then attending his mother's party on Friday.

"Have you heard anything new about the case from your friend at the TCPD?" I asked.

"No. It appears that Ray and Bailey are certain they have the right guy. I suppose it doesn't help that Captain Moe's brother is currently serving time in federal prison."

"That's not fair."

"I know, but keep in mind that Doug is there at the station, and he's still looking for suspects."

"But is he actively working the case?"

"As actively as the rest of us are," he said.

I went to bed that night feeling rather dejected for Captain Moe.

Yet I rose this morning with renewed optimism.

The rest of us—me, Ted, Vera, Paul, Doug, Veronica, and Riley—*were* working as hard as we could to get justice for our friend, and we'd get him exonerated. I knew we would. Whether that affirmation remained with me throughout the rest of the day remained to be seen, but I set off for the Seven-Year Stitch feeling hopeful.

Angus seemed hopeful, too . . . or, at least, frisky. He raced into the Stitch as soon as I opened the door, grabbed his Kodiak bear, and tossed it into the air. He played like that for several minutes until he wore himself out and lay down on his bed beneath the counter.

I was cross-stitching an angel Christmas ornament when Riley came through the front door with a drink carrier and a bag from MacKenzies' Mochas. She went to the sit-and-stitch square and put the bag on the coffee table.

"I have a mint mocha and a cinnamon latte. I love them both. Which would you like?"

"I'll take whichever one you want the least," I said.

Without looking to see which was which, she took one coffee out of the carrier and handed it to me. It was the mint mocha, and it was wonderful.

She took two huge cinnamon rolls out of the bag and handed me one of those.

"You know how you're not an alcoholic if you don't drink alone?"

"Okay." I dragged out the word.

"Well, I'm not depressed if I have breakfast with a

friend rather than stuffing my face and crying in my office, right?"

"Okay."

"Stop saying that and eat your cinnamon roll."

At the smell of cinnamon roll and coffee, Angus came out from under the counter, sniffing curiously.

"You can have a bite of mine in a few minutes," Riley told him. "That way I'll only have to run on the treadmill an extra hour rather than an extra hour and a half."

Thankful that I'd set my cross-stich work on the seat of the red club chair when Riley came in, I tore a piece off the sticky cinnamon roll and popped it into my mouth. It, too, was wonderful.

"Is it Captain Moe's case that's got you down?" I asked.

"I'm not down. I'm merely having breakfast with a friend. But, yes, the case could be going much better."

"Do you want to talk about it?"

She sipped her latte. "Cam Whitting can't be here in person. He's working on a case in Seattle that has him tied up for the next few weeks. But at least he has agreed to consult."

"What advice is he giving?"

"Nothing I didn't know already. He says not to give an inch to the Tallulah County Police Department. All the evidence against Uncle Moe is circumstantial. And Uncle Moe had no motive to kill Sandra Vincent. Cam also told me I need to hire a private investigator to look into Ms. Vincent's personal life."

"Goodness, don't say that in front of Vera," I said.

"Why not? Do you think she'd recommend someone? I mean, maybe she knows someone really good."

"She thinks she *is* someone really good. She's already been snooping at the hospital."

"Oh, gee." Riley stuffed a huge bite of the cinnamon roll into her mouth.

"In the interest of full disclosure, I have to admit that I've been doing some snooping, too, and so have Ted and his mom and Ted's friend on the TCPD."

She chewed thoughtfully and swallowed. "Turn up anything?"

"We've uncovered a few shady characters, but we haven't been able to make a direct connection to Sandra Vincent and her murder yet."

She sighed. "I wish Dad was here."

"What advice is he giving you?"

"He says he'll bet me dollars to doughnuts—of which he currently has neither—that there's an ex-husband or boyfriend in Ms. Vincent's recent past. Find him, Dad says, and we'll find our killer."

"So, do you have a private investigator on the case?" I asked.

"Only our usual guy, but this is not his forte. His typical day involves tailing cheating spouses or phony workers'-compensation claimants, not looking for killers."

"If you'd like, I'll ask Ted if he knows anyone."

"I'd appreciate that. Thanks."

I sipped my mint mocha before changing the subject to one I knew would lift Riley's spirits. "How's Laura doing?"

Riley's face immediately relaxed into a smile. "She's so precious. And growing so fast. Look at this photo I snapped of her just yesterday." She took out her phone and pulled up the photo.

"Oh, my goodness! Look at those eyes," I said. "She's absolutely gorgeous."

I'd called Ted before lunchtime to ask him to bring me only a Cobb salad for lunch and to ask him if he knew of any private detectives he'd trust with Captain Moe's case. He said he'd look into it and bring me some news when he brought our lunch.

When he arrived, he'd brought me the requested salad, plus nachos for himself. I offered to trade him a bite for a bite, but he declined.

"Are you sure?" I asked. "It has ranch dressing."

"I'm positive. I was in the mood for nachos today. Would you like a nacho?"

"Just a teensy one." I took the smallest—albeit cheesiest—one on his plate. "That's delicious."

He sighed. "Do you want to trade?"

"No, but I'm flattered that you love me enough to offer. You should've seen the size of that cinnamon roll Riley brought me for breakfast. She was indulging in some emotional eating, and she dragged me down with her."

"Poor baby."

I laughed. "Okay, so she didn't have to twist my

arm. I'm a good friend. Friends don't let friends eat their depression alone."

"You said she wants to hire a private investigator. I have a name for you: Harvey Gordon. He's a retired police officer who opened his own investigations firm in Coos Bay a few months after leaving the force. He couldn't handle sitting around doing nothing."

"So, you think he can find out who killed Sandra Vincent?"

"I think he's Riley's best shot at turning up another suspect and at least throwing more reasonable doubt onto Captain Moe," he said.

As I drove to the hospital that evening, I thought about Ted's suggesting Harvey Gordon. Riley had been pleased with the recommendation and had said she'd call Gordon right away. I hoped he'd be able to help Captain Moe. It was Captain Moe who *should* be brightening these children's day. Marcy the Elf was a mere liaison to the North Pole. Captain Moe was Santa himself.

I pulled into the parking lot and found an available space not terribly far from the building. I was dressed in the elf costume, but I'd brought clothes to change into so I could leave the costume with Carrie Monahan.

I had my head down and was putting my keys into my purse when two big hands shot out and took me by the shoulders. I gasped and looked up into the face of Charlie, the security guard.

"Sorry. I didn't mean to startle you. I was just preventing a collision."

"That's okay." My voice came out more normal that I'd expected, given the fact that my heart was racing.

"Hey, I know you. You're the elf who was here on Sunday."

"Right. And you're the security guard who was standing at the door. Thank goodness you didn't let me into that room. I might've had a heart attack, and you'd have had two bodies to deal with."

He shook his head. "That was the scariest thing I'd ever seen. I understand they arrested that guy who was playing Santa. Is he a friend of yours?"

I nodded. "I heard you were the first to arrive. Did Mr. Patrick call out to you or did he phone the front desk?"

"He yelled when he found her. I was close enough that I heard him and went running to see what was going on."

"Did he look guilty to you when you went into the room?"

"Nah. To be honest, he looked as scared as I felt."

"So you don't think he did it?"

He shrugged. "That's not my job to say."

"I'm talking completely off the record. Do you think that man killed Sandra Vincent?"

"Well, I'm not a police officer. I'm only a security guard. So I'm not trained like they are. But I'd imagine if he'd killed her, he'd have had some blood on him. Right?"

"That's right." I hadn't heard anyone mention anything about blood, but it stood to reason that if Captain Moe had stabbed Sandra Vincent, he'd have had blood on his clothing. "Did Ms. Vincent have any enemies you were aware of, Charlie?"

"I'm not really sure. I'm not too privy to the opinions of the board members."

"Well, thanks, Charlie. I'd better get in here and read to the kids."

"Yeah. That's awfully nice of you. And about what I said . . ."

"It won't come back to bite you."

He smiled. "Thanks."

I went inside. Since I'd been slowed down by talking with Charlie, I took the elevator rather than the stairs up to the pediatric ward. I went to the nurse's desk. Carrie Monahan was engaged in an intimate conversation with a muscular man leaning familiarly across the desk.

"Hi," I said. "I'm sorry to interrupt, Carrie, but I just wanted to let you know I'm here."

"Sure thing! Marcy, this is my fiancé, John Martin. He's part owner of Martin Brothers Construction, the crew that built our cancer ward. Have you visited the new ward yet?"

"I haven't. It's nice to meet you, Mr. Martin."

John Martin nodded an acknowledgment.

"You really should see the cancer ward," Carrie said. "It's state-of-the-art."

"Maybe I can get over there before I leave this evening."

"Why don't I see if they're ready for you? If they're not, then John and I can walk over there with you right quick before you go in."

"Are you sure that's a good idea?" I opened my arms and looked pointedly at my costume. "I'd hate to scare the patients or make them think they were hallucinating."

Carrie laughed. "I guess you have a point there. Maybe you *should* wait until you're in your street clothes before going over there. I'll show you around when you're done reading." She turned to Mr. Martin. "The kids adore Marcy. Give me a second to show her into the playroom, and I'll be right back."

Again, Mr. Martin merely nodded. It appeared he was a man of few words . . . or maybe no words.

When I went into the playroom, I saw a couple of new faces and many of the same ones. One pale child with dark circles beneath his eyes sat front and center. He seemed to be struggling to remain upright and awake.

"Hi." I stooped down in front of him. "I'm Marcy. What's your name?"

"Brendan."

"Brendan, what would you like for me to tell Santa you want for Christmas?"

He shrugged his bony shoulders.

Carrie pulled me aside. "Good job. Do you know his family?"

"No. Why?"

"They're the Carstairs," she whispered. "His dad's on the hospital's board of directors. He'll appreciate that you were kind to Brendan."

But, like Captain Moe, I hadn't intended to single anyone out. I was going to be kind to all of these children. It was the reason I was here.

Chapter Fourteen

Instead of going straight home, I went to Ted's apartment. His complex consists of three identical chocolate-and-tan, two-story buildings, each sectioned into four individual units. The buildings were named the Lincoln, the Somerville, and the Westchester. Ted lived in the right corner unit of the Westchester building. I was glad the complex was well lit as I navigated the beige stepping stones to Ted's door.

Ted, wearing navy plaid lounge pants and a white T-shirt, answered my knock. He closed the door behind me and took me in his arms. "Are you all right?"

"Yeah. I just needed to see you."

"I'm glad." Leaving one arm around me and still holding me close, he walked me over to the long, black-leather sofa that was the centerpiece of his living room. "Want me to turn on the fireplace?"

I shook my head. "Thanks, but I'm fine."

We sat down on the sofa, and I nestled against him.

"So, what's on your mind?" he asked.

"I ran into Charlie the security guard as I went into the hospital this evening. He pointed out that Captain Moe didn't have any blood on him when Charlie entered the conference room."

He turned his mouth down at the corners. "I hadn't heard that. I'll check with Doug and see what the official report says about it."

"If the security guard who was the first on the scene doesn't think Captain Moe killed Sandra Vincent, then he'd be an excellent witness, wouldn't he?"

"Did he tell you he doesn't think Captain Moe killed her?"

"Well, the way he put is was that he isn't trained like police officers, but he thought Captain Moe would've had blood on his clothes had he killed Ms. Vincent," I said. "You don't think that would be helpful to Captain Moe's case?"

"I don't think the security guard would be very helpful other than to admit that he didn't see Captain Moe stab Ms. Vincent, but Captain Moe not having blood on his clothing is a strong plus in his defense."

I gazed at the beige brick fireplace across from us. "Talking with Charlie wasn't my only interesting encounter. I also got to meet one of the infamous Martin brothers."

"Really?"

"Really. He's apparently engaged to Carrie Monahan, the head nurse of the pediatric ward. She introduced us and bragged about what a terrific job his company did on the cancer ward," I said. "She wanted me to let the two of them show me around the ward right then and there, but it was time for me to go read to the children. I did go with Carrie when I was finished reading, though."

"What did you think?"

"It *looks* impressive. But after everything I've heard about Martin Brothers Construction, I had to wonder if it was all style and no substance."

He inclined his head slightly. "I'm not sure they could get away with subpar building practices on something as important as a hospital cancer ward. Maybe they just strong-arm the competition out of the way but then do an adequate job on the actual construction."

"Maybe. But it's usually been my experience that if someone is unethical in one area, they will be in another."

I went on to tell him about meeting Brendan Carstairs.

"He was such a heart-rending child that I went right over to him. Carrie took me aside afterward and congratulated me on fawning over Dr. Carstairs's son. But I didn't single him out. I just went to him first."

"I know, babe." He lifted my chin and kissed me. "You're wonderful."

We sat in easy silence for a few minutes.

"I spoke with Tiffany today," he said. "She and Mark really are considering leaving Washington."

"Do you think they'll move to Tallulah Falls?"

"I don't know, but I doubt it. Portland would be more their cup of tea. But it would be nice to have them closer."

"It would . . . especially for you and Jackson. It's clear that you adore each other," I said.

"That's true. And you might be surprised to hear this, but Tiffany is really starting to like you."

On Friday morning, Angus and I were kinda droopy when we first got to the Seven-Year Stitch. Well, I was, anyway; I hadn't slept well the night before. Angus often takes his cues from me, so if I'm tired, he's tired. I flopped onto a red club chair and propped my feet on the ottoman. I held the Christmas ornament currently in progress—a puppy with a bone tied up in red ribbon—but I didn't feel like working on it just yet. The coffee was still percolating, and I was impatiently waiting for it to finish and infuse me with some energy.

"So, how was your night, Jill?"

I knew good and well that my mannequin couldn't speak, but I talked to her sometimes, anyway . . . especially when I was feeling particularly goofy and/or hadn't had a restful night.

It was fantastic. I caught up on some reading, and then I stood here looking out the window. There were some interesting people at the Brew Crew last night—ask Todd about it—and later, I was startled by a raccoon leaping off our roof.

"Wow. Was the raccoon okay?"

Oh, sure. They're pretty keen little acrobats, I think. So, why are you so drowsy this morning? Did you and Ted have a night on the town?

"No. Actually, it's this case that's keeping me awake. Did you know that Captain Moe didn't have any blood on him when he was discovered standing over Sandra Vincent?"

Hmm. Let me play devil's advocate here, Marce. If he'd killed her, he wouldn't have called for help upon "finding" her until he'd cleaned himself up, right? I mean, say I was going to do such a nefarious deed. I'd have a change of clothing on hand—which he did. I'd kill my victim, go wash up in the restroom, change clothes, and then go back to the body and start screaming my head off.

"You've got a good point there. But what about the bloody clothes you'd have taken off?"

Good question. I'd have stashed them somewhere so I could destroy them or dispose of them later. You know, like in an incinerator or something.

"But where could you have put them that the police wouldn't have found them?"

I have no idea. Has Captain Moe been back to the hospital since he was first questioned about the murder?

"Jill! You don't think Captain Moe could be *guilty*, do you?"

I don't think anything! I'm talking through your imagination. Do you think he could be guilty?

"No, I definitely don't. I'm just tired, that's all." I got up and went to see if my coffee was ready.

I'd had two cups of coffee and was feeling much more alert when a customer came in and asked if I could show her how to do a turkey stitch.

"In embroidery or knitting?" I asked.

"There's turkey stitching in knitting?" The woman's eyes widened behind her large round-framed glasses, giving her a comical expression.

"Yes, but it's actually called a Turkish stitch. It's a lace stitch. So, I take it you want to learn the embroidery stitch."

"Yes, please. It's on a pattern I'm using, and I have no idea what it is," she said.

"Turkey work is generally used to make something fuzzy. Does that make sense with your pattern?"

"It does. There's a teddy bear where the pattern indicates turkey work."

"Did you happen to bring your project with you?"

"I did." She reached into her tote bag and brought out the embroidery hoop containing her work and her pattern.

"Let's go over here to the sit-and-stitch square, and I'll help you."

The rest of the day passed in much the same way. Customers came in to buy supplies and to get help with their projects. Vera dropped in to say hello. Ted brought lunch—I requested nachos this time.

It was a mild day, so after work Angus and I went to the beach for a walk before heading home. Our walk made me feel less guilty about leaving him all evening to go to Dani's mom's visitation and to the party at Veronica's condominium complex.

I chose to wear a black V-neck dress with lace sleeves. I hoped it would be somber enough for the funeral home and yet festive enough for the party.

Ted arrived to pick me up. He looked scrumptious in a black suit with a crisp white dress shirt.

I kissed Angus on the head and promised him we'd be back as soon as possible. I left the living room and kitchen lights on for hi, and then looked around to see if there was anything else I needed to do before we left. There wasn't.

"You're dreading this, aren't you?" Ted asked, as he walked me out to his car.

"Yeah. It's awkward going to pay my respects to a woman I never even met. But given the way I found Dani on Tuesday evening—or, rather, the condition she was in when she found me—I feel obligated to go. We'll just say a quick hello and then be on our way."

"All right."

"I have to admit, I'm kind of dreading the party at your mom's place, too." I sighed. "All those high-society people . . ."

"Marcy Singer, you grew up around some of Hollywood's A-listers. You're worried about a few members of the country-club set?"

"I know it seems silly, but the Hollywood A-listers were our friends or, at the very least, our acquaintances. These people are your mother's friends, and I'm afraid that anything I do or say wrong will reflect badly on her."

"You let Mom worry about what her friends think." He chuckled. "In fact, she's the one who'll tell them what they think if they start to get out of line, so don't worry about that."

Our first stop was the funeral home. It was a brick

building with white trim. Ted parked and came around to open my door and escort me inside. Solemn ushers greeted us kindly as we walked up the ramp to the front door.

We went inside, and I desperately hoped Dani's mom was the only person for whom services were being held this evening. I had no idea of either of their last names. There was a sign directing us to THE SPENCER FAMILY.

We strode down a green-carpeted floor until we came to a room that was austere despite the decorator's attempts at creating a comforting atmosphere. The focal point of the room was an ornate white fireplace with a faux floral arrangement and a small mountain landscape painting over the mantel. In front of the fireplace sat a Victorian-style sofa in a floral print. Solid light blue chairs sat on either side of the fireplace, and the sofa was flanked by end tables with lamps that cast soft light into the room.

The room was full of strangers—to us, anyway. And judging by their expressions, they were wondering who Ted and I were. I spoke to an elderly woman who seemed especially kind.

"Hi. I'm looking for Dani."

She shook her head. "I don't believe I know a Dani."

"Of course, you do, Mother." A woman in a gray suit put her arm around the elderly lady. "She's Emma's daughter." She turned to Ted and me. "Dani is right over there in the corner."

"Thank you."

I headed over to where Dani was talking with a man in khaki pants and a blue-striped dress shirt.

"Marcy!" she cried when she saw me. "Thank you so much for coming. This is my husband, Joe."

Ted and I exchanged pleasantries with Joe.

"I realize I didn't know your mom, and I barely know you," I told Dani, "but I wanted to pay my respects."

"I'm so glad you did. I told Joe how kind you were to me the other night."

"I was afraid for her to drive before she'd had an opportunity to calm down a little," I said.

"I appreciate your looking out for her."

We made small talk for a few more minutes, and then I told Dani to let me know if there was anything I could do to help.

We were leaving when I spotted Charlie the security guard.

"Charlie, hi," I said. "It's me—Marcy . . . the Elf."

"Marcy, yeah, sure! How are you?"

"I'm fine." I introduced Charlie and Ted.

"How did you know Emma?" Charlie asked me.

"I didn't. I know her daughter, Dani. She's, um, a patron at the Seven-Year Stitch, my embroidery shop."

"Dani's a real nice girl. I know she's devastated by her mother's death. I sure was."

"You were close to Emma?" I asked.

"Oh no. I mean, I knew Emma, but what I intended to say was that I was devastated when my own mom died a couple of months ago. She was on the list for a heart transplant, and she never got it."

"I'm sorry to hear that."

"Anyhow, that's how I came to know Emma and

Dani. Emma had been waiting for a liver." He shrugged. "It's a strange thing for people to bond over. But when you're searching for a way to help someone you love, you share information."

I lowered my voice. "Dani said her mother was supposed to have received a transplant but got bumped down on the list."

Charlie's face darkened. "That happens more often than you know. It's a shame."

"Who makes the call to bump someone in favor of someone else?" Ted asked.

"At Tallulah County General, it's the hospital administrator. I hope they put Carrie Monahan in the job this time. She promised us she'd be making some changes to the program when she applied for the position the last time, but somehow Sandra Vincent knocked her out of the job."

"How'd she do that?" I asked. "Was Ms. Vincent more qualified?"

"My guess is that she knew someone on the board of directors who wanted her to have the position, for whatever reason."

Chapter Fifteen

Ted and I left behind the somber ambiance of the funeral home for the festive atmosphere of the condominium complex. Bill, the doorman, greeted us happily and told us how wonderful we looked. Ted tipped him, and he looked even happier.

Ted, who'd reluctantly been to parties here before, led me to the ballroom. Whereas the funeral-home décor had been designed to comfort, the ballroom had been designed to impress. Three ornate crystal chandeliers hung from the center of the ceiling, there was a polished wooden floor for dancing, and upon a stage sat a gleaming black baby-grand piano. Round tables covered with long white linen tablecloths lined the dance area. Six plush burgundy chairs circled the tables. In front of each chair was an exquisite place setting of white china, crystal water and wineglasses, and elegant silverware wrapped in a burgundy linen napkin.

As soon as we walked into the ballroom, Veronica met us and propelled us to the side of the room where two sophisticated-looking couples were standing with Tiffany, Mark, and Jackson—who, by the way, had on the cutest little suit I'd ever seen.

"Ted, Marcy, I'd like you to meet Harold and Constance Carstairs, as well as their son, Dr. Bellamy Carstairs, and their daughter-in-law, Melanie," Veronica said.

So these were the snooty Mr. and Mrs. Carstairs, their influential son, and their despised daughter-in-law. Harold was a tall man whose paunch spilled over the top of his pants. He unabashedly looked both Ted and me up and down, from the tops of our heads to our shoes, so, I imagined, he could make an informed judgment about us based on how we were dressed. Constance was petite and had silvery blond hair, and her pale blue eyes were forever flying to her husband's face so she could tell how she was supposed to be feeling or what she was to be thinking at any given moment.

Melanie was an attractive, athletically built brunette who gave us a warm smile when we were introduced but looked back at her in-laws as if she wished the floor would simply open up and swallow her . . . or them. Bellamy had his father's height and his mother's blond good looks. Had I asked him, I'm sure he would have assured me that he was chiseled perfection. Yep. Chiseled out of cold, slick marble.

He sandwiched my hand between both of his in a gesture that would've seemed warm if offered by a person who appeared to be more sincere than Bellamy Carstairs. "Marcy . . . That's not a very common

name around here. You wouldn't happen to be Marcy
the Elf, would you?"

"Yes, I have dressed up as an elf for the hospital on
a few occasions."

"You're too modest." He turned to the others in our
little group. "This woman is far too modest. Head
Nurse Carrie Monahan told me about how Marcy lav-
ished attention on our little Brendan on Thursday
night and made him feel very special." He turned
back to me. "I appreciate that."

"You're welcome," I said. "But I have to say that
entertaining those children and being able to make
them laugh and forget about their problems for a little
while meant as much to me as it did to them."

He squeezed my hand before letting it go. "You
aren't looking for a job as a nanny, are you?"

I realized he was joking, but I wasn't quite sure
how to answer. So I merely said, "I'm afraid not. I own
the Seven-Year Stitch—the embroidery specialty shop
in town—and there's no one to whom I can hand the
reins of that job."

Dr. Carstairs laughed. "Well, you must at least
come to our home and visit Brendan. I understand
that when you were with the Santa Claus last Friday
evening, you brought a large dog with you. Brendan
found him quite amazing."

I smiled. "Yes, that's Angus. And he is an amazing dog."

"So, what do you say?" he continued. "Would
Marcy the Elf please bring her furry friend from the

North Pole to visit Brendan on Sunday? His doctors have him stabilized, and he's coming home tomorrow."

"That's wonderful," I said.

"Yes. And we'd love to have you and—Angus, did you say?—come and welcome Brendan home on Sunday. Wouldn't we, darling?"

Melanie Carstairs chimed in for the first time since being introduced. "Of course."

"So what do you say?" he asked.

I hesitated, and Dr. Carstairs's parents jumped in to help persuade me.

"Brendan is an absolutely charming little boy," said Constance. "I know you'll be completely enamored of him once you get to know him."

"We'll be happy to pay you for your time," said Harold.

"Payment certainly isn't necessary," I said. "But, you see, I can't be Marcy the Elf because I turned the costume back in to Carrie Monahan last night. I guess we could tell Brendan it's the elf's day off."

Bellamy Carstairs didn't laugh. Instead he looked smug. "I've got you covered, my dear. I rented that costume this morning and had it dry cleaned. It's in our hall closet, awaiting your arrival."

"Wow. You've thought of everything. How did you know you could even find me?" He was pretty sure of himself, too.

"I knew Carrie had your number, and I was planning to call you first thing tomorrow morning," he said. "Brendan is everything to us, isn't he, darling?"

Instead of giving Melanie a chance to answer, he continued. "So, will you come?"

"How could I refuse such a generous invitation?" I looked at Ted. He read my pleading expression perfectly. Unlike Bellamy, however, I didn't want to back anyone into a corner, so I didn't voice my entreaty.

"Would you like me to come with you and help out with Angus?" Ted asked.

I nearly kissed him right then and there, but I restrained myself. Instead I turned back to the Carstairs. "Yes. I think that's a wonderful idea, don't you?"

"Splendid! Then it's settled." Bellamy reached into his inside breast pocket and took out a business card. He flipped it over, took out a pen, and scribbled something. "I've written our home address on the back. Could you please be there around eleven o'clock Sunday morning?"

"That'll be great." I took the card and dropped it into my purse.

"Listen, babe. They're playing our song." Ted held his hand out to me. "If you'll excuse us, we really have to dance to this one."

He led me onto the dance floor.

I expelled a sigh of relief. "Thank you. Although I didn't realize 'Baby, It's Cold Outside' was our song."

He twirled me around the dance floor. "'Chattanooga Choo Choo' would have been our song if that's what the band had struck up. I was dying to get away from the Carstairs, and I could tell you were, too."

"How'd we get talked into going to their house tomorrow?"

"It was a clear case of manipulation. He put you in such a position that you could hardly refuse."

"True," I said. "But we can turn this into a win-win situation. I can make Brendan happy and we can see what we can find out about the Carstairs that might help Captain Moe with his case." I began to sing along with the song. "I ought to say no, no, no, sir."

Ted knew the words, too. "Mind if I move in closer?"

I threw back my head and laughed, and he kissed my throat.

I gave a little yelp. "Your mom might be watching."

"So?" He laughed and then whispered in my ear. "I love you, Inch-High."

Minutes after we'd finished our dance, dinner was served. I was relieved that once Ted, Veronica, Tiffany, Mark, Jackson, and I were seated—including a high chair for Jackson—there wasn't room for the Carstairs. And I was doubly relieved to see that they were within waving distance but not speaking distance.

The food was fancy. I worried at first about Jackson not being able to eat what was on the menu, but I shouldn't have. Veronica had already spoken with the chef, and Jackson was served a special toddler-friendly meal. He had macaroni and cheese, mashed potatoes, small bites of breaded chicken, and apple slices. Frankly, I thought his meal looked better than ours. I wasn't terribly froufrou at heart. We had a house salad, roasted chicken breast with mushrooms, mashed potatoes, and steamed Brussels sprouts. The meal was good, but I'd have seriously traded Jackson my Brussels sprouts for a single bite of his mac and cheese.

Near the end of dinner, Jackson started to get fussy.

Mark sighed. "I'll take him up and try to get him settled down. I think all this excitement has been a little much for him."

I could see that neither Mark nor Tiffany was finished with dinner. "I'll take him back up to Veronica's condo . . . if no one minds."

"I wouldn't want to impose on you like that," Tiffany said.

"I would," Mark said. He answered his wife's glare of disapproval with a shrug. "I'm sorry, but I'd be thrilled if Marcy would take Jackson upstairs for us. Do you realize how long it's been since you and I have danced together?"

Tiffany relented. "Are you sure, Marcy?"

"Positive." I leaned toward her and lowered my voice. "It'll keep me out of the Carstairs' line of fire."

"I'm dreadfully sorry about that," said Veronica. "I didn't know the doctor would ask you to come to his home and give a performance."

"Would you like for me to come up with you?" Ted asked.

I shook my head. "Not yet. Dance with your mom first."

He raised my hand to his lips and kissed it before I pushed back my chair.

"Jackson, wanna go play?" I asked.

"Play!" He stretched his arms out toward me.

Tiffany gave me her key, and Jackson and I ducked out of the ballroom and into the elevator.

"The party is over for us, right?" I asked.

"Party over."

"I'm glad we can go play now."

"We play. We like play."

"Yes, we do."

As soon as we got into Veronica's condo, I slipped off my black platform pumps.

"Hurt a toes?" Jackson asked.

I smiled. "They were starting to hurt my toes. What do you say we get you out of that suit?"

"Yeah."

I didn't know whether or not to give Jackson a bath, so I merely changed him out of the suit and into some pajamas. Then we went back into the living room, sat down on the sofa, and watched a video of animated characters singing songs. They were pretty simple, and the words were displayed on the screen with a ball jumping from word to word, so I sang along. Jackson did, too . . . kinda. Other than dancing with Ted, this was the highlight of my evening.

After about half an hour, Jackson lay down and dozed off. I turned off the television and covered him with his blanket. Then I went to find Clover. She was in Veronica's bedroom, confined by a baby gate. I reached over the gate and lifted up the large brown-and-white bunny, and she snuggled beneath my chin. I returned to the living room, sat at the end of the sofa opposite Jackson, and stroked Clover's soft fur.

The door opened, and Tiffany came in. When she saw that Jackson was asleep, she asked, "How'd you do that?"

"We sang ourselves to sleep. Well, we sang Jackson

to sleep. I just got a little drowsy. And the bunny is putting me over the edge." I stifled a yawn.

She smiled and sat on the chair nearest me.

"I didn't give him a bath," I said. "You didn't mention it, so I just changed him into his pj's."

"That's fine. I bathed him before putting him into his suit, so we're good." She paused. "I'm sorry you had to leave the party. If it's any consolation, you aren't missing much . . . except Ted dancing with Mom. That was sweet. Not as sweet as watching him dance with you, but not bad."

"He's an excellent dancer," I said, hoping the dim light hid my blush. "Growing up, my mom would sometimes throw parties or we'd be invited to parties much like this one, and I'd usually end up finding a quiet corner to hide out."

"Mom told me your mother is a costume designer. So I guess you could do some major name-dropping about the parties you've attended."

"I suppose. But those events weren't parties as much as they were negotiations. Everyone was there to see who they could meet and what they could take away from that meeting."

"Sounds a lot like Bellamy Carstairs," said Tiffany dryly.

"Exactly like that. *Dance, monkey, dance!* Dr. Carstairs commands. And I'll go dance . . . but only for Brendan. And for Captain Moe. I was so relieved when Ted volunteered to go with me."

"It wasn't hard to read that desperation in your eyes. If he hadn't spoken up, I would have."

I laughed softly. "Thanks."

"You love my brother, don't you?"

"More than I can say."

She smiled. "I never saw him look at Jennifer the way he looks at you."

We heard voices in the hallway.

"Looks like they're back," I said. "I guess I should return Clover to her room."

"Not yet." Tiffany reached for her. "Let me hold her for a few minutes first."

"She is wonderfully therapeutic."

Veronica, Mark, and Ted came through the door.

Mark looked at Jackson sleeping peacefully on the sofa and then at me. "What form of magic is this?"

"Apparently, it was a singing spell," said Tiffany.

Mark stepped closer to his wife and ran a hand over Clover's soft head.

"Marcy, you know you don't have to take your shoes off here," said Veronica.

I admitted I hadn't taken them off to avoid soiling the carpet, and then I relayed Jackson's "hurt a toes" question. That made everyone laugh so hard that the child stirred in his sleep.

"Shhh!" Mark hissed. "Don't wake the dragon. Or Marcy'll have to sing all night."

"And dance on Sunday," Tiffany said with a grin.

"What's that?" Ted asked.

"Inside joke," she told him.

Chapter Sixteen

On Saturday morning, I was surprised that the first customer to come into the Seven-Year Stitch was Melanie Carstairs. She had her dark brown hair swept back into a ponytail, and she wore jeans and a yellow sweater. She looked much more comfortable—in every way—than she had last night.

"Mrs. Carstairs, what a pleasure to see you again."

"Thank you," she said. "Please call me Melanie. I heard you say last night that you own this place, and I've been wanting to learn some form of embroidery—something that isn't too hard—that I can do when I'm sitting with Brendan while he's playing or sleeping."

I took her over to the shelves and showed her beginning cross-stitch kits. "Or, even simpler, you could do some hand embroidery." I handed her a book called *Stitch the Halls!* by Sophie Simpson. "There are several projects in here, and the author lets you know the difficulty level and the estimated time of completion for each."

"Oh, this looks like fun." Melanie thumbed through the pages. "I think I could do this."

"I'm certain you can. Would you like to get started?"

"You mean you'll help me?"

I smiled. "Of course."

She bought the pattern book, a wooden hoop, some embroidery needles, some canvas, and a variety pack of floss. Then we went over to the sofa and got started.

Melanie hadn't shown much interest in Angus when she'd come into the shop, so he merely remained by the window, where he watched the world go by as Melanie and I began her first embroidery project. I was able to get her well on her way before another customer came in. When I returned to the sofa, I was pleased by how much progress Melanie had made and told her so.

"Thanks. I'm enjoying this. It's relaxing."

"I admire you. I know it has to be tough being a full-time caregiver," I said.

"I admire Brendan. The poor baby has been through a lot." She blinked back tears. "And I know he's getting the best possible care. His doctors are wonderful. But I wish I could do more to help him."

"I'm sure you're doing everything you can."

"As a mom, yes. But I want to be on the front lines, you know? For Brendan and for other sick children. I applied for the hospital administrator position when it came open earlier this year. I'd hoped to make some inroads at Tallulah County General. But the job went to someone else."

"Aw, I'm sorry that didn't work out for you."

"Thanks." She went back to working on the Christmas ornament she was stitching.

"I met the hospital administrator—Ms. Vincent. She's the one who got the job over you?"

Melanie nodded. "It wouldn't have been so bad if Sandra had been more qualified than I, but she wasn't. In fact, she was *less* qualified. I have a master's degree in health administration. She only had a bachelor's degree in business administration."

"Then how in the world did she get the job over you?" I asked. I already knew the answer, but I needed to play dumb.

She shrugged. "Bellamy's best guess is that she knew someone on the board who was able to sway a majority of the members to vote her way."

"I'm so sorry. I think you would've been great in that position."

"I know I would have. Brendan doesn't need me at home all that much. He has a nanny or a teacher with him during most of the day now, so I'm merely on hand in case of emergencies. If I'd got that administrator position, I could've been making policy changes and budgeting and hosting fund-raisers to get our researchers the funding they need to help these sick children."

"I hate to be indelicate, but the job is open again, right?"

"It is."

"Are you going to try again?"

"I might," she said softly. "I want to feel useful.

There's not a more desperate feeling in the world than having a sick child and not being able to cure him."

Vera came into the shop not long after Melanie had left. By then, I was working on my own Christmas ornaments. She came over and sat down beside me, peering over at my cloth to see what I was making.

"Oh, it's a little church. I love it!"

"Consider your hint dropped, Ms. Langhorne."

She laughed. "Thank you. Subtlety is my strong suit."

"Oh yeah." I laughed, too. "How are you this morning?"

"I'm great. I slept in. It was a pretty fun party last night, don't you think? Or did you? You seemed to disappear awfully early."

"Jackson was getting sleepy, so I took him upstairs so Mark and Tiffany could enjoy themselves a little longer."

"Making nice with the in-laws." She winked. "Good strategy."

"They aren't my in-laws. But I do feel like I made a little headway with Tiffany last night."

"That's wonderful, hon. I knew she'd come around if she'd just allow herself to get to know you."

Angus ambled over to greet Vera. She scratched his head and talked with him for a couple of minutes before turning to me again.

"Did you find out anything interesting from the Carstairs?"

I set aside my cross-stitch project so I could give Vera my full, splayed-hands expression of disbelief.

"Are you ready for this? Dr. Carstairs *rented* the elf costume. And he wants me to put it on tomorrow to visit with Brendan, who's coming home from the hospital later today."

"Wait, wait, wait. You're going to have to back up on this one. The man went out and rented an elf costume for you?"

"No. He rented *the* elf costume for me." I waved my hands. "All right. I'll start at the beginning." I explained how Veronica had introduced us and how Dr. Carstairs had insisted that I bring Angus for a visit with Brendan tomorrow as a welcome-home deal. "I told him I'd returned the elf costume, and he said he'd rented it and had it dry cleaned and that it would be waiting for me at their house to put on when I arrive."

She blinked. "Okay, is it just me, or is that borderline creepy?"

"I think it steps over the border a little bit. I couldn't come to the house as Marcy? I *have* to be an elf? I even suggested we tell Brendan that it was my day off from the North Pole."

"Talk about your control freaks. Dr. Carstairs is going to have his way or else, isn't he?"

I nodded. "So, Angus, Ted, and I are going over there tomorrow. Ted offered to come along right in front of Dr. Carstairs, so the good doctor couldn't exactly refuse. Ted can help me wrangle Angus, and I believe he intends to do some snooping while I entertain Brendan."

At the mention of his name, Angus thumped his tail against the floor.

"I do have something interesting to tell you," I continued. I went on to inform Vera how Melanie Carstairs had been in this morning to buy some embroidery supplies. "She began talking with me about the hospital-administrator position while we worked on her project. She really should've had that job, Vera. If what Melanie says is true, she was more qualified than Sandra Vincent."

"But you and I know, thanks to Veronica, that Bellamy Carstairs was the reason Melanie didn't get the job."

"Right. She's thinking of applying again, now that the job is open. I don't know how Bellamy will keep her from getting it this time."

"Marcy, the man rented an elf costume and insisted you wear it. He'll find a way to keep his wife home and out of his business."

"True. I just think it's a shame. They're married and they have a sick child. I'd think he'd want to work with his wife, not against her." I sighed. "So, did you find out anything interesting at the party?"

"I did. You know that Martin Brothers Construction company?"

"Please tell me they didn't build Veronica's condominium."

She smiled. "No. At least, not that I'm aware of. But one of the women who was at the party has a daughter who's a nurse at Tallulah County General. She was very proud of the fact that her Carrie was engaged to one of the Martin brothers."

"Wait. Did she give her daughter's last name?"

"No, why?"

I told Vera about meeting John Martin at Carrie Monahan's desk on Thursday evening.

Her eyes widened. "So, one of *the* Martin brothers is dating the head nurse of the pediatric ward . . . who also applied for the hospital-administrator position."

"Right. And if Carrie and Melanie Carstairs are the only applicants for the position this time, I'd say Carrie will be awarded the job."

"And then Martin Brothers Construction will be sitting pretty for any other construction projects that open up."

"True. But they already are," I said. "Maybe it's the other way around. Maybe it's the Martin brothers who got Carrie as far in the application process as she got the first time around."

"And maybe one of them did in Sandra Vincent to allow his girl to aspire to her lofty career goals."

Ted called around noon to tell me that he wouldn't be able to leave work and come for lunch today. I was disappointed, but I understood.

"How about tonight I take you to Zefferelli's?" he asked.

Zefferelli's was our favorite Italian restaurant.

"That sounds wonderful," I said. "And, in that case, I'm glad we're not having a big lunch."

He chuckled. "Be thinking about what you want."

"I already know. The chicken parm."

"Me, too."

We said our good-byes, and then I locked the front door and walked down to MacKenzies' Mochas for a cappuccino and a small salad.

I'd just paid and was getting ready to walk out of MacKenzies' when John Martin walked in.

"Oh, hi," I said.

He didn't give me any indication that he recognized me.

"I'm Marcy. Better known at Tallulah County General as Marcy the Elf."

"Yeah. How are you?" His voice was flat. He didn't care how I was.

"Fine, thanks. You?"

"Busy."

"That's too bad. I was hoping that since I ran into you, I might ask you about a project I'm thinking about." I gave a shrug of nonchalance. "But that's okay. My mom's a costume designer in Hollywood. I'm sure she can recommend someone to come out and give me a quote."

It was shameless, I know. But, as expected, dropping the fact that Mom was a costume designer in *Hollywood* made the man see dollar signs.

"I guess I can spare a couple of minutes. Grab us a table while I get my coffee."

"Great." I smiled. "Thanks." I hoped Blake would take his time getting Mr. Martin's order ready. I had to come up with this fictional project I'd apparently been thinking about.

I stepped back over to the counter and told Blake I was going to sit down for a few minutes rather than taking my salad to go.

He gave me a funny look and then told me that was fine. I stared at him hard, trying to communicate with him telepathically. *Stall him.* Blake looked confused. I gave him a tight smile and then sat down at the nearest table. It was a small table with only two chairs, and I sat where Blake and I could easily see each other. If things went south, Blake would probably bail me out. He'd been like a big brother to me since I'd been Sadie's college roommate, and I knew he'd keep an eye on me.

Mr. Martin got his coffee and came over to the table. He sat down and gave me a level stare. "Tell me about this project."

"I'd like a gazebo," I said. "Now, I know your company deals in large projects like the hospital's cancer ward, but I hoped maybe you could recommend someone local."

"We do all kinds of different things, not only big jobs." He tasted his coffee. "You said your mom was a costume designer. Was she with that movie crew that was here a few months ago?"

"Yeah. Sadly, that whole affair ended tragically, but she was part of the crew."

"That must have been cool."

"It had its moments." I smiled. He didn't.

"You think they might consider coming back and resuming work on the film?" he asked.

"I don't believe so. That project has been scrapped . . . for the time being, anyway."

"That's too bad. I mean, I figure the set designers might hire local contractors to help with their construction," he said. "I've got a cousin up in Portland who does lots of movie and TV work."

"That's nice."

"Yeah. Good work if you can get it."

"I'll mention you to Mom if the studio does decide to revive the film," I said.

"Thanks. About that gazebo: I couldn't have anyone get to it until the spring. But how big you want it?"

"I'm not sure. Nothing too big. Just something to picnic in—that sort of thing." I gave a light laugh. "Nothing like the size you and Carrie would need for a marriage ceremony."

He didn't laugh. He just drank more coffee.

"Have you set the date yet?" I continued.

He shook his head. "I guess she'll take care of all that. The ceremony tends to mean more to the woman than it does the man, right?"

"I guess it does." I dug my fork around in my salad and tried to make my question seem offhand. "Wow, wasn't that terrible about the hospital administrator at Tallulah County General? I haven't had a chance to talk with Carrie about it much."

"Why would you?"

"Well, just to get her thoughts on it. You know. It was terrible. I hope it doesn't make her afraid. I know she works some pretty late hours."

"Why would it make Carrie afraid?"

I shrugged. "Ms. Vincent was killed right there in the hospital during the day. I think that's frightening, and I'd be terrified if I worked at that hospital, knowing there was a killer on the loose."

"The guy's not on the loose. He got arrested."

"But what if he's not the guy?"

"He's the guy."

"How can you be so sure?" I asked. "Why would a guy hired to play Santa Claus kill the hospital administrator? He had no motive."

"Maybe she stuck her nose where she didn't have any business." With that, John Martin slid his chair back from the table, got up, and left.

Blake came out from behind the counter and over to my table. "What was that all about? Are you okay?"

"I'm fine," I said. "But one thing's for certain: I don't want that guy anywhere near my gazebo."

"But you don't have a gazebo."

"Exactly."

Chapter Seventeen

When I got back to the Seven-Year Stitch after lunch and after walking Angus, I gave Vera a call. I didn't call Ted because I knew he was swamped today.

"Hi, hon. What's up?" she asked when she answered.

I told her about John Martin and my ruse about wanting a gazebo built.

"Oh, a gazebo would be darling. Are you sure you're not considering it for real? I mean, you didn't simply pull the idea out of thin air."

"Well, it might be nice, but I'm actually calling to tell you about Mr. Martin."

"Of course," she said. "Go on."

"I asked him about quoting a price on a gazebo, and then I said he probably didn't take on small projects like that, given the fact that his company had built the cancer ward onto Tallulah County General. And then, since I'd worked the conversation around to the hospital, I asked him about Sandra Vincent's murder and whether or not his fiancée, Carrie, was afraid to work there, knowing there was a killer on the loose."

"Good job. What did you get out of him?"

"He said that he's convinced the police arrested the right guy. And when I asked him what possible motive the Santa hired by Ms. Vincent for an event would have to kill her, he said that maybe she stuck her nose where it didn't belong."

There was silence on the other end of the line for so long that I said "Hello" to make sure Vera and I hadn't been disconnected.

"Yeah, hon. I'm here. The way you said that made it sound like a threat to me."

"The way John Martin said it to *me* made it sound like a threat, too. So I must be getting close to a nerve, right?"

"You could be. And from everything I've heard, those Martin brothers are nasty guys," she said. "Let Ted and the rest of the police handle them. Stay away from them."

"I will. But I'm wondering if maybe Sandra Vincent or the board of directors had been wooed over to some new construction company and was dumping Martin Brothers Construction. If so, there's a plausible motive for one of the Martins to murder her."

"Let Paul and me look into it and see what we can turn up. In the meantime, be careful."

"I will," I promised.

Later that afternoon, I was helping a woman pick out a scroll-frame starter kit for her niece when Riley and Laura came in. Riley had the baby bundled up in a coat and a pink knit hat with a flower on the side.

"What a beautiful baby!" the woman exclaimed.

"Thank you," said Riley.

Angus came up to snuffle at Laura's feet, and the baby looked at her mother with a smile.

"Mama," said Laura.

And then she said a bunch of gibberish that apparently only Riley understood because Riley responded with, "I know!"

The customer paid for her purchases, fawned over Laura one last time, and then left.

Riley sat on a stool and placed Laura on the countertop in front of her. I played with the baby while Angus sat on the floor beside Riley and looked up at the child longingly. He whimpered now and then.

"What do you think?" Riley asked. "Is it time to introduce them?"

"That's entirely up to you."

She patted the counter, and Angus eagerly propped his paws up on top to get a better look at the baby.

Laura reached out and touched his head, then drew back her hand and laughed. She did it again and again.

"I think she likes him," said Riley.

"And the feeling is obviously mutual."

After a few minutes, Angus got tired of standing on his back legs and went back to the window to look out. Riley took a wipe from her diaper bag and quickly washed Laura's hands before they wound up in her mouth.

"Did you give that private investigator, Harvey Gordon, a call?" I asked.

"I did. Although he hasn't been able to turn up much yet."

"Mmma, mama ma-maa," said Laura.

"I'm sure Mr. Gordon has his own way of investigating, and I certainly don't want to interfere," I began.

"But?" She knew I was holding back. "Marcy, if you know something that might help Uncle Moe, please tell me. I'm running out of ideas, and he's running out of time."

"I've got a bad feeling about John Martin and Carrie Monahan." I told her what we'd learned about the construction company, how I'd found out that John and Carrie were engaged, how Carrie was one of three finalists for the hospital-administrator job, and about my encounter with John Martin over lunch.

"What a jerk," she said. "I agree, though: that is suspicious behavior."

Laura babbled some more, and Riley kissed the baby's plump cheek.

"I'll talk with Harvey about Martin Brothers Construction and about Carrie Monahan," said Riley. "I'll give him the information you've given me and ask him to see what he can turn up."

I glanced out the window and then drew in a breath.

"What is it?" Keeping one hand firmly on Laura, Riley turned to look out the window.

"That guy standing on the sidewalk in front of the Brew Crew. The one staring over here. That's John Martin."

He was leaning against the wall outside of the pub with his feet crossed, and he was watching the Stitch.

"I'm going to let him know I see him." I came around the counter, went over to the window, and waved. I tried to make it look like a friendly greeting, but John Martin raised his hand as if he were pointing a pistol and then lowered his thumb. *Bang.*

I tried to look nonchalant as I turned my back and headed toward the counter, but my heart was racing. "D-did you see that?"

"Yep. And I'm positive he intended his gesture as a threat, although in a court of law, he could say he meant the gesture in a harmless way."

Mr. Martin turned and went into the Brew Crew.

"It's almost time for you to close up shop," said Riley. "I'll take Laura on out and put her into the car, and then I'll drive around to the back where your Jeep is parked. Don't go out the door until you see that I'm there."

"That's not necessary. I just saw him go into the pub. He's not going to be waiting for me in the alley."

"Probably not, but I want to be sure. And so does Laura. Don't you, Doodlebug?"

Laura said a few garbled words as seriously as she could.

Riley grinned. "See?"

She took the baby and left. I glanced at the clock. I still had ten minutes until closing, but I was a little freaked out, and I doubted anyone would be coming by this late. I went ahead and locked the front door. I gathered my purse and tote bag from beneath the counter and called to Angus. He trotted beside me to the back door.

I opened the door slightly and saw that Riley's dark blue Mercedes was idling right behind my Jeep. I locked the door and went on outside. After putting Angus and my things into the Jeep, I went over to Riley's car.

She put down her window. "Be careful, okay? Tell Ted about this creep."

"I will. And you tell Harvey Gordon about him. Hopefully, your PI can dig up something that will help Captain Moe."

"From your mouth to God's ear."

I was driving home when Todd called my cell phone.

"Hey, there."

"Hey, yourself." He was speaking so quietly, I could barely hear him.

"Can you speak up a little?"

"No. I'm in the Brew Crew office. There's a guy at the bar asking about you, and I don't like it."

"I think the guy you're talking about is John Martin, and I don't like it, either. What kind of questions is he asking?"

"For one thing, he wants to know if you bring that big dog to work every day," said Todd. "He was talking with Will. When Will said that you *do* bring Angus to work with you just about every day, the guy asked if the dog bites."

I groaned. Will was Todd's day manager and bartender, and he was also one of the sweetest guys on the planet. I was certain he'd told John Martin that Angus was as friendly as could be. "Todd, I'm scared of this guy. Please tell me Will didn't—"

"No, it's okay," Todd said. "He thought there was something fishy about the guy's questions, so he said that the dog seems all right but that he wouldn't push it. And Will said he was careful not to give the guy Angus's name."

I breathed a sigh of relief. "Thank him for me."

"I will. I'm going to slip out the back and come over while you lock up and—"

"I'm way ahead of you," I interrupted. "Although I do appreciate the thought, I'm on my way home already. Riley was here when John Martin was standing outside the Brew Crew. He was watching the Stitch, so I went over to the window and waved."

"Marcy! If you think somebody is dangerous, you don't antagonize him!"

"I know. It was a friendly wave. But instead of waving back, he pretended to shoot me."

"I don't like this."

"I'm not crazy about it, either," I said. "On the bright side, though, maybe he's the one who killed Sandra Vincent."

"Oh yeah, that's a really bright side."

"It would be if we could prove it and get Captain Moe off the hook."

He blew out a breath. "At least tell Batman that the Joker is in town, would you?"

"I wonder if Ted is flattered by all these sweet nicknames you give him. I'll have to ask."

"That's not an answer to my question," Todd said.

"I'll tell him. And Riley is putting her private investigator on this guy's trail, too. If he *did* kill Sandra Vincent, maybe Mr. Gordon can find the evidence to put John Martin away."

By the time Ted arrived to take me to Zefferelli's, I had fed Angus, changed into a brown leather skirt and a coral sweater, and had touched up my makeup.

"Wow, you look beautiful."

"Thank you," I said.

I hadn't really planned on telling Ted about John Martin until we were comfortably ensconced at our table at Zefferelli's with a basket of breadsticks between us. But then he noticed that I left the television on for Angus . . . as well as a few extra lights. I always left a couple of lights on for Angus, but I seldom turned on the TV. On top of that, Ted saw me looking around furtively as we walked to the car.

"What are you doing?" he asked, as he opened the passenger's-side door for me to get in.

"Just looking around."

He shut the door and came around to the driver's side. "I know better. You never just look around."

"Are you saying I'm not observant? Admittedly, I don't have the laser focus that you do, but I think I'm fairly observant."

"Marcy."

"It's nothing . . . probably."

This time he merely gave me *the look*. It's a serious look that kinda says he's through playing games.

I took a deep breath and started with lunch. "You know how you called and told me you couldn't get away for lunch? Well, I went down to MacKenzies' Mochas for a salad, and while I was there, I just happened to run into John Martin. So I came up with a pretend project—a gazebo—to ask him for a ballpark quote on."

"In other words, despite his surly demeanor when you met him on Thursday, you decided to pick his brain about Sandra Vincent."

"Pretty much. And when I *did* try to pick his brain about Sandra Vincent, he said that Captain Moe probably killed her because she stuck her nose where she had no business," I said. "And then he left without giving me an estimate on my gazebo."

"Do you really want a gazebo? I could probably build a gazebo."

"I don't know. It might be something to consider later on. But I haven't finished my story about John Martin."

He glanced at me. "What else did he do?"

I told Ted about Mr. Martin standing across the street at the Brew Crew, pretending to shoot me, and then asking Will whether or not Angus would bite.

"Either he thought Will would tell you or he really wanted to know if he should be careful of Angus." His voice was cold and hard. "Regardless, he wanted to scare you."

"I can't honestly say he doesn't intimidate me at all, but I do hope that if he killed Sandra Vincent, he left enough evidence for Harvey Gordon to find."

Ted didn't say anything to that, and I noticed that a muscle in his jaw was working.

I placed my hand on his forearm. "Please don't let what I just told you ruin our evening."

He took a deep breath, and I could see it took some effort for him to relax. "All right."

Chapter Eighteen

Ted drove Angus and me to the Carstairs' home in the Jeep. I was a little nervous about the entire affair and preferred that Ted drive so I could steel myself for whatever I was about to encounter. Along the way, his phone buzzed. He'd received a text message.

He nodded toward the phone, which lay on the console between us. "Would you read that message for me, please?"

I picked up the phone and looked at the screen. "It's from Tiffany. It says, 'Tell Marcy to dance, monkey, dance.'" I burst out laughing.

"I don't get it."

"I basically told Tiffany on Friday night that Dr. Carstairs had made me feel like a performing monkey and that if it wasn't for Brendan and the fact that we could possibly uncover more information to help Captain Moe, I'd have turned him down flat."

"You're a good person. Most people would've told him where to get off."

"Would you have?" I asked.

"Probably. But, then, I haven't met the boy."

"Yeah. It makes a difference. You'll see. Plus, Melanie is nice." I told him about Melanie coming in to learn some basic stitches and to get supplies so she could do something useful while Brendan is sleeping. "It's a shame she didn't get the hospital-administration job. I think could've done some good work."

We pulled up to a wooden and metal gate with an intercom about four feet in front on the driver's side. Ted put down his window, and when prompted announced that we were there to see Brendan at Dr. Carstairs' request. The gate slowly swung open.

The curving, paved driveway was beautifully lined with boxwoods, cedars, hellebores, and Lenten roses. We rounded a bend and the drive opened up into a circular parking area. Ted maneuvered the Jeep into a spot where we wouldn't be blocking the garage door, should anyone in the house need to leave while we were there. He got out and snapped Angus's leash onto his collar.

I took a couple of deep, calming breaths before I got out of the Jeep. I didn't care for Dr. Carstairs, and I wasn't particularly thrilled to be seeing him again.

Ted and Angus were waiting for me at the back of the Jeep.

"You ready, babe?"

I nodded. "As ready as I'll ever be."

We walked around to the front porch, and I rang the bell. A tall blond woman wearing a light blue pin-striped dress and a white apron answered the door.

"Hello. I'm Barbara, Brendan's nanny. Right this way, please."

She led us to a den off the massive, high-ceilinged foyer. "Sir, you and your dog may wait here. Ms. Singer, your costume is in the bathroom—the door is there, to your right. Please put on the costume, and we'll all go together to greet the family."

As I went into the bathroom, Ted sat stiffly on a tan leather chair. Angus sat as close to Ted as possible, and Barbara stood emotionless by the door. What a lively atmosphere. They were sure to have a ton of laughs while they waited for me to change. I hurriedly slipped into the silly elf costume, reminding myself all the while that I was doing this for a sick little boy and that he'd be delighted to see me.

I came out of the bathroom, and Barbara immediately said, "This way please."

Brendan's room was obviously the master suite. There was a gas fireplace at one end of the room, and an array of toys decorated the mantel. The bed was on the right side of the room, and a seating area was on the left. There wasn't much of a play area. I didn't know whether the Carstairs had another room designated for the playroom or if Brendan was simply too ill to need one.

Three large windows faced out onto the bay. Brendan reclined on a love seat and looked outside. My heart clenched a little. I imagined the boy would love to have the energy to run and play in the yard.

"Hi, Brendan," I said softly.

He raised his head and looked wearily in my direction. But when he saw the costume—and Angus—his face brightened. "Marcy the Elf and Angus!"

"That's right," I said. "We heard you came home from the hospital yesterday, and we wanted to drop in and say hello on our way back up North. Is that okay?"

"That's great!"

"This is my friend Ted," I told Brendan.

"Is he from the North Pole, too?"

"I am. I'm Santa's head of security," said Ted. "Sometimes the South Pole elves try to get into the workshop and steal our toy ideas. I'm there to make sure that doesn't happen."

"Whoa." The little boy's blue eyes widened.

Dr. Carstairs and Melanie were sitting on a larger sofa near Brendan.

"Hi," I said, mainly to Melanie. "How are you?"

"I'm great," said Melanie. "I finished my first Christmas ornament last night, and I've already started another one."

"I can hardly wait to see," I said.

"However, this is Brendan's time," said Dr. Carstairs.

"Of course." Melanie lowered her eyes.

"So, what would you like to do?" I went over and sat at Brendan's feet. The child was covered up to his chin with a fluffy white blanket.

"Can Angus come over and sit with us?" he asked.

"Sure."

Ted unleashed Angus, and I called him over. He went up to Brendan's face and snuffled the child's ear.

Brendan laughed. "He's funny." He patted the cushion, and Angus climbed up over the child and lay down with his head on the boy's chest.

Angus's tail was wagging near my face, and I made exaggerated contortions to try to escape getting a mouthful of hair. Brendan laughed until he was out of breath.

I moved onto the floor and sat cross-legged. "Do you have a favorite book I could read you?"

He nodded and pointed to one that was at the top of a stack. It was about a boy detective.

"Dr. Carstairs, why don't you show me around the grounds?" Ted asked quietly.

"Of course." Dr. Carstairs seemed relieved for the excuse to leave the room.

I'd only been reading for about twenty minutes when Brendan fell asleep. Angus quickly followed suit.

"How sweet they are," said Melanie. She used her phone to snap a photo. "Poor Brendan is still exhausted from his latest trip to the hospital. His condition is improving, though."

"He and Angus are precious together. Have you ever thought about getting Brendan a dog?"

"I have. But pets are a lot of work. And we have so much to deal with already, given Brendan's condition."

"I understand. Well, anytime you'd like to schedule a playdate with Angus, just let me know." I smiled. "So, how about that embroidery?"

Melanie reminded me of a child herself as she proudly displayed the red-and-white gift box she'd embroidered. "What do you think?"

"You did a beautiful job!"

"Thank you." She then showed me the one she'd started this morning while Barbara was giving Brendan his breakfast. It would eventually be a Christmas tree with red-and-white French knots and a silver satin-stitch garland. So far, Melanie had the outline of the tree.

"This is terrific," I said. "Do you know how to do the French knots?"

"I think so. If I have any trouble, may I call on you tomorrow at the Seven-Year Stitch?"

"Of course you may."

"Mrs. Carstairs, don't you think we should put Brendan in his bed?" asked Barbara.

"Yes." She looked over at her son. "He looks so comfy that I hate to move him, though."

"I know, but Dr. Carstairs won't like it if he returns and finds the boy like this."

Melanie nodded. "Marcy, can you get Angus?"

"Sure." I went over and spoke softly to Angus.

The dog raised his wiry gray head and looked at me. Then he flopped it back down as if to say, *Why are you bugging me? I'm taking a nap here.*

"Come on," I said.

Angus reluctantly got up and hopped off the love seat.

Melanie cradled Brendan's head and shoulders,

and Barbara got his feet. They managed to get him to the bed without disturbing him at all. The child must truly have been exhausted.

"If you don't mind, I'll go ahead and change," I said.

"I'll show you the way," said Barbara.

It wasn't necessary, but I didn't want her to feel unwanted. Angus plodded along behind us.

"In Brendan's room, you said Dr. Carstairs wouldn't like Brendan being asleep on the love seat," I said when I was sure we were out of Melanie's range of hearing. "Why is that?"

She lifted and dropped one slender shoulder. "Dr. Carstairs likes things a certain way—that's all. As his employee, I must see that his requirements are met."

"And what about Mrs. Carstairs?"

"She is my employer also."

"But you work primarily for the doctor," I said.

"Everyone in this house is here at the doctor's discretion—including you." She nodded toward the den. "Please leave the costume hanging in the bathroom, so it will be here the next time you come."

I felt like telling her that I was here at my own discretion and that I wouldn't be back, but I didn't. I merely changed my clothes and left the elf costume hanging on the hook on the back of the door.

When I emerged from the bathroom, only Angus was awaiting me in the den. I was glad. Barbara might be the perfect employee for Dr. Carstairs, but I was ready to get away from both of them.

I hugged Angus and stepped out into the foyer. Dr. Carstairs, Melanie, and Ted were standing there talking. I was a bit surprised that they weren't sitting in the living room, and I decided that Ted must be every bit as ready to leave as I was.

"Thank you for having us come to visit Brendan," I said. "He's a sweet boy."

"Thank you for coming, Marcy," said Melanie.

"He's truly enamored of your dog," said Dr. Carstairs.

"Isn't everybody?" Ted snapped the leash onto Angus's collar.

"What would you have to have for him?" the doctor continued.

"Excuse me?" I asked.

"Bellamy!" cried Melanie.

"Name your price for the dog."

"Angus is not for sale." I stepped closer to Ted and Angus. "He's family."

"So's my mother," said Dr. Carstairs. "But for a cool million, she's yours." He laughed. "Five hundred thousand? Anyone?"

I managed a tight smile and hoped it didn't look as if I were snarling at the doctor. "Again, thank you for your invitation. I hope Brendan is better soon." I walked out the door and headed for the Jeep.

"Well, if you reconsider about selling the dog, let me know!" Dr. Carstairs called.

"Just keep walking," Ted muttered under his breath. "Just keep walking."

"Are you talking to me or to yourself?"

"Both."

*   *   *

On the drive home, I asked Ted what he and Dr. Carstairs had talked about while they'd been alone.

"At first, of course, we talked about his land. He told me where the property lines were, that he had over five acres, blah, blah, blah."

"But you were finally able to turn the conversation to the hospital?" I asked.

"Of course I was. Manu doesn't pay me the big bucks for *not* getting people to talk." He winked.

I smiled. "Man, it feels good to be out of that oppressive house! Poor Brendan. That toxic atmosphere can't be healthy for him . . . or for Melanie, either, for that matter."

"The Carstairs' home is a castle. Bellamy Carstairs is king of that castle. The hospital is a kingdom. Bellamy Carstairs is the ruler over that kingdom. That was the gist of our entire conversation."

I gave a low growl, forgetting that Angus was in the backseat. He poked his head over the seat to see what I was growling about. I kissed his nose and told him I wasn't angry with him.

"Bellamy Carstairs is an obnoxious bully. Is it possible he killed Sandra Vincent?" I asked Ted.

He shook his head. "He'd never get his hands dirty like that. Besides, he's a surgeon. He'd have carved her up with precision."

"Ted, that's awful!"

He chuckled. "Sorry. That guy brings out the worst in me. But, no, I don't think he killed Sandra Vincent.

Why would he? He had her in his back pocket. She'd do anything he wanted her to do."

"Sounds like Barbara, the nanny. It's clear she works for him and that Melanie is just an after-thought . . . or another child Barbara has to tend to. Did Dr. Carstairs say anything about Martin Brothers Construction?"

"As a matter of fact, he did. I asked him about his deck—I could tell it had been built recently, probably this past summer. He said Martin Brothers did the job and that I can rest assured that they won't be doing any more work for him."

"Really? Did they do the deck before or after the cancer ward was completed?"

"I don't know, but if I'd have to make a bet, I'd say the two projects were going on at around the same time. In fact, what made Carstairs angry with the Martin brothers was that they didn't have their best team on his deck. That crew was working at the hospital."

I scoffed. "And his deck is more important than a hospital cancer ward?"

"In his world it is."

"So, it's possible that the cancer ward was the last project that Martin Brothers Construction will be doing for Tallulah County General," I said. "I wonder if the Martins know that."

Chapter Nineteen

On Monday morning, Sadie dropped in to ask how everything was going with Captain Moe's case.

"I honestly have no idea," I said. "I know that Riley has a private detective on the case, but Ted's insider at the Tallulah County Police Department says that the detectives who made the arrest feel they have their killer."

"Of course they do. They don't know Captain Moe like we do."

"Exactly. Which is why we're trying to find other suspects to at least provide the jury with reasonable doubt."

"Any luck?" she asked.

"The list of people who could've possibly had it in for Ms. Vincent just keeps growing, but I do have one suspect who's standing out in my mind." I told her about John Martin.

"What a creep! Is he the guy you were talking with in the coffee shop the other day?"

I nodded. "And then he was standing outside the Brew Crew, looking over here, so I waved to let him know I saw him. He gestured as if he was shooting me."

Sadie gasped.

"But that's not all," I continued. "He asked Will whether or not Angus was aggressive."

"What's Ted saying about all this?"

"He's warned me to be careful." I nodded toward a police cruiser driving slowly down Main Street. "And that doesn't surprise me. That's the third time this morning, and I've only been open an hour and a half."

"I'm glad he's got his patrolmen looking out for you."

I smiled. "He worries about me."

"So do I. That Martin guy sounds like a serious threat."

"I think he's just trying to scare me," I said. "Hopefully, Harvey Gordon—that's Riley's PI—will be able to connect him to Sandra Vincent's murder somehow."

"I hope so. Keep me posted."

She was getting ready to leave when Tiffany, Mark, and Jackson came into the Seven-Year Stitch.

"Hey, guys!" I said.

Angus happily loped over to Mark, who was holding Jackson.

"It's good to see you again," Sadie said. Then she lowered her voice. "If it would be okay for Jackson to have a sugar cookie, stop by MacKenzies' Mochas and I'll fix him up."

"Heck, *I'd* like a sugar cookie," said Mark. "And it

would be wonderful to get some goodies for the trip home."

Tiffany shook her head. "Go on, then." She turned her attention to Sadie. "Please cut Mark off at two bags of food, please. It's only a five-hour trip."

Sadie laughed. "All right. Be safe."

Tiffany and I watched the trio tramping down the street, talking animatedly. Angus went to the window and paced back and forth, hoping, no doubt, that Mark would bring him back something.

"I imagine Sadie is telling Mark and Jackson all about the goodies she spent the morning baking," I said.

"And Mark is probably saying he'll take at least one of each."

"Then he and Jackson will be gone a few minutes. Come on over and have a seat."

She followed me to the sit-and-stitch square, sat on a red club chair, and stretched her legs out on the ottoman. She closed her eyes. "I might not be able to get back up."

"Didn't you sleep well last night?"

"Not particularly. I was wondering if I had everything packed, what time we should get on the road—that sort of thing."

"I know. It's so hard sometimes to shut out the world and have a peaceful night's rest."

She opened her eyes. "What about you?"

"Oh, I slept fine."

"That's not exactly what I meant. I know you're upset about your friend's murder charge. And Ted told me about that creep who was watching you on Saturday."

"It's nothing," I said. "I'm not worried about that guy." Of course, I was, but I didn't want to admit that to Tiffany. If she knew how scared I really was, she'd probably call her brother and talk him into taking off work to come babysit me.

"Yes, you are worried. I can tell."

"Maybe a little. But if you sit here more than twenty minutes, you'll see a police cruiser rolling slowly by."

She nodded. "He really does love you."

"And I really do love him."

"I know." She gave me a slight smile. "I was prepared not to like you at all. In fact, I looked for things to *dislike* about you. Prissy little bohemian who runs an embroidery shop . . . *Bound to be an airhead*, I thought."

I laughed. "You might not be far off the mark there."

"No. You sell yourself short. Um . . . no pun intended. You're brave and thoughtful and devoted to my brother. You make him happy. How could I *not* like you?"

"Thanks."

"You're welcome." Her smile widened. "Just know that my feelings can change in a Seattle second if you hurt him."

"Point taken."

"Somehow I think it's a shame you didn't have any siblings. I believe you'd make someone a good sister."

I laughed. "Well, Todd Calloway and Blake Mac-Kenzie have both insinuated themselves into the role of my big brother, so I guess you'd have to ask them. And, naturally, they'd both tell you I'm a brat."

"What you need is a sister."

"Maybe I'll have one someday," I said.

I was refilling the floss bins when the bells over the door signaled an arrival. "Be right out!"

"Take your time."

I didn't recognize the female voice that had called to me and that I now heard talking softly to Angus. When I stepped out of the aisle and around the corner, I saw that it was Dani.

"Hi, Dani." I placed my basket of floss on the counter and gave the young woman a hug. "Where's Nicole?"

"She's with my aunt today. I just wanted to stop by and thank you again for coming to Mom's visitation Friday night. That was so sweet of you."

"Would you like a cup of coffee?"

"Please." She sat on the sofa.

Angus sat by her side, tail thumping, as she continued petting his head and telling him what a good boy he was.

I went into the office and made us up a coffee tray. When I returned to the sit-and-stitch square, I put the tray on the table and sat on the sofa across from Dani.

As she helped herself to her coffee, she said, "I guess I'm still kinda numb, you know?"

I nodded. Actually, I didn't know. I couldn't bear the thought of something happening to Mom and had no idea how I'd deal with it.

"I mean, we were sort of prepared for it," she continued. "But we were also thinking that any day that donor would come through, and Mom would have the transplant and get better."

"I saw Charlie—one of the hospital security guards—at your Mom's visitation. He said you two had bonded over your mothers both awaiting transplants."

"Yeah. Charlie's mom was on the list for a heart transplant, I believe. She died just a few weeks ago."

"That's what he told me," I said.

"Wanna hear the saddest part? The day she died, the heart came through for her. Of course, she was dead, and the heart went to the next person on the list. But to be that close . . ." She shrugged. "I suppose it wasn't meant to be."

"Is there some sort of support group at the hospital for people whose loved ones are on the transplant list?"

"Yes. The group meets at the hospital. It's for people on the list and for their families, too," she said. "The people on the list who are well enough to attend meetings get to share their fears and concerns with those who have the same feelings, as well as with those who've undergone successful transplants."

"Oh, that's good. I didn't realize people who'd already had transplants were part of the group."

"They are. And they're terrific. They give those on the wait lists—and their family members—hope that everything will work out. Or, you know, that it *can*."

"I'm sorry it didn't in your mother's case," I said.

"So am I."

*   *   *

I'd gotten in a shipment of cross-stitch kits and was hanging them up when Ted arrived with lunch. He'd brought us chicken tikka masala from a nearby Indian restaurant. Since we didn't want to give Angus any of the spicy food, Ted had stopped at the pet store first and got Angus a bag of beefy treats.

"You think of everything." I kissed Ted before putting the clock on the door.

He and Angus went on back to my office. Ted was taking our food out of the bag when I got there.

"Tiffany, Jackson, and Mark stopped by on their way through town this morning," I said, as I took two sodas from the mini fridge.

"Did they?"

"Uh-huh. Sadie was here when they arrived, and she took Mark and Jackson down to the coffee shop to load up on food for the drive back to Seattle. Tiffany told Sadie to cut Mark off at two bags."

Ted grinned. "Let me guess—he brought back two bags filled to the brim."

"Yes, he did." I laughed. "And he also had a small, disposable cooler that Blake had fixed up for him. Mark said that the cooler didn't count because it wasn't a bag and that, besides, he didn't want to have to stop for lunch."

"Oh, of course not. I mean, they'll be trekking across the wilderness for days, right?"

"Tiffany said you told her about John Martin. That surprised me."

He shrugged and took out his plastic utensils. "It was on my mind. You haven't seen or heard from him, have you?"

"No. It's like I told Tiffany—he isn't going to do anything. He just wanted to scare me."

"And my Inch-High Private Eye doesn't scare easily." He winked.

"That's right. Especially when I have a patrolman driving by my shop every twenty minutes or so."

"You noticed that?"

"Um, yeah. I noticed that. And thank you."

"You're welcome."

"Did Tiffany or Mark say anything else to you about possibly moving closer to Tallulah Falls?" I asked.

He arched a brow. "No. Why? Is their moving to Oregon something you'd like or totally hate?"

"I think I'd like it," I said. "I believe that although we started out on rocky ground, Tiffany and I are starting to hit it off. How about you? Would you like for them to live closer?"

"I would. It'd be good for Mom, for Jackson, for Tiffany. And I wouldn't mind seeing more of Tiff, now that she's older and has more sense."

I laughed and shook my head. From what I knew of siblings, this was typical of the banter between brothers and sisters.

Ted's cell phone rang. He glanced at the screen and saw that it was Manu. He answered using the speaker.

"Hey, Manu, what's up?"

"I know you're having lunch with Marcy, but I

need you to take care of something as soon as you're finished."

"Sure. We're about to finish up. I can take off in a couple of minutes. What's going on?"

"Someone threw a brick through Melanie Carstairs's windshield," said Manu.

I drew in a breath. "Oh, my gosh. Is she hurt?"

"Luckily, she wasn't driving the car at the time, Marcy. She was inside the bank. The car is still there. There is a unit there, but they're waiting for someone else to get there before they start to canvass the area to see if anyone saw anything. You're the closest person I have to the bank right now."

"I'm on my way."

Ted ended the call, gave me a quick kiss, and left me to wonder who was trying to send Melanie Carstairs a message.

Chapter Twenty

Angus and I were coming back from his after-lunch potty break when Vera pulled into a parking spot near the Stitch. She got out and waited for us.

"Paul heard about the incident with Melanie Carstairs's car," she said, pushing the button on her key fob to lock her BMW. "He's gone over to the bank to get the full story. So, do you think it was random or that she was targeted?"

"I have no idea. Manu called Ted during lunch, and he went over to talk with Melanie." I pushed open the door and took the leash off Angus.

He trotted to the office to get a drink of water. I put the leash under the counter.

"May I get you some water or coffee or something?" I asked Vera.

"No, hon, I'm fine. How'd it go yesterday?"

"It went fine. I really like Melanie. And Brendan is precious. You should've seen him and Angus cuddled up on the love seat. But Dr. Carstairs seems to be a weird control freak."

"Hmm. Makes you wonder how he and Melanie wound up together, doesn't it? I mean, was he always that way? Was *she* always the way she is now? Maybe she was as nasty a person as her husband until she had a child."

"Could be." I went over to the red club chair where I'd left my current Christmas ornament project. "I just wonder if throwing a brick through Melanie Carstairs's windshield isn't the kind of thing John Martin might do to warn her off of reapplying for the hospital-administrator job."

"That's right. They'll have to fill the position fairly quickly," she said. "And I imagine Mr. Martin would want to eliminate the competition. . . . And that he has plenty of bricks lying around."

"Plus, scaring people seems to be right up his alley."

"Still, I don't know how he could get away with throwing a brick through someone's windshield in a bank parking lot in the middle of the day. Someone is bound to have seen him."

"Yeah. I'd imagine *lots* of people saw him and that the security cameras did, too. How in the world did he get away?"

"I'm looking forward to hearing what Paul finds out. I mean, surely in this age of cell phones and viral videos and whatnot, someone captured the incident— or at least got the guy's license plate."

"You'd think," I agreed. "I hope it *was* John Martin and that he was dumb enough to have thrown that brick himself rather than hiring someone else to do it.

At least that would give Ted a reason to haul him in and question him."

"Yeah. We need to find Sandra Vincent's killer quick. If we don't, poor Captain Moe is going to be sunk. So, in addition to John Martin, who else might've wanted to bump off Sandra Vincent?"

"I might say Carrie Monahan, except she seems genuinely sweet. Also, I'd imagine a nurse would use some sort of medication rather than a knife to the chest to kill someone."

Vera turned down the corners of her mouth. "Maybe if the murder was premeditated, but what if she acted in the moment?"

"But why would a pediatric nurse be carrying around a butcher knife from the hospital's kitchen?"

She gave this some thought. "One of the kids could've had a birthday cake they needed to have cut."

"I guess that's a possibility." I stretched my legs out on the ottoman and examined the toes of the wingtip flats I'd worn today. "What about the people on the transplant list? From what I've heard, Sandra Vincent had either the authority or the means—or both—to manipulate that list."

"Having the power to basically decide who lives and who dies is going to make you a few enemies. Do they have some sort of support group for patients and their families?"

"They do. Dani—the woman whose mother died last week—told me about it earlier. She and Charlie, the security guard, met at a support-group meeting. Charlie's mother was awaiting an organ transplant, too."

"We should go to the next meeting."

I frowned. "And do what? Stand up and say, 'Hi, we're Marcy and Vera, and we're here to find out if any of you killed Sandra Vincent'?"

"No, of course not. Who'd volunteer any information if we did that? We can pretend we're there gathering information for Paul for an upcoming article." She shrugged. "I mean, he might really do the article if I supply enough good information."

"That's not a bad idea. Find out when the next meeting is," I said at last. "You know I can't possibly go on Wednesday."

"I know that, dear." She took out her phone and called the hospital. After being transferred what must've been ninety-two times, she asked about the support-group meetings and then turned to me with a triumphant smile. "The meeting is this evening at seven o'clock. We're going."

After Vera left, I called Ted.

"Hey, babe," he answered.

"Hi. Any chance you caught John Martin with the smoking brick?"

"Considering that the smoking brick was in the driver's seat of Melanie Carstairs's station wagon, that would be a no. Furthermore, nobody saw anything except a big guy wearing a ski mask. After throwing the brick, the man drove off in an older-model pickup truck that had mud obscuring the license plates."

"Oh no. You've got basically nothing, then."

"Right. And the bank's surveillance footage backs up the witnesses. Burly guy wearing a ski mask drives an old pickup truck right up to Mrs. Carstairs's car, gets out, hurls the brick, and drives away."

"But at least you know now that it wasn't a random act. He deliberately chose Melanie's car. Is she scared?"

"She seemed to be handling it fairly well, all things considered. Officer Moore drove her home, and we had her car towed to the closest body shop to be repaired."

"Do we have any plans this evening?" I asked.

"Actually, I meant to talk with you about that over lunch. I've promised Mom I'd take her Christmas shopping this evening. You're welcome to come along."

"I'd like to, but I kinda made plans with Vera."

"Why do you sound so uncertain about these plans, Inch-High?"

"Well, I think you just hit that nail right on the head with your nickname, because we're going snooping." I told Ted about Vera's idea for us to infiltrate the organ-transplant support group as reporters.

I'd fed Angus and allowed him to go out into the backyard. When Vera arrived, I was having trouble getting him to come back inside.

"Bear with me," I said. "Angus is enjoying his off-the-leash freedom, and I can't get him back inside."

"Let me try." She flung open the back door, bent over, and put her hands on her knees. "Come see me, my sweet boy!"

Angus galloped inside and nearly knocked her down in his enthusiasm. I quickly rescued Vera and then shut the door before Angus could run back out.

"Are you all right?"

"Sure," she said with a laugh. "I could probably use a lint roller before we head out, though."

I fished a lint roller out of one of the kitchen drawers, and she got the dog hair off her slacks and sweater.

"There." She smiled. "Good as new."

I locked up, leaving lights as well as the television on again.

"Still afraid that nasty John Martin might come calling?" she asked.

"Yeah. I don't want to take any chances."

"I don't blame you. Paul said they weren't able to narrow down a suspect in the vandalism on Melanie Carstairs's car."

"Ted said the same thing."

"What's he doing tonight? I hope you didn't have to break a date so we could attend this support-group meeting."

"He's taking his mother Christmas shopping," I said. "He invited me along, but I told him what we were doing."

"Did he strongly encourage you to go shopping, or did he say something along the lines of *you can come with us if you'd like?*"

"Um, it was more like that last thing, but since I'd already asked him about his plans, he probably knew I had something in mind that I wanted to do."

She nodded. "That's what I thought. He's shopping for you, and so he didn't *really* want you to come along."

"I think had that been the case, he'd have said so."
She looked smug. "We'll see."

"What's that supposed to mean?"

"I bet he'll get you a fabulous gift."

"I'm sure he will," I said. "He knows me very well.
Anything he picks out for me will be perfect."

We walked into the conference room. It was a different room from the one that had served as the North
Pole. Of course, that room would probably be out of
commission for a long time. This was a smaller room
on the first floor.

There was a table against one wall with Styrofoam
cups, hot water, instant coffee, tea, and sweetener. A
few people were gathered around that table, and others were sitting in metal chairs that formed a circle.

Vera and I went over to the chairs and sat down.

"When are you going to tell them what we're doing
here?" I whispered.

"As soon as everyone gets here."

Charlie, the security guard, burst into the room.
"Sorry I'm late, folks. If everybody's ready, we'll get
started."

He sat down on the middle chair at the top of the
circle. "I believe we all know each other." He looked
surprised when his gaze fell on me. "Marcy?"

"Hi, Charlie."

"What're you doing here?"

Vera stretched her hand out to Charlie. "I'm Vera
Langhorne. My boyfriend, Paul Samms, is with the

newspaper. He couldn't be with you this evening, so I'm here to do an article on your group and the plight of organ recipients and their families. Hopefully, it will bring more awareness to the community about organ donation and how people can help."

Charlie shook her hand. "Thank you."

"I hope we can help," she said.

"Just pretend we aren't here," I said.

"Right," said Vera. "I hope you don't mind Marcy bringing me. She's the one who told me about your group."

"I don't mind at all," Charlie said. "I just ask that you don't use anyone's actual name."

"Of course not. We'll certainly respect everyone's privacy."

Charlie introduced us to the rest of the group and then got on with the meeting. "I imagine most, if not all, of you have heard about Ms. Vincent's passing."

There was a murmur of consent from the group.

"I'm sorry for what happened to her," said a young woman with her red hair in a fishtail braid. "But I'm not sorry that woman is through meddling in our lives. Grandpa was moved down on the list three times thanks to her. He'd have had a heart by now if she hadn't been overseeing the transplant list."

Vera and I shared a glance as other members of the group said the same types of things.

"I think the main thing we need to do as a group is petition the board of directors to make Carrie Monahan the new hospital administrator," said Charlie.

"She's a good, caring person. She's worked with children for years. She's compassionate. And she'll be our advocate."

I wondered why Charlie was so adamantly going to bat for Carrie Monahan, especially since any decisions she might or might not make were too late to help his mother.

Chapter Twenty-one

Ted came over later that evening. He brought a pint of vanilla ice cream, chocolate syrup, and peanuts. Was it any wonder that I adored this man?

We went into the kitchen, where I scooped the ice cream into two glass dessert bowls. I put a spoonful into Angus's bowl, and he gobbled it up before I could get back to the table. Ted and I sat down and added the extra goodies to ours before digging in.

"So, how'd it go?" he asked. "Did you and Vera have an enlightening time at the support-group meeting?"

"Well, the main thing we learned was that the people in that group didn't care for Sandra Vincent. I don't know whether it was truly her fault or not, but they all blamed her for their loved ones getting knocked down the list. One woman said her grandfather was bumped three times in favor of someone else."

"I have to wonder if that responsibility would be left up to the hospital administrator alone. I'd imagine the patients' doctors would be in the best position to determine what patients were in the greatest need," he said. "I'd think it would be a group decision."

"I agree. I think they're simply looking for a scapegoat." I took a bite of my ice cream. "But, for some reason, they think Carrie Monahan would do a much better job."

On Tuesday, I was helping a woman find a beginner's ribbon-embroidery kit for her daughter when Melanie Carstairs came in. I excused myself and allowed the woman to browse on her own while I attended to Melanie.

"Hi, Melanie. How's everything going?"

"Good. I'm really enjoying making those Christmas ornaments. And I think I'm getting better at it."

"That's great."

"In fact, I'm here for more embroidery floss," she said.

"Well, let me know if I can help you find anything."

The other customer chose her ribbon-embroidery kit and brought it to the counter. I rang up her purchase and put it and a flyer about upcoming classes and events in a periwinkle Seven-Year Stitch bag. When she left, I noticed Melanie was accumulating quite a handful of flosses, so I took her the basket I used to transport items from the storeroom to the floor.

"I thought you might need this."

She took the basket. "Thanks. Actually, I wanted to talk to you about something."

Oh no. Not again.

"Could you please stop by after work to see Brendan for a few minutes?" she continued. "I know things ended awkwardly last time with Bellamy trying to buy your dog and everything, but he won't be home until late."

Still, I hesitated. It wasn't Melanie or Brendan that was the problem; it was the entire situation. And I'd promised myself after Sunday that I wouldn't go back.

"And you don't have to wear that silly costume," Melanie continued. "We'll tell Brendan that it's your day off from the North Pole. He just enjoys you and . . . and Angus so much. And I can show you the ornaments I've made."

I got the feeling this visit was as much about Melanie needing a friend as Brendan needing a visit from an elf. "All right. I can't stay long, but I'll drop by."

"Thank you." She beamed. "Thank you so much."

At lunch, I told Ted about Melanie's visit and that I was planning to stop by there for a few minutes after work.

"Well, good luck," he said.

"She promised me that Dr. Carstairs wouldn't be there—and that I wouldn't have to wear the stupid costume. I really got the feeling that she needs a friend."

"I'll trust your judgment."

"You don't think I should go, do you?" I asked.

"I think you should do whatever you feel like doing."

"Brendan is a good kid. He can't help that his dad is an obnoxious jerk."

"Are you trying to convince *me* or yourself that you're doing the right thing by going this afternoon?"

"Both, I guess." I shook my head. "You know good and well that I'd vowed to never go back after Sunday."

"Yes, I seem to recall having heard that over and over and over and over on the drive home."

I laughed a bit self-consciously. "I was firm in my resolve until Melanie Carstairs stopped in and implored me to visit. And then I caved. Are there any new leads on who vandalized her car, by the way?"

"No. I had a slow morning, though, and I ran John Martin's name through the computer. He has a history of assault. I still have patrolmen driving by here regularly—"

"I noticed. Thank you."

"—but be especially vigilant when you're walking to and from your car. And make sure you aren't being followed when you're driving."

"Got it."

He checked his watch. "I need to get back, but I'll walk Angus before I go."

I had to admit, Ted's protectiveness did have its advantages.

As I wound my Jeep around the curves leading up to the Carstairs' home, I complained to Angus that I was probably losing my mind for agreeing to come back to this house.

"Or, at best, I'm losing my spine. I'll probably turn

into a puddle of goo right here behind the wheel. If I do, can you jump up here and pull us safely to the side of the road?"

He woofed.

"Or if you can't, simply burrow down in the back-seat and cover your head. Then call Ted to come and rescue you."

Angus didn't respond to that remark. He just cocked his head as if to say, *Hello? No thumbs!*

I caught a glimpse of something on a dirt path between two of the boxwoods lining the driveway. It was a vehicle. I slammed on the brakes, causing Angus to fall forward slightly.

"Sorry, sweetie."

Again he merely looked at me, decidedly thinking that I really was losing my mind.

The vehicle was a pickup truck. It was pulled in so I couldn't see the front, but the back license plate was caked with mud.

I took out my cell phone and called Ted.

"Marcy, are you all right?"

I smiled slightly. He'd obviously been concerned about my driving out to the remote Carstairs home alone.

"I'm fine, but I see something strange." I told him about the pickup truck partially hidden on the Carstairs' property. "There's no one inside the truck. Do you think that whoever vandalized Melanie's car is here? That they plan to hurt her? The guy on the surveillance tape was driving an old pickup that matched this description."

"Where are you now?"

"Sitting in the driveway, looking at the truck."

"Get out of there. I'll get the closest possible units out there immediately, and I'll be there as soon as I can."

"I'm staying. I can't just leave wondering if something has happened to Melanie or Brendan."

"Marcy, please. We—the police and I—will handle this."

"Fine. I'll back out of the driveway and stay by the side of the road. If I see anyone leaving the property, I'll lie down in the seat or something."

"Marcy—"

"You're wasting time."

He gave a growl of frustration before telling me to be careful. Then he ended the call.

I did as I'd promised, although I realized that backing around those curves wasn't going so well. I pulled into the dirt path where the truck was parked and turned around. Then I drove back out to the road, pulled over, and shut off the engine.

I called Melanie Carstairs.

"Hello, Marcy. Where are you?"

"I'm nearby." I was trying to be cagey, in case Melanie's would-be attacker was listening. "Is everything all right?"

"Um, yes. Everything is fine. Why?"

"Is there anyone there with you?"

"Brendan and Barbara are here. Marcy, is something wrong?"

"Can anyone hear what I'm saying to you right now?"

"No. Why? You're scaring me."

"I've called the police, and they're on their way. I spotted a pickup truck half-hidden just off your driveway. It could be the same person who threw the brick through your windshield. If he's there already, say something to let me know."

"Oh, goodness. I wish you hadn't called the police."

"Are you being threatened?" I asked.

"No. That truck belongs to our gardener, Luis."

I closed my eyes. "I'm sorry. The license plate was all muddy, and I was afraid it was the guy who'd vandalized your car. I'll call Ted back and—"

Too late. I heard the sirens and then saw the patrol car speeding toward me.

"They're here," I said. "The police are here. I'll follow them down. Ted's gonna kill me."

The squad car pulled into the driveway. I called Ted and explained.

"I'm almost there. I want to take a look at that truck and see if it's the same one from the surveillance tape. Who's to say Melanie Carstairs's gardener doesn't have a grudge against her?"

After speaking with Ted, I started the Jeep, did a U-turn, and once again headed down the Carstairs' driveway. I pulled in, making sure I didn't block the police cruiser, and got out of the Jeep. I snapped Angus's leash onto his collar, and we walked to the door.

Barbara let us in, albeit grudgingly. She glared at me as if I had brought down some sort of plague upon the Carstairs family.

Melanie was in the living room with the two uni-
formed officers. They were two young men I'd never
met. Melanie was in tears.

Ted arrived very shortly. "I've examined the truck
parked on the dirt path between the two boxwoods,
and it is indeed the truck I saw in the bank's surveillance footage."

Melanie gasped. "I don't think so. That truck
belongs to our gardener. The truck on the tape only
looks like Luis's truck."

"That may be," said Ted. "But I need your gardener's full name and address. We need to pick him up
and question him about vandalizing your car."

"Please don't!" She looked from Ted to me and then
back to Ted before she burst into tears. "I did it! I paid
Luis to wear the mask, come to the bank, and throw
the brick through my windshield!"

My jaw dropped. "Why?"

Melanie's head whipped around toward me. "So
Bellamy would fight for me to get that job. He didn't
the last time I applied, but I wanted him to be my
champion this time. The only way to do that was to
make him think someone definitely didn't want me to
have it."

"So you're saying that you arranged to have your
own car vandalized?" Ted confirmed.

"Yes. All right? I did. Luis is innocent, so leave him
alone!"

"Did it work?" I asked. "Did Dr. Carstairs agree to
try to influence the board on your behalf?"

"Yes. Although it doesn't make any difference now,

does it? I told Bell that when I got home from the bank, someone called our home phone and warned me not to apply for the job as hospital administrator." She hung her head. "He said we'd see about that. I believe he was truly going to help me get that job."

Ted shook his head and wrote Melanie a citation for filing a false police report, a Class A misdemeanor.

Chapter Twenty-two

Ted went back to the police station to do his paper-work, and I took Angus home. I fed him and let him go out into the backyard to play while I started dinner for Ted and me. I decided on spaghetti, meat-balls, and breadsticks, because I had all the ingredients on hand.

By the time Ted got to my house, I was putting din-ner on the table. He hung his suit jacket in the foyer and loosened his tie. I could see how tired he was.

"I wish I'd suggested meeting you at your place," I said. "You're exhausted."

He shook his head. "It's just been a frustrating day. I'm fine. Thank you for dinner. It looks wonderful."

"How about I give you a back rub after we eat?"

"Now, *that* would be fantastic." He smiled as he sat down at the table.

"And we'll make cookies. And we'll fling that tie across the room."

"Let's not get carried away," he said. "This is one of my favorite ties, and anything flung around here winds up being shaken vigorously and chewed up by a certain woolly beast."

"Okay. We'll neatly fold the tie and put it someplace where Angus can't get to it."

"Thank you. The back rub and the cookies do sound great, though."

"Then we'll get on that right after dinner." I kissed him and filled his wineglass.

He twirled spaghetti around his fork. "I can't believe Melanie Carstairs's gall. I thought she was the nice one. And yet she sent our police force on a wild-goose chase for something she orchestrated herself."

"I know. I thought she was the nice one, too." I still did, but, then, maybe she was simply the lesser of two evils. "I do think it's a shame, though, that making it look as if she were being threatened was the only way she felt she could garner her husband's support."

"Yeah. That is sad. But that's *their* problem and not the responsibility of the Tallulah Falls Police Department."

I tore a breadstick in half. "About those cookies . . . What kind are you in the mood for?"

"Whatever you have the ingredients for." He took a sip of his wine. "I'm sorry. I'll let it go. I refuse to let the Carstairs ruin our evening."

"Thank you."

We wound up making peanut butter cookies shaped like teddy bears. I even took red icing and made bow ties for them. They were adorable *and* delicious—a combo that can't be beat. In fact, the rest of the evening was unbeatable.

It was good that Ted and I ended up having such a wonderful night because I needed those warm fuzzies to carry me through the rough morning I had the next day.

I'd barely gotten my purse and tote bag stowed under the counter and my coat hung up when Bellamy Carstairs stormed through the front door.

"Ms. Singer, you've certainly got nerve!"

"Excuse me?"

At my side, Angus stiffened.

"How dare you come to my home and make trouble for my family?"

I blinked. Twice. I was trying to gather my composure before I spoke. "I was invited to your home by your wife, and I had no intention of causing trouble for anyone."

"Your idea of not causing trouble was calling the police on my wife?" His face was red, and he reminded me of a squealing piglet, standing there in his brown tweed jacket, spouting accusations.

"I called the police because I saw a truck half-hidden on your property. It fit the description of the truck used by the vandal who threw a brick through Mrs. Carstairs's windshield. I was afraid she and Brendan might be in danger."

"Somehow I doubt that."

"Your opinion doesn't concern me, Dr. Carstairs. I'd appreciate it if you left now."

He took a step toward me, and Angus growled.

The bells over the shop door jingled, and Todd burst into the Stitch.

"Hey, there! Marcy, I was heading to MacKenzies'

Mochas and wanted to see if you need anything." He put himself between Dr. Carstairs and me. "Hi, Angus. How're you doing, buddy?"

The dog didn't move. He continued to watch Dr. Carstairs.

"Dr. Carstairs was just leaving," I said.

Dr. Carstairs jabbed a finger at me. "You stay away from my family." He turned and left.

Todd put his hands on my shoulders. "You're trembling."

"I'm okay now. He's gone."

He led me over to the sofa. "I could tell things were tense in here. That's why I came in. Want to tell me what was going on?"

I sat down, and he sat beside me. Angus came and leaned against my right leg. I patted him reassuringly as I explained to Todd what had happened yesterday.

"That's messed up," said Todd. "A wife has to make it look as if she's being threatened in order to gain the support of her husband?"

"I agree. But there's a reason Bellamy Carstairs doesn't want his wife to have any insight into his life at the hospital. I'd love to know what that reason is."

"I think it's best that you just let it go. That man is obviously a bully, and one bully having you on his radar is plenty, don't you think?"

"You're talking about John Martin."

"Yes, I am. Have you heard anything from him?"

"No. I think he believed me to be sufficiently scared away from whatever it was he was trying to hide."

"That's good." Todd leaned his head back against the sofa. "Man, you get yourself into a lot of trouble."

"I know. It's a special skill."

"Why not try oil painting or something less hazardous?"

"Oil painting can be dangerous, breathing all those fumes."

"I was seriously on my way to MacKenzies' Mochas," he said. "Would you like something? On me?"

"No, thanks. I do appreciate your saving me from the evil Dr. Carstairs, though."

"Anytime."

I got my tote, moved to the sofa facing the window, and then worked on my Christmas ornaments.

Riley Kendall stopped by on her way back to the office from court. She was dressed in a red suit with taupe heels, and she looked impressive and lawyerly. I told her so.

"Gee, thanks . . . I think. I'm making some lace ornaments," she said, as she sat her brown leather briefcase on the counter. "I need some white floss."

"How many skeins do you need?"

"Better make it ten."

I got her ten skeins of white embroidery floss and returned to the counter. "So, any new developments in Captain Moe's case?"

"I'm afraid not. We've got all these shady characters—like John Martin—but nothing that ties them to Sandra Vincent's murder."

"It's actually amazing how many shady characters

there are involved with Tallulah General Hospital, isn't it?" I told Riley about my visit to the Carstairs' home yesterday and then Dr. Carstairs coming by here earlier.

"That's scary. I'm glad Todd happened to be walking by."

"Me, too. I doubt Dr. Carstairs would've tried to hurt me, but who knows?"

"Dr. Carstairs . . ." She drummed her fingertips on the counter as she looked up at the ceiling. "Bellamy Carstairs . . . That name rings a bell with me for some reason."

"He's apparently a big deal with the hospital."

"No, that's not it. It involves a case. An old one." She shook her head. "You've kicked my curiosity into overdrive. I'll have to call Dad. He never forgets anything." She took out her wallet and paid for the floss. "Thanks, Marce."

"If your dad does remember something about Dr. Carstairs, will you let me know what it is?"

"Of course," she said.

She hadn't been gone more than half an hour when she called me. "I just got off the phone with Dad. Bellamy Carstairs stood trial about fifteen years ago for the drugging and sexual assault of a med student. It was Dad's partner's case. I remember it because I saw the photo and thought Dr. Carstairs was handsome."

"I suppose he was back in the day," I said. "Or even before I realized he was such a jerk."

"Hey, I was fifteen. I didn't have the best taste back

then. And, of course, I probably thought he was inno-cent," she said. "I thought just about everybody was innocent when I was that age."

"What happened in the case?"

"He was found not guilty. A nurse named Carrie Monahan provided him with an alibi for the time of the alleged incident."

"Carrie Monahan?" I echoed.

"Yeah, why?"

"Carrie Monahan is the head pediatric nurse at Tallulah General."

"Huh. Well, now. Isn't *that* interesting?"

When Ted arrived at around one, I was decorating a small live Christmas tree that Vera had brought in earlier.

"Isn't it adorable?" I asked. "Vera said I needed something to *spruce* up the place, and then she laughed and laughed at her play on words."

He leaned closer. "That *is* a spruce. At least she knows her trees. It smells good. Did she bring the ornaments, too?"

"Yes, except for the ones I've made."

"Cute."

"What smells so yummy?" I asked.

"Clam chowder and sourdough bread."

Angus had already come over and was snuffling the bag.

"We'd better get into the office and dig in before Angus takes it away from you." I put the cardboard clock on the door that said I'd be back in twenty minutes.

I went into the office, where Ted was taking our food out of the bag and placing it on the desk.

"I had some interesting visitors today," I told him.

He froze. "Who?"

"Todd. Riley. Dr. Carstairs."

His mouth formed a grim line. "What did he want?"

"If by *he*, you mean Dr. Carstairs, he wanted me to stop butting into his family's business. If you mean Todd, he came to check on Angus and me while Dr. Carstairs was here. He passed by on his way to get a coffee and thought the situation looked tense, which it was."

"He told you to stop butting into his family's business? They're the ones who keep insisting you come visit and play elf to their little boy!"

"Well, I'm not sure exactly how he phrased it, but he didn't appreciate my calling the police on his wife yesterday."

The muscle in Ted's jaw worked.

"Please stop grinding your teeth and eat," I said. "We are not going to allow Bellamy Carstairs to ruin our lunch, just like we didn't allow him and his wife to spoil our evening yesterday. Remember?"

Nothing.

"I do have some interesting news," I continued. "Fifteen years ago, Bellamy Carstairs was accused of sexual assault, and his alibi was provided by a young nurse named—wait for it—Carrie Monahan."

"Are you serious?"

"Yes. Riley came in to buy some white embroidery floss and while we were talking about the unsavory people involved in Captain Moe's case, Dr. Carstairs's name came up. She thought it sounded familiar from a case her dad had once worked on. She called him, and, sure enough, that was it."

"And Carrie Monahan provided the alibi?" he asked.

"That's what Riley told me."

"Huh." He leaned back in his chair. "If Dr. Carstairs would have been found guilty, had Ms. Monahan not testified on his behalf, then he owes her a huge debt of gratitude, doesn't he?"

"Yes, he does. Do you . . . Do you think he was guilty of the assault?"

"I don't know. From what I've learned about Dr. Carstairs, I wouldn't be terribly surprised. But, either way, he owes Carrie Monahan. I'll call Riley when I get back to the office and have her get Harvey Gordon to dig a little deeper into both of their pasts."

"I'd imagine she's already done so," I said. "But it won't hurt to give her a reminder and have her fill you in on more of the details of the case."

"In the meantime, if Dr. Carstairs ever comes back in here, call me. I'll have him arrested for trespassing."

"But this is a public place," I said.

"It's *your* place, and he's not coming in here to buy embroidery supplies; he's coming in here to harass you."

"You worry too much, sweetheart. Angus and I can handle Bellamy Carstairs . . . and anyone else."

"*You* overestimate yourself. You aren't ten feet tall and bulletproof."

"Neither are you," I pointed out.

"Marcy, please just humor me." He took my hand. "I don't want that jerk anywhere near you."

I kissed him. "If he comes back, I'll call you."

"Thank you."

Chapter Twenty-three

After work, I rushed home and heated a container of tomato soup in the microwave while I fed Angus. There were some snow flurries outside, so I walked Angus rather than let him go into the backyard after he ate. Back inside, I was more than ready to taste that warm soup. I took a drink, then kissed Angus on the head and left.

I finished the soup on the way back to the Seven-Year Stitch. Amazingly, I didn't spill a drop onto my white jacket. I was extremely proud of myself.

Vera was the first to arrive at the crewel class. "The tree looks lovely."

"Yes, it does. Thank you so much for bringing it in."

"You're welcome."

"I'd been meaning to get a tree for the shop, but I simply hadn't gotten around to it yet," I said.

"It's not like you haven't had a lot to deal with." She took a seat in the sit-and-stitch square. "So, what's new?"

I told her about the entire Carstairs fiasco.

"I just heard about Melanie being responsible for the brick through her own windshield. Paul learned about that from the police blotter." She shook her head. "As you well know, John Langhorne was a first-class heel, but I don't think I'd have had to pretend to be terrorized in order to get his attention."

Vera's late husband *had* been a heel. But she was right: he'd have at least pretended to support her in anything she set out to do. "Here's something I don't understand," I said. "Melanie was one of the three finalists for the hospital-administrator job when Sandra Vincent was hired. Had Dr. Carstairs not wanted her to have the job, why did she make it so far in the hiring process?"

"I don't know. Maybe he didn't want her to know that he was crushing her efforts."

"True. But then why would she make it seem she was being pressured *not* to apply for the job this time in an attempt to gain his support?"

"I have no idea," said Vera. "It seems to me that the Carstairs are both playing a lot of stupid games."

The bells over the door jingled, and my eyes widened. "Muriel, what are you doing out in this snow?"

Tiny Muriel was about ninety years old and couldn't have heard a foghorn from five feet away.

"Yes, only three more weeks to go!" she said cheerily, coming to sit on the sofa by Vera. She patted Vera's shoulder as she sat. "I like Christmas, don't you?"

"I sure do."

*   *   *

I got home and sank into a warm bath. Like a toddler waiting on his mom, I could hear Angus waiting outside the bathroom door.

"We'll watch a movie when I get out," I called to him.

His tail thumped against the wall in response. The hallway was a tight squeeze for such a large dog.

My cell phone, which was on the hamper, began playing "(I've Had) the Time of My Life." It was Ted. I changed Ted's ringtone as often as I did Mom's, and this was his flavor of the month.

I got out of the tub, retrieved the phone, and got back into the warm water. "Hi, handsome."

"Hello, beautiful. Did you have a good class?"

"Yes, it was nice. And what've you been up to?"

"I spoke with Doug after lunch today. Then he and I met for dinner in Depoe Bay. After I told him about Carrie Monahan and Dr. Carstairs, he began to look into the history of both at Tallulah County General Hospital."

"Let me guess," I said. "Carrie came to work there soon after Dr. Carstairs?"

"Yes, and she came up through the ranks fairly quickly. She beat out another nurse who'd been there for ten years for the head pediatric-nurse position."

"That's not fair."

"No, it isn't. The nurse who had seniority left after Carrie got the job."

"I wonder if it was voluntary or if she tried to fight Carrie's promotion over her."

"There was nothing Doug could find about a lawsuit or complaint lodged against Tallulah County General over it," said Ted. "But that doesn't mean she didn't complain, only to realize how futile her protests were. By the way, it wasn't until Carrie Monahan started working at the hospital that Martin Brothers Construction began winning bids there."

"But if Carrie has so much pull, why didn't she get the hospital-administrator job? She *was* one of the three finalists."

"I don't know. I get the feeling somehow that Dr. Carstairs sees himself as a master chess player and that everyone around him is merely a pawn in his game. He moves them wherever he'd like and knocks them out of the way when he doesn't need them anymore."

"Did Doug find any solid connection—outside the hospital, I mean—between Dr. Carstairs and Sandra Vincent?"

"Not yet, but he's looking."

"This whole thing is so bizarre. And there's poor Captain Moe, right in the middle of it all." I sighed. "Could we have dinner at his place tomorrow night? I'd like to check on him."

"Sure, babe."

"I have a Christmas ornament to take him. It's Santa Claus sitting on a dock, fishing. Do you think he'll like it?"

"He'll love it."

*   *   *

I got up early Thursday morning because I wanted to get some Christmas shopping done before opening the Seven-Year Stitch. I left Angus with the promise to either pick him up before going in to work or to have Ted pick him up at lunchtime.

I drove to the Tallulah Falls Mall and was glad to see that it wasn't terribly crowded. I thought I'd probably picked a good time to go. The weekends were bound to be a nightmare by now for those—like me—who didn't like to shop surrounded by a crush of other people.

I had only about an hour and a half before I had to get to the Stitch, so I needed to shop strategically. I stopped in at the jewelry store to see if I could find something for Sadie. I smiled to myself as I thought that Blake would probably have me in here with him on Christmas Eve to help him pick out something for her. Maybe my gift should complement whatever I was going to suggest to him. After mulling over the displays for a good twenty minutes, I didn't find anything that suited me for Sadie, but I did find a lovely necklace for Veronica. I'd show it to Ted at lunchtime to see if he thought she'd like it.

I wandered on through the mall, hoping something in a store display would catch my eye as the perfect gift for someone on my list. I shouldn't have waited so late. I always started stitching early so I could decorate my wrapped gifts with handmade ornaments. But it was buying the actual gifts themselves that was my problem. It was always so hard to figure out who might like what.

The signs—SALE, HALF OFF, SPECIAL—promised deep savings inside each store. As I walked around, I began humming along to the music being played over the loudspeaker—in this case, "Jingle Bell Rock." I could smell gingerbread and vanilla as I passed the candle store. Reggie liked candles. I should go in there to see what scents they had.

As I turned to go inside the candle shop, I spotted Carrie Monahan at a table in the food court, drinking coffee. Someone was with her, but his back was to me. I could tell the man wasn't Bellamy Carstairs or John Martin, and that was good enough for me. I went over to say hello.

"Hi, Carrie," I said brightly. "How are you?"

"I'm fine." She nodded toward the chair to her right. "Won't you join us?"

"Sure." As I sat, I noticed that the man was Charlie, the security guard. "Oh, hi, Charlie."

"Good morning, Marcy."

"That's right," said Carrie. "You two know each other from . . . from that awful Sunday."

I nodded.

"And Marcy and her friend Vera came to the organ-transplant support group the other night," said Charlie.

Curious as to how Carrie would react to my mentioning Dr. Carstairs, I got to the heart of my reason for coming over. "But I doubt I'll ever be able to visit the hospital again."

"Really? Why?"

I drew in a deep breath, inhaling the rich scent of their coffee as I did so. "I'm afraid Dr. Carstairs is furious with me. I imagine you know that Melanie Carstairs had applied for the hospital administrator's job at the same time as Sandra Vincent."

Carrie and Charlie exchanged glances.

"I'd heard something about it, yes," said Carrie.

"Well, apparently, she didn't feel she had her husband's full support, so she made it look as if someone was threatening her to keep her from applying for the job now that Ms. Vincent is, well, no longer the administrator."

"How'd she do that?" Charlie asked.

"She had her gardener come to the bank and throw a brick through her windshield, and then told her husband someone called and threatened her not to apply for the job," I said. "The next day, Mrs. Carstairs came to my embroidery shop and asked me to stop by and see Brendan that afternoon. When I went to the Carstairs' home, I saw a pickup truck half-hidden in the driveway."

I looked at both Charlie and Carrie to see if I could hazard a guess as to what either was thinking. I had no clue.

"My boyfriend is with the police department, so I had a general description of the truck that had been used by the vandal of Mrs. Carstairs's vehicle," I continued. "When I saw the truck, I was afraid that the person who'd thrown the brick through the windshield was threatening the Carstairs. So I called the police."

"That's when Mrs. Carstairs had to come clean

about having the gardener throw the brick," Charlie said.

I nodded. "Then yesterday morning, Dr. Carstairs came by my shop and was angry that I'd caused trouble for his family. I can assure you that wasn't my intention."

"I know it wasn't," said Carrie. "And when Dr. Carstairs has time to think it over, he'll realize it, too. I imagine that, more than anything, he was embarrassed by his wife's actions."

"Do you know Dr. Carstairs very well?" I asked.

"Not very," said Carrie. "But he's infamous for his quick temper."

"I don't think I've ever met the man," said Charlie. "But I can believe he'd be humiliated and looking for someone else to blame for his wife's behavior. Anyone would."

"I just don't understand why she'd feel the need to go to such extremes to either get his attention or have him help her get the hospital-administrator job," I said. "And I wonder if her actions will have the opposite effect and he'll now refuse to help her out at all."

"I hope so." Charlie raised his coffee cup in a salute to Carrie. "I think we've got the perfect hospital administrator sitting right here."

"That's right." I feigned sincerity. "You mentioned that the other night at the support group meeting. How could I have forgotten?"

"Oh, I don't know, Charlie. I'm sure there are a lot of qualified candidates for the job," said Carrie.

"Still, wouldn't it be wonderful if you got the job

this time?" I asked. "Charlie said at the meeting that you have some great ideas for the organ-transplant list."

"Well, that certainly would be a pet project of mine." She smiled. "And I'd like to think I could make the hospital a better place overall."

"Just seeing how you deal with the children on the pediatric ward, I'm sure you would." I turned to Charlie. "Have you seen that playroom up there?"

"No, I haven't," he said.

"Oh, you've got to get up there. It's fantastic. The kids love it."

I smiled at Carrie. "Good luck. Maybe the hospital-administrator job will be an early Christmas present for you."

"I hope so. I know they need to move on it quickly."

"I'd better get back to my shopping," I said. "I'm sorry to have disturbed the two of you."

"No problem." Carrie waved my concerns away with a flick of her wrist. "I'm glad you stopped by. Don't worry about Dr. Carstairs. He'll come to his senses and probably stop in to apologize within the next day or so."

"I hope you're right," I said. "I enjoyed reading to the children."

"And they love it." She placed her hand on Charlie's forearm. "You should see them, Charlie. It's like she casts a magic spell over them. They adore her."

I laughed. "They adore *Angus*. He's my Irish wolfhound," I told Charlie.

He nodded. "I'm sure they like you both a lot."

"Would you like for me to talk with Bellamy?" Carrie asked. "I mean, Dr. Carstairs? We all call him *Bellamy* behind his back. It's such a pretentious name." She chuckled.

"Oh no," I said. "I wouldn't want to get you into any trouble with him. Maybe when you're the administrator, you can put in a good word for me then."

I told them good-bye and went into the candle shop. As I browsed the rows and tried to distinguish one scent from another, it occurred to me that Carrie Monahan wasn't wearing an engagement ring. Had she been wearing one the other evening at the hospital? Maybe the nurses weren't allowed to wear jewelry. Either way, it was easy to see that Charlie was smitten with her. I wondered if he knew she was engaged to John Martin.

Chapter Twenty-four

I didn't have time to pick up Angus before going to the Seven-Year Stitch, so I called Ted as soon as I got there.

"Hey, sweetheart. What's up?"

"I went to the mall this morning and didn't have time to pick Angus up before getting here. Would you mind swinging by for him at lunchtime? I'll get our lunch from MacKenzies' Mochas."

"All right. That sounds great," he said. "How'd your shopping trip go?"

"It was interesting. I did find your mom a necklace—I'll show it to you at lunchtime—but then I ran into Carrie Monahan and Charlie, the security guard."

"At the mall?"

"Yeah. They were having coffee in the food court."

"Did it strike you as odd?"

"Actually, it did," I said. "I kinda doubt it was a coincidence that they ran into each other at the mall, so why not have coffee at the hospital?"

"Unless they didn't want anyone at the hospital to know they were meeting."

"Right. Something else I noticed was that Carrie wasn't wearing an engagement ring, even though she introduced me to John Martin as her fiancé. It makes me wonder if she's simply stringing Charlie along in order for him to support her in her bid for the hospital-administrator job, or if she just doesn't wear jewelry."

"Do you know the security guard's last name?" Ted asked.

"No. I don't think anyone has ever mentioned it."

"It should be in Sandra Vincent's file. He is the person who came to Captain Moe's aid, after all. I'll have Doug see who this Charlie is."

"Okay. Would Caesar salads be all right for lunch?" I asked. "Since we're having dinner at Captain Moe's, I thought we might want something a little lighter for lunch."

"Salads will be terrific."

We had said our good-byes and ended the call when I spotted a familiar-looking woman heading toward the Seven-Year Stitch.

When the woman came inside the shop, I recognized her as Jane, the woman whose contractor husband was blackballed by Martin Brothers Construction.

"Hi, there! How's the stump work going?"

"It's going well," she said. "In fact, I finished Grandma's ornament and enjoyed making it so much that I want to do some more."

"Good. Do you need my help finding anything?"

"Nope. I think I remember where everything is. If

I need you, I'll let you know." She looked around the shop. "Where's your dog today?"

"My boyfriend is bringing him in at lunchtime. I did a little shopping before work this morning."

"That's nice. I hate going on the weekends now, but it's about the only time I can get away long enough to really browse. I've been doing a lot of my shopping online this year."

"I enjoy doing that, too. You can find some of the neatest things online." I was looking for a good way to segue into asking Jane about Martin Brothers Construction. "And, of course, you can find some cool things in specialty shops, too. I think they have some neat ones in Lincoln City, don't you?"

"I do."

"I am sorry your husband was blackballed in Tallulah County and you had to move there, though," I said. "I think it's a charming town, but no one wants to be *forced* to make a move."

"It *is* a charming town." She smiled slightly. "We like it. My daughter has already made new friends at school. Everything's good."

I looked around to make sure no one was about to walk into the Stitch. "Was it Martin Brothers Construction that was responsible for your husband's problems in Tallulah County?"

Jane took a sudden keen interest in the embroidery floss directly in front of her.

"I'm not asking just to be nosy." I explained to Jane how I'd met Mr. Martin at the hospital when I'd gone to read to the children. "I ran into him again at the coffee shop down the street, and I asked him about Sandra Vincent."

"She's the woman who was found stabbed to death in the conference room, isn't she?"

"Yes. He basically told me to mind my own business, and then acted all creepy—standing on the other side of the street, making shooting motions in my direction, asking the people at the Brew Crew if Angus was an aggressive dog."

"Don't write him off as a kook." Jane turned and took me by the arms. "John Martin is dangerous. Yes, he blackballed Aaron with other construction companies, but the real reason we left our home—the dream house we'd built when we first married—was that John Martin threatened our lives. *All* our lives."

I gasped. "Did you call the police?"

"No, Marcy. We were scared. We still are. We left the man alone, and we're finally feeling secure again. Take my advice: don't cross John Martin."

When Ted and Angus arrived for lunch, I'd already gone down to MacKenzies' Mochas and picked up our salads. I'd put them and two sodas on the desk. Blake had, as usual, sent Angus a peanut butter cookie. I had that sitting out, too.

I spoke to Angus but went straight into Ted's arms, holding him as tightly as I could.

"What's wrong?" He pulled away slightly to look down into my face. "Did something happen?"

I shook my head. "Just let me hold you for a second."

"We'll hold each other for as long as you'd like. I'm just worried about you."

Angus wedged his nose between us.

I laughed. "Somebody's feeling left out." I bent and hugged him.

"Ready to talk about it?"

"It's not that big of a deal, really. I guess."

"Marcy."

"Okay. Jane, the woman whose husband is the contractor that John Martin ran out of town, was in here earlier. I told her about Mr. Martin's creepy behavior, and she told me not to cross the man. She said he threatened the lives of their family."

"Did she contact the police?"

"No. She was afraid to. She said they left John Martin alone, and everything has been fine for them." I gave Angus his cookie. "But, Ted, that's scary. He even threatened their child."

He sat down at the desk, his face like granite. I hated when he got like this.

"Please say something."

"I'm just angry, babe, and I'm trying to sort this all out." He ran his hands through his hair. "On the one hand, I understand why your friend and her husband didn't file a police report. It would've been their word against Martin's unless they had some sort of proof. Either way, it was too risky."

"I agree."

"And I understand why you're scared." He patted

his thighs, and I gratefully took a seat and snuggled against him. "But I will protect you."

"I know you will," I said. "I'm not really even afraid of John Martin . . . not really." Okay, I was, but I didn't want to admit it. "I just got to thinking after Jane left about running into Carrie and Charlie at the mall this morning. What if she decides to mention to John Martin that she saw me, and he thinks I'm making trouble?"

"That won't happen. You said yourself that it appeared that the security guard was smitten with her and that she was enjoying his attention. She's not going to tell her fiancé anything about their meeting."

I nodded slowly.

"And I promise you that John Martin is not going to hurt you. He's not going to threaten you. He's not going to stand across the street and scare you. He's not going to step one foot into this store. He's not going to call you. Because if he does any of that, I'll throw him in jail so fast, he won't know what hit him."

I took his face in my hands and kissed him deeply. "Thank you."

I was showing a customer a redwork pattern book when Melanie Carstairs came into the Seven-Year Stitch that afternoon.

"Hello, Mrs. Carstairs," I said. "I'll be right with you."

"Take your time. Hi, Angus."

Angus got up and walked over to her, and Melanie patted his head. "Brendan is sorry he missed you the other day."

Inwardly, I groaned. There was no way I was going to visit the Carstairs' home ever again. I'd been banished by Dr. Carstairs—alias the king—himself.

"Maybe you can bring Brendan in to see Angus sometime," I said brightly. I returned my attention to my customer, who'd decided to buy the book.

"I love your little tree," said the woman, leaning closer to look at the ornaments. "Did you make these?"

"I did."

"Would you be willing to sell one or two of them?" she asked.

I said I'd be happy to do so, and she added two of the ornaments to her purchase.

She left, and I asked Melanie if there was anything in particular I could help her find.

"No," she said. "I'm here to apologize for my behavior and for Bellamy's, too. He told me he came in yesterday morning. He said he instructed you never to come to our home again, and I can imagine he was quite brutish about it."

"He certainly didn't hem and haw."

"I truly am sorry, Marcy. I know you didn't intend to cause trouble for us when you called the police on Tuesday. You saw the truck and became concerned."

"I did. I thought that whoever had vandalized your car had come to your house and had hidden in the bushes. I was afraid he was there to attack you."

"I know, and I appreciate your concern. The whole affair wasn't your fault—it was mine. But Bellamy can't accept blame for anything himself, and, by association, he won't let me accept blame, either. I have tried, though."

"It's none of my business, of course, but I have to wonder why you'd do such a thing. Why would you have your gardener throw a brick through your windshield?"

"To make Bellamy care."

"Did it work?" I asked.

She sighed and rubbed her temples with her fingertips. "I don't know. In a way, I guess."

"Would you like to have a seat?"

She nodded, and we went to sit on the sofa.

"I know he didn't try terribly hard to help me get the hospital-administrator job when I first applied for it."

"I understand that you *were* one of the top three contenders."

"I was," she said. "But then I lost out to Sandra Vincent. Bellamy said she knew someone on the board . . . was *cozy* with him. He wouldn't tell me who. I felt that if he'd pushed a bit harder, I could've gotten that job and used it to do some good in this community, not only for Brendan, but for a lot of people."

"Do you think he'll back you this time?"

"I'm not sure. I hope he will." She threw her head back against the sofa cushions. "I simply can't understand it. We want the same things. I know we do. We want to help our son. We want to make sure that sick children get the best possible care. We want to see to it that the people on the organ-donor waiting list are treated as equitably as possible. Together Bellamy and

I could reform Tallulah County General into one of the best hospitals around!"

"I'd love to see that happen."

"Charlie Emerson told me that you brought your friend to do an article on the support group and the concerns of those awaiting organ donors. That was really nice of you. Charlie's mother, Mary, and I were friends."

"Really." I said it flatly, a statement rather than a question.

"Yes. I know it's unusual to be friends with someone with such a marked age difference as there was between Mary and me, but we just hit it off."

"How did you meet?"

"At one of the meetings. I began attending them when I applied for the hospital-administration position. I didn't go as much after the job was awarded to Sandra Vincent, but I still went now and then. And, of course, I kept in touch with Mary until her death."

"That's sweet of you."

Chapter Twenty-five

Ted called a few minutes later to tell me that he'd heard from his friend Doug. Apparently, the security guard—Charlie Emerson—had applied for a position with the Tallulah County Police Department but had been unable to pass the examination.

"That's kinda sad," I said. "He'd have probably been a good police officer."

"Maybe."

"You don't sound so sure."

"He didn't pass the exam. That probably means he wasn't cut out for a career in law enforcement."

"You might be right. In fact, I'm beginning to think he's more suited to a career as a gossip columnist." I told him about Melanie's visit and her being glad I'd brought Vera to do an article about the group.

"Why is the security guard talking with Melanie Carstairs about the organ-transplant support group? I was under the impression that he wanted Carrie Monahan to get the job."

"He came right out and said as much at the meeting," I said. "He was asking patients to petition the board of directors to instate Carrie as the hospital administrator. I think either he mentioned it to Melanie in passing because she was friendly with his mother or he's talking to Melanie to see where she stands with regard to the position."

"So he can report back to Carrie Monahan."

"Right. That's the only reason I can think of that he'd pretend to be on both their sides."

"But maybe he feels that Bellamy shot his wife down before and will again," said Ted. "What does it hurt to keep Melanie posted on things if it makes no difference in the long run?"

"Or, it could be that he's keeping his options open," I said. "He doesn't know which woman will eventually end up with the job, so he wants them both to think of him as an asset."

"And yet you said he seemed smitten with Carrie when you saw them together this morning."

"I do think he has a crush on her. Still, he could simply be hedging his bets with regard to the job. After all, whoever gets the hospital-administrator job could fire Charlie if she so chose."

"I guess that's true enough."

"But enough about Tallulah County General," I said. "Do you think your mom will like the necklace I got her?"

"For the thousandth time, she'll love it. And she'll also love the cross-stitch Clover you're making for her. She cares a great deal about you, you know."

"I care a great deal about her. And I honestly

believe Tiffany was beginning to thaw toward me before she left for Seattle. I felt a bit of genuine warmth blow my way as she headed out the door." I neglected to add her threat about how quickly her feelings would change if I ever hurt Ted. It was a nonissue anyway. I would never hurt Ted.

"The more she gets to know you, the more she'll like you," he said. "So, I'm looking forward to Captain Moe's later. Aren't you?"

"Yes. Has your salad already worn off?"

"Pretty much."

"How do you think he's holding up?" I asked.

"He's tough. I believe he's doing fine."

"Fine? Or as well as can be expected?"

"That last one."

"Could we go by the mall after dinner?" I asked. "I was really in the mood to shop this morning before I ran into Carrie and Charlie."

"Sure. After all, I need you to help me pick out something for Angus."

"You know he'll love anything you get him."

"Maybe, but I want it to be something special."

I laughed. "You're something special."

"So are you. See you soon."

I was helping a man choose an advanced cross-stitch kit for his wife when Vera came into the Seven-Year Stitch.

"Hi, Vera. I'll be with you in a few minutes."

"Take your time," she said. "I'm in no hurry."

The man chose a wintry Victorian scene, and we returned to the counter.

"If she doesn't like it, can she return it?" he asked.

"Of course." I rang up his purchase and slipped his receipt and a flyer into the bag.

He thanked me and left.

"Are you offering gift certificates?" Vera asked, as I joined her and Angus in the sit-and-stitch square.

"Yes."

"Well, you need to print off a little sign or something and put it on the counter so people will know. I can do calligraphy—I took a class in it once. Give me a marker and a piece of thick paper, and I'll make the sign while we talk."

I went into the office and got Vera a fine-tipped marker and a piece of card stock.

"So, what's the latest?" She turned the paper this way and that, as if deciding what she wanted to do with it.

I told her about seeing Charlie the security guard and support-group facilitator over coffee with Carrie Monahan, and then I informed her about Melanie's visit. "I think maybe Carrie is taking advantage of Charlie because he has a crush on her."

"Poor Charlie. Maybe we should go to another meeting just to let him know Carrie is trying to pull him around by the nose."

"Don't you think we might be pushing our luck? You haven't written that first article yet, you know."

"No, but Paul is looking over my notes." She didn't look up from the sign she was making. "Get out your phone and see when the next meeting is scheduled."

Since she was making me a gift-certificate sign, I decided to humor her.

"The next meeting is set for tomorrow morning at eight o'clock."

"Good. We can go before you open the Stitch."

"Do you really think that's a good idea?" I asked. "What are you planning on telling Charlie about Carrie? How will you even bring that up?"

"I don't know. I'll think of something. He seems like a nice guy. I don't want to see him being taken advantage of. Do you?"

"Well, no, but—"

"Here. What do you think?" She turned the sign around.

ASK ME ABOUT OUR GIFT CERTIFICATES

"That looks terrific," I said.

"Good." She smiled. "I'll pick you up at seven thirty in the morning. I can be there at seven, if you'd like to swing by MacKenzies' Mochas and get some coffee and a scone."

"Seven thirty will be fine."

Ted and I arrived at Captain Moe's at around quarter past six that evening. I was glad to see that the parking lot was just as full as ever. Then a disturbing thought occurred to me.

"Do you think all these cars belong to Captain Moe's regular customers or that some of these people might be reporters or people who just came because they wanted to get a look at someone accused of murder?"

"I have no idea," said Ted. "But if any reporters or lookie-loos are here, they're in for a good meal."

"I know."

He put his arm around me and hugged me to his side. "Don't worry about Captain Moe. He's a strong guy. He can take care of nosy people."

We walked inside to find Eric Clapton's "Layla" playing on the jukebox.

Captain Moe waved at us and then had a server show us to a table. Ted and I sat and ordered our drinks. Before the waiter could return with our sodas, Captain Moe came over to say hello.

"How are two of my favorite people doing this evening?" he asked.

"We're fine," I said. "How are you?"

"I'm good."

"Marcy was afraid the place might be infiltrated with reporters or rubberneckers," Ted said.

"Ah, Tink, their money spends as well as anyone's." He winked.

"I know. I just don't want anyone harassing you—that's all."

Captain Moe's eyes sparkled as he addressed Ted. "What was it the Bard said in *A Midsummer Night's Dream*? 'Though she be but little, she is fierce.'"

Ted laughed. "It's like he had a crystal ball."

"Ain't it the truth?"

The waiter arrived with our sodas, and Captain Moe left so the man could take our order. He promised to come back and check on us again soon.

"So, what do you think?" I asked Ted when the waiter had walked away.

"I think you *are* fierce."

I huffed. "About Captain Moe?"

"Well, I doubt he's as fierce as you are, but—"

"Ted, you know what I mean!"

He leaned forward and lowered his voice. "Babe, how were you when you were a murder suspect?"

"That was different. I wasn't actually *arrested*. Had I been, I think I'd have been in much more of a panicked state."

"No, you wouldn't have. You'd have done as Captain Moe is doing and tried to go on with your life while praying that Riley and the detectives on the case found the real killer."

"I just wish there was something we could do."

"There is. Didn't you see how Captain Moe's face lit up at the sight of you? Knowing he has the support of his friends means a lot to him."

"Have I told you tonight how wonderful you are?" I asked.

"Not since we were in the car. I was beginning to doubt."

"Never doubt."

We were almost finished eating when Captain Moe was able to get back to our table. He pulled up a chair and sat down.

"So, what are you two doing for the rest of your evening?" he asked.

"We're going shopping. I went this morning, but I didn't get very far before running into Carrie Monahan and Charlie Emerson. She's the head nurse on the pediatric ward, and he's a security guard at Tallulah County General."

"I don't think I've met her, but I do remember Charlie. We had . . . an unfortunate encounter."

"I know," I said. "I shouldn't have even brought him up, but I wanted to ask you about Carrie." I looked around to make sure most of the other patrons were either out of earshot or not paying any attention to us. "Do you know anything about John Martin?"

Captain Moe shook his head. "No. Why?"

"We get the impression he's something of a bully," said Ted. "He's engaged to Carrie Monahan, and she was a finalist for the hospital-administrator position."

"You think he bumped off Sandy so Carrie could have the job?" Captain Moe stroked his beard. "Doesn't seem likely. Why would a bully—who would likely be controlling—want his fiancée working longer hours?"

"Why would she be working longer hours?" I asked. "I'd have thought the hospital-administrator job would be the easier of the two."

Captain Moe shook his head. "Not from what I could see. It seemed like Sandy was on call all the time. Every little fire that sprang up, someone was calling to have her put it out."

Given the weight of the arrest on everyone's mind, it was easy to overlook the fact that Captain Moe and Sandra Vincent had been dating. "How are you doing—dealing with her loss, I mean?"

"I'm coping with it. I'm ashamed to say that her death has taken a backseat to the other matter at hand."

"It's easy to see why," said Ted. "You didn't do it,

and you're desperate to find out who did so you can be exonerated. No shame in that."

"None at all," I agreed.

"Thanks for coming in, guys. I appreciate your stopping by."

As we drove to the mall, I ticked off my seatbelt by leaning over against Ted's shoulder. The belt protested by becoming tight and uncomfortable, but I didn't care.

"You okay?" Ted asked. "If you're not up to going shopping, we can go on home."

"I'm okay. Just thinking about Captain Moe. Are you up to going shopping?"

"I'm up to going shopping. Tell me what you're thinking about Captain Moe."

"I'm just thinking about what he said about Carrie Monahan and John Martin," I said. "It hadn't dawned on me that someone as big a bully as John Martin wouldn't want his fiancée putting in longer hours at the hospital. He might not want her to have that job."

"Unless her having the job would pave the way for Martin Brothers Construction on future projects."

"True. But if Bellamy Carstairs was angry about the work Martin Brothers did for him, and if he truly has as much sway with the board as everyone seems to think he does, then maybe Martin Brothers Construction is out of luck with the hospital, no matter who gets the job as hospital administrator."

Chapter Twenty-six

Vera picked me up at seven thirty on Friday morning. She had already gone by MacKenzies' Mochas and got us lattes and scones.

"Just try not to get crumbs in my car," she said. "But if you do, don't worry about it. I'll just take it by the detailing shop and get them vacuumed out."

"I'll do my best not to be crummy."

"And please try to hurry and drink that before we get to the hospital. We probably shouldn't take our own refreshments inside, since they have coffee there."

"Maybe so, but theirs is nasty."

"That's why we shouldn't take ours inside, dear. Somebody might turn vicious on us and try to take our coffee."

I merely shook my head at Vera. But I did finish my latte before we went into the hospital, and so did she.

As we walked inside, Vera asked me to take her arm. I did so. The steps were wet and slippery because it had been raining off and on since last night. It was currently only sprinkling, but the dampness and chill hung heavily in the air.

Charlie Emerson came over to join us. "Ladies, may I have a word with you in the hallway before we begin?"

"Of course." I looked at Vera.

Charlie offered his meaty forearm to Vera. She took it but gave him a reproachful look.

"How old do you think I am?" she asked.

"Just being polite," he said.

"What would you like to talk with us about?" I asked.

"I'm just wondering when your article will be out."

"That's why we're back today: to take more notes," Vera said. "I've already turned my first set of notes over to Paul, but he needed more information before writing his article."

"I think you've likely got all the information you need from these people," he said. "I imagine you need to talk with some of the doctors and other staff to round out your article. I'll try to get you a list of the people you should speak with."

"That's kind of you." Vera patted his arm. "How sweet of you to help us this way."

"I don't mean to pry, but you looked so happy with Carrie Monahan yesterday morning."

"And?" His face hardened.

"It's just . . . You know she's engaged, right? To John Martin?"

He squinted. "Are you sure?"

"She introduced him to me as her fiancé, but I might've misunderstood."

"I'm sure you did."

I placed a hand on his arm. "You seem like a really nice person, and I don't want you to get hurt."

His face remained like granite. "I won't. But thank you for your concern. I should get back inside."

My first customer of the day was Muriel. But she wasn't there to buy anything. She'd sewn herself to her latest embroidery project and couldn't figure out how to save both her sweater and the stitches she'd so laboriously put into her project.

"I think the only way out of this predicament is to undo the stitches that have attached your work to your sleeve."

"Thank goodness," she said. "I knew if anyone could fix it, you could."

If you'll recall, Muriel is the one who doesn't hear well.

I retrieved a long embroidery needle with a blunt end from my office. I didn't want to accidentally hurt Muriel should she jerk against the needle. Then I sat on the sofa beside her and began gently pulling out the stitches.

She lurched backward. "What're you doing? I thought you could fix this without hurting either my work or my sweater."

"No, I told you that the only way to get you untangled without damaging your sweater was to take out the stitches."

She shook her head, setting her white curls to bobbing. "No, of course you can't cut the sweater. It's one of my favorites. You'll have to think of something else."

"Yes. I'll have to remove these stitches."

"I can't take off my sweater! I don't have anything on under it except my bra."

I raised my voice. "How about this? I'll take out the stitches that connect your sleeve to your embroidery project, and then I'll put the stitches back in. Will that work?"

"You'll fix it?"

"I'll fix it!"

"Okay. Thank you."

I carefully removed the stitches. Muriel had obviously worked for at least an hour before realizing she was attached to her project. Finally, I got her loose. Neither the sweater nor the project was the worse for wear—except, of course, the project was now missing some stitches, which I'd told Muriel I'd put back in.

She was relieved to be free. She stretched her arm this way and that.

"It might take a little while for me to replace the stitches. Would you like for me to bring you the project later, or do you want to wait?"

"I'll wait," she said. "I don't have to be anywhere. Is that coffee I smell?"

"It is. May I get you a cup?"

"Please."

I was getting her coffee when the bells over the door jangled.

"Be right out!" I called.

"Take your time."

Something about that voice sent a chill down my spine. I stepped into the shop and saw that it was John Martin.

"Good morning, Ms. Singer."

"H-hi. May I get you some coffee?" I asked, trying to pretend that I wasn't disturbed by his presence.

"Her coffee isn't anywhere near as good as you can get at that place down the street, but hers doesn't cost anything!"

Thank you, Muriel, for that glowing review.

"I'm not here for coffee," said Mr. Martin.

"What can I do for you, then?"

"I thought I'd made myself clear to you once: I don't like people intruding into my concerns. You apparently thought I was joking."

Angus emitted a low, menacing rumble.

"I wasn't aware that I'd been intruding into your business, Mr. Martin."

Todd burst through the door with a baseball bat. Blake was right on his heels.

"What's going on here?" Blake asked.

"Oh, mercy!" Muriel clapped her hands together. "I haven't played softball in *years*! I don't even know if I can anymore. But if you need me, I'll give it a try."

John Martin looked a bit bemused by Muriel, but then looked at Todd and Blake. "So, who are you clowns? The bodyguards?"

"We're the stand-ins," said Todd. "The main bodyguard is on his way."

"With backup," Blake said. "Not that any of us will need help to mop the floor with you."

I worked my way into the midst of the three men. I didn't want there to be any bloodshed here in my shop today. Poor little Muriel might have a coronary. And so might I.

"Everything is fine," I said. "Mr. Martin and I have apparently had a misunderstanding, wherein he thinks I'm trying to meddle in his business. Mr. Martin, I couldn't care less about your business, your romance, your aspirations, or anything about you. And I'll most definitely find someone else to build my gazebo."

"You're building a gazebo?" asked Todd. "I could probably do that."

"Yeah, gazebos are easy, Marce. Todd and I could knock out a good-sized gazebo in a weekend."

I looked up at these two men that I was beginning to see more and more as brothers. I was kinda sorry I'd missed out on siblings growing up, but I was certainly appreciating them now. Tears pricked my eyes, more from being touched by their protectiveness than from fear of John Martin. But that's not how Todd and Blake saw it.

Blake pushed me behind his back, and Todd stepped forward.

"You need to get out of here and never come back." He half raised the bat. "Got it?"

At that point, Ted entered the shop. Thank goodness he didn't have his gun drawn, but he did have his jacket pushed back and his hand on his hip so he could bring it out if necessary. Like Blake, he put himself between John Martin and me.

"How many boyfriends have you got, lady?"

"Don't speak to her," said Ted. "You're under arrest for trespassing and criminal threat."

"Hey, I'm going," said Mr. Martin. "I just don't want your girlfriend here nosing around in my business."

"You have the right to remain silent," said Ted.

"I said I'm going!"

"Just let him go, Ted," I said. "You can arrest him if he ever comes back. Okay?"

Ted gave me a hard stare and then jerked his head at John Martin. "Get out."

Mr. Martin stormed out the door.

"Thank you," I said.

Ted took me by the shoulders. "Are you all right?"

"I'm fine."

"She was in tears," said Blake. "What did he say to you?"

"I wasn't in tears. Not really. And he just told me to mind my own business."

Ted hugged me. "Thank you both for getting here so quickly and for calling me."

"Anytime," said Todd. "And she was in tears. I saw it, too."

"Martin had just better be glad I was the one took Todd's call instead of Sadie," said Blake. "He wouldn't have left here in one piece if she'd been here."

The mental image of Sadie thrashing John Martin made me giggle. "That's true."

"Gotta get back," said Todd. "Will and I are just across the street if you need us."

"Same for Sadie and me." Blake patted my back. "We'll check on you later."

They left, and Ted walked me over to the sofa across from Muriel.

"Do you think they'll want me to play in the soft-ball game?" she asked.

Chapter Twenty-seven

When Ted returned with lunch that afternoon, we laughed—pretty much—about the morning's events.

"I finally had to tell Muriel that the softball team wouldn't need her until the spring," I said. "Hopefully, she'll forget all about it by then."

"I'd say she forgot about it by the time she got back home. Did you repair her project?"

"I did. It took about an hour, but it wasn't hard. Poor Muriel. How in the world did she manage to sew her sweater to her embroidery?"

"I guess stranger things have happened."

We were having chicken strips with mashed potatoes today, and Angus was getting impatient for a taste. I cut off a bite of my chicken and put it in his dish. It took him longer to turn around than it did to inhale the food.

"I'm glad your neighbors were so quick to react to John Martin's arrival," Ted said. "I'm glad Calloway was paying attention."

"Even if he hadn't been, I'd have been fine, you know. I'm not some little hothouse flower."

"You *are* a hot little flower."

I pressed my lips together to show him that I was serious. "I can take care of myself a lot better than you guys give me credit for."

"I give you credit, babe. But John Martin is a bully, and I don't want him anywhere near you. You shouldn't have to worry about being threatened in your own shop."

"You face threats in your job on a daily basis."

He gave me the face that said *give me a break*. It made me lean over and kiss his cheek.

"You're so gorgeous," I said.

"Don't change the subject. I want you to call me immediately if you ever see John Martin headed your way again."

"I will. I didn't see him headed my way *this* time, though. I just looked up, and there he stood."

"What prompted his visit?"

I shrugged. "I'm not sure. Todd and Blake got here before we could really discuss it."

Ted gave Angus another bite of chicken. "I'm sorry if I seem overprotective at times."

"I don't mind. It's way better than underprotective."

He chuckled softly. "Yeah, I guess it is."

Just after lunch, Charlie Emerson came by the shop. He was wearing jeans and a sweatshirt and carrying a duffel bag

"Hi, Charlie. I almost didn't recognize you out of uniform." I was standing at the counter, and Angus was lying on his bed. I didn't invite Charlie to sit.

"Yeah. I just got off work and came up here to check on Dani before heading to the gym. She told me where your shop was, so I stopped in to apologize if I made you and your friend feel unwelcome at the meeting this morning."

"You didn't make us feel unwelcome. How is Dani?"

"She's doing as well as can be expected. Having Nicole to take care of probably helps. When you're busy, you can't sit around and dwell on your loss—at least, that's what I learned after Mom died. That's when I got more involved with the support group and other things at the hospital."

"That's good."

"Is everything all right?" he asked. "You look a little down."

"I just had kind of a disturbing visit this morning from a friend of Carrie's."

"This friend . . . was it John Martin?"

I nodded. "He's not a nice person. Or, at least, my encounters with him haven't been pleasant."

"And you wonder what Carrie sees in him."

"Well, yeah."

"I hate to say this, but I think Carrie is stringing him along," said Charlie. "I knew she'd been out with him a time or two, but I didn't think anything of it until you said she'd introduced him to you as her fiancé."

"I'm sorry about that. I might've completely misunderstood."

"No, I don't think you did."

"But you think Carrie is playing Mr. Martin?" I asked.

"Yeah. See, she wants this hospital-administration job really bad, and John and his company have a lot of influence with the board of directors."

"Are you sure? Dr. Carstairs mentioned to my boyfriend that Martin Brothers Construction did some work on his deck and he wasn't happy with it at all. He said he wouldn't be using them again."

Charlie's eyebrows shot up. "Really? Then maybe John Martin doesn't have the pull that Carrie thinks he does."

"Maybe not." Either way, employment advancement was a horrible reason to get involved with someone, but I didn't mention that to Charlie.

"I guess Mrs. Carstairs is a shoo-in for the job, then, if Martin Brothers Construction has fell out of favor with the board," he said.

"I don't know. I heard that Dr. Carstairs didn't want his wife to get the job when she applied the first time. If that's true, it isn't likely he'd change his mind so quickly."

"I don't blame him for wanting his wife to stay home with Brendan. Carrie is always telling me what a good kid he is. If both parents don't have to work, then why shouldn't Mrs. Carstairs stay at home with their child? She should cherish her time with him."

"Do you have any children, Charlie?" It was an awkward attempt at changing the subject, but it was the best I could do under the circumstances.

"Not yet. But I hope to have one or two someday."

On that note, Charlie finally left.

"He's a nice guy," I told Angus, "but something about him makes me uncomfortable, especially after this morning. He was awfully anxious about the article, and he didn't think we needed to sit in on another of his meetings."

Jill decided to put in her two cents. *Yeah, I mean, why wouldn't you guys be welcome at the meeting? It's not like you don't have a legitimate reason to be there. Oh, wait.*

"I know, I know. Maybe that's why I feel ill at ease around Charlie: because Vera and I lied to get access to the transplant people because we thought maybe one of them had killed Sandra Vincent."

And yet you still don't know much about Sandra Vincent, do you? You don't know who liked her, who didn't like her, her hobbies, her political affiliations. . . .

"No, I don't know much about Sandra Vincent. Maybe Riley's private investigator has found something out about her." I moved over to the sit-and-stitch square and flopped onto the sofa. Jill was right. I had nothing to go on to help Captain Moe out of this predicament. And I'd been trying so hard to help. It was depressing.

Angus came over to sigh and look sad and commiserate with me.

At around three-thirty, Carrie Monahan walked into the Stitch.

"Hi, Carrie. What's up?"

Hearing my guarded tone, Angus came to stand beside me.

"Charlie called and told me that John came in here this morning and was bullying you. I just wanted to apologize. I'm afraid my fiancé can be a real hothead."

First Dr. Carstairs and now John Martin. Was there anyone Carrie knew who *didn't* have a reputation for being a hothead?

"I didn't intend to put my nose where it doesn't belong or to interfere with you or Mr. Martin in any way. And I haven't meant to meddle in your affairs." I paused. "I suppose that I sometimes speak without thinking first, and that gets me into trouble once in a while."

"I plan to talk with John and see what this is all about."

"Please don't," I said. "He's angry enough with me already. I don't want to make any waves, and I just want him to stay away from me. I wish Charlie hadn't said anything to you about it."

"Charlie's sweet."

"I think he's got quite a crush on you."

"He'd probably get a crush on any girl who smiles at him," she said. "Better be careful, especially if he's already coming by your shop to see you. He gets a little . . . I don't know . . . stalkerish. But in a nice way."

I didn't want to mention to Carrie the reason for Charlie's visit. "Maybe so, but I believe his heart still belongs to you." I laughed.

"Well, hey, I need to be going. If you'd like to come by and see the kids again, we'd love to have you."

"I'll take a look at my schedule and get back to you."

As much as I'd enjoyed reading to the children—and as much as they'd liked having me there—I felt I'd pretty much worn out my welcome at Tallulah County General Hospital. Both John Martin and Bellamy Carstairs had made that as clear as crystal.

After Carrie left, Angus strolled back over to lie by the window.

I pulled up Riley Kendall's contact information on my phone and called her office. Julie, her administrative assistant, answered the phone.

"Hi, Julie. It's Marcy. Is Riley busy?"

"Actually, she's in court right now. Is there anything I can help you with?"

"I don't know. I was thinking about Captain Moe and his case, and I was hoping Riley's PI might've been able to turn up another viable suspect."

"Well, the guy is turning up dirt left and right—on Ms. Vincent, on the hospital's board of directors, on Ms. Vincent's friends and associates—but it seems that everyone except Captain Moe has an alibi."

"What sort of dirt is Mr. Gordon finding?" I asked.

"The usual. Most of it's hearsay, but people have told Mr. Gordon that Ms. Vincent accepted bribes for one thing or another, that she showed favoritism to board members, and that she put her own interests ahead of the hospital's."

"Yeah, Vera and I both have heard whispers like that floating around the hospital. But, as you say, it isn't going to help Captain Moe very much, is it?"

"I'm afraid not. Still, all the evidence against him is circumstantial, so that's something."

Before I could respond, Julie said she had another call coming in and asked if I'd hold. I told her I'd let her go and would talk with her later.

This case was so frustrating. There had to be evidence either exonerating Captain Moe or condemning someone else in Sandra Vincent's murder. I simply wasn't seeing it. I remembered the way Ted set up the evidence board in his apartment. Maybe I could make my own evidence board. Only I'd put it on my laptop instead of the wall.

While I was en route to the office to retrieve the laptop, a customer came in and bought some canvas and floss. As soon as she left, I grabbed the laptop and returned to the sit-and-stitch square. I sat on the sofa facing the window so no one walking in could see what I was doing before I had time to close the laptop.

I decided to make a chart. I had an app on my computer that made it easy for me. In the center of the chart, I put *Murder of Sandra Vincent*. From there, I linked Captain Moe and wrote everything I knew about his finding the body.

Captain Moe: Dating the victim. Found the body with a knife in her chest. Was wearing white gloves; no blood was found on his suit or his person. Charlie Emerson came to his aid almost immediately. Charlie called the police.

I made another link from the center of the chart to a box detailing everything I knew about Sandra Vincent: *Dating Captain Moe; could have also been dating a member of the board of directors. Rumored to have put her interests ahead of those of the hospital. Accused of moving people on the organ-transplant list to suit her agenda. Catered to members of the board.*

I made boxes for Melanie Carstairs and Carrie Monahan, since both had been finalists for Sandra Vincent's job and it was likely one of them would be given the position now that Ms. Vincent was deceased.

It was almost five o'clock by the time I had finished and saved my evidence chart. I doubted I was any farther along in my search for Sandra Vincent's killer, but at least I had my evidence chronicled in an orderly fashion and I could add things to the chart as I saw fit. Plus, I'd share it with Ted this evening to see what he thought about it.

Chapter Twenty-eight

I was getting ready to lock up when Dr. Carstairs came in. I stepped back and slid my keys into my pocket.

"Good afternoon, Dr. Carstairs. What can I do for you?"

"My wife informed me that I owe you an apology."

"You don't owe me anything," I said. "But I do accept your apology."

"Very good. Would you please accept our invitation to come over and visit Brendan this weekend?"

Is he kidding me? I studied his face for a moment. No lips twitching to suppress laughter. No crinkling at the corners of his eyes.

"I'm sorry, but I'm busy this weekend." And then I couldn't resist. "Besides, aren't you worried I'll meddle in your business while I'm there?"

"I knew you'd bring that up. Look, when I came by here that morning, I was furious with Melanie. Do you have any idea what that little stunt of hers will end up costing us? There'll be the legal fees, court costs, not to mention having the windshield repaired, and I have no idea how much she paid Luis to throw the brick."

"I honestly didn't mean to cause problems for your family. At the time, I had no idea that Melanie was responsible for the vandalism to her car. I was truly afraid for her—and for Brendan—when I arrived."

"I know that now. I knew it then. I was just so angry at Melanie. I should've been honest with her in the first place and told her that I didn't want her to apply for the hospital-administrator position. I feel that her place is with Brendan."

"I understand." I could've argued on Melanie's behalf, but I figured she already had and, besides, it was none of my business.

"Are you really busy this weekend, or were you making an excuse not to come?"

"I am busy. Brendan is a charming boy, and I enjoy spending time with him, but I really can't this weekend."

"Very well. Another time, then."

"Another time." As much as I hated to do it to Brendan, Angus and I wouldn't be visiting him again.

Sadie rushed into the Stitch, looking from Dr. Carstairs to me and back again. "Hi, everybody. Almost closing time, huh? I guess I got in right under the wire."

"I'll let you tend to your customer," said Dr. Carstairs. "Have a pleasant weekend, Ms. Singer."

"You, too."

As soon as Dr. Carstairs left, Sadie whirled toward me. "Was that him? That wasn't him, was it?"

"Him who?"

"John Martin! The guy who threatened you earlier. I'd stepped outside to add something to the easel out front and saw this guy come in. I thought about it for a second, and then I got my butt up here just in case. But that wasn't him, was it?"

"No. That was Bellamy Carstairs."

She turned down the corners of her mouth. "Bellamy, huh?" She affected a British accent. "Hellew, Ai'm Bellamy Carstairs. How wonderful to make your acquaintance."

I giggled. "What's Blake putting in the cappuccino today?"

"Ai'm sure Ai don't know."

"Give it up, Sadie. Lady Mary Crawley you're not."

"Oh, well. A girl can dream, can't she? I was ready to go all Muhammad Ali on that chump." She raised her fists and danced around. "Float like a butterfly, sting like a bee . . ."

Her antics excited Angus to no end. He scampered around her legs, barking and jumping.

"Now see what you've done! You've got Mr. Foreman all keyed up."

"We'll take him out, won't we, Jumpin' Joe?"

I rolled my eyes. "Jumpin' Joe? That's DiMaggio. The baseball player? Even Jill is shaking her head over that one. What's gotten into you today?"

"I'm just sorry I missed out on all the excitement

earlier today. Although I hear that Muriel now wants to be on Todd's softball team."

"That's true. I told her they don't start practicing until the spring."

Sadie threw back her head and laughed. "Oh, well. I'd better get back to the shop. Blake will wonder what's happened to me."

"Why don't the two of you come over for dinner tomorrow night?" I asked. "It'll be fun."

"Sounds good. I'll check with Blake and see if he has any plans. And if he says he does . . ." She went back to shadowboxing.

"Go get 'em, champ!" I looked down at Angus. "She's a wild woman today, our Sadie. She went from jolly old Brit to a former heavyweight boxing champion in thirty seconds flat."

Angus woofed. I took that to mean, *I know, right?*

I took the laptop containing my evidence chart home with me. After feeding Angus and letting him out into the backyard, I went into the living room and pulled up the file. I was eager to compare notes with Ted when he got here.

My phone buzzed, letting me know I had a text message. It was from Ted. He was in a meeting and would be late. Oh, well. I'd see what I could put together before he got here.

In the center of the chart was the victim, Sandra Vincent. Leading from her were all the people that I knew had been involved with her in some way—Captain Moe (I couldn't leave him out and present a fair portrait), Dr. Carstairs, Melanie Carstairs, John Martin, Carrie Monahan, and Charlie Emerson. I had broken links from Sandra to various groups—the board of directors and the organ-transplant families—but since no one particular suspect had emerged from these groups, I decided to focus on the people with whom I was most familiar.

Captain Moe had been romantically involved with Ms. Vincent, but they'd been known to argue, as well. Were people aware of their romantic entanglement? Had the killer attempted to set up Captain Moe to take the fall for the crime, or had his finding the body simply been a happy accident?

Dr. Carstairs didn't have a strong motive to murder Sandra Vincent. After all, she did whatever he wanted her to. The only reason I could see that he'd want her removed was if he'd done something that he needed to ensure remained covered up. Maybe he was afraid he couldn't trust her not to talk. As I'd seen earlier today, money was a big concern with Dr. Carstairs. He was more worried about the money it would take to get his wife out of trouble than he was about their reputation. I'd have thought a man in his position would have paid any price to try to salvage his family's reputation. As things stood, Melanie came across a little nutso.

Melanie Carstairs had let her crazy show when she'd hired her gardener to vandalize her car. And she wanted Sandra Vincent's job. How far would she go to get it? Would she have murdered the woman in order to take the job? But if she had, how would she have made her getaway? The killer *had* to have been someone thoroughly familiar with the hospital. I didn't know whether Melanie was or not, but I rather doubted it. Plus, if she was psycho enough to kill someone, she'd have simply let the gardener take the fall for the vandalism instead of confessing to it right away. She hadn't been able to condemn an innocent man in order to save herself, so I didn't see her murdering Sandra Vincent.

On to John and Carrie. Given what I'd seen of John Martin, I could easily imagine him stabbing someone in the chest. But other than wanting his fiancée to have Ms. Vincent's job, I couldn't see any real motive in his murdering Ms. Vincent. She couldn't sway the board to hire Martin Brothers Construction for upcoming projects, especially if the company had already alienated Bellamy Carstairs.

As for Carrie, I couldn't see her killing Sandra Vincent to take over her job, either. Yes, she had intimate knowledge of the hospital and could likely make a quick getaway from the crime scene. But someone would surely have noticed if she was two floors away from her typical post and covered in blood. And what excuse would she have given for taking a knife from the kitchen? Admittedly, although Doug had reported that the murder weapon had been identical to the knives used in the hospital's kitchen, I didn't know that anyone had yet established that it had, in fact, been taken from there. I supposed I could call up detectives Ray and Bailey to ask, but I doubted they'd be happy to hear from me.

But back to Carrie Monahan. Was there a way she could have legitimately wound up with a knife from the hospital's kitchen? *Oh, hi. I'm Carrie. I'm the head pediatric nurse. I'm going to borrow this butcher knife to cut up a birthday cake.*

Here's a spatula! Wouldn't that be better?

No, thanks. I don't think a spatula would do this job.

Pretty suspicious.

My eyes fell on the name Charlie Emerson. Charlie could go anywhere in the hospital without anyone questioning him. He could've been in the kitchen, picked up a knife, and hidden it. Plus, Charlie seemed innocuous. Had someone noticed him in the kitchen, he or she would've probably thought, *There's Charlie getting some lunch.*

His mother had died recently. Like the families of many of the people on the organ-transplant waiting list, he felt that Sandra Vincent was responsible for manipulating that list. It was possible—even probable—that he thought Ms. Vincent was at least in part culpable in his mother's death.

He had a major crush on Carrie Monahan, and he thought she cared about him, too. Given his feelings for both women, was it possible he had stabbed Sandra hoping to both avenge his mother's death and provide a dream job to the woman he loved?

And he had that duffel bag with him today. . . . *Wait. The duffel. A change of clothes.*

I took out my phone and called Riley. My call went to voice mail, but I left her a message.

"Hi, Riley. It's Marcy. I've been mulling over this

case, and I really think you should look a little closer at the security guard, Charlie Emerson. He had means, motive, and opportunity. I know that given Charlie's aw-shucks demeanor, it's a hard sell, but just question him again and see what you can learn. Plus, he was in here today with a duffel bag, which means he could've killed Sandra and changed out of the bloody clothes before anyone saw him. I just have a gut feeling about him."

As I ended the call, I heard a car pull into the driveway and Angus start barking.

Thank goodness. Ted was here. I could go over my theory with him and see if he thought I was totally wacko.

I put my phone and the laptop on the coffee table and hurried to the front door. I flung it open only to see Charlie Emerson standing on the porch.

I felt my eyes widen in alarm.

"Did I scare you?" he asked.

"N-no. No! You just surprised me, that's all. I was expecting my boyfriend, Ted. He's supposed to be here any second. He's a detective, you know, and he was in a meeting, but he's on his way now."

"Then let's you and me take a ride."

"No, thanks. Let's wait for Ted." I didn't even ask where the man wanted to go. I had a feeling I already knew enough.

"This can't wait. It's something we need to do right away."

"What is it?" I could literally feel my heartbeat pulsing at the base of my throat.

"We need to talk with Carrie."

"All right. We'll call her."

"We're going to talk with her now." He reached out and grasped my shoulders. "Please don't make me hurt you. You're small, and it wouldn't take much."

I thoroughly resented that remark even while I recognized the validity of it. Still, I kicked at him, and he plucked me off the ground. He took my wrists in one hand and took my ankles in the other while he bent and flung me over his shoulder. I screamed and thrashed, but it didn't do me any good. I hadn't fully realized what a bear of a man Charlie was. "If you don't shut up, I'm going to knock you out. I can't have you screaming while I'm carrying you outside. Now I'm going to set you back down and pull out my gun. If you make a sound, I'll knock you out with the butt of the pistol. Got it?"

I stilled. Then I nodded. I couldn't think if I was knocked out. I needed to remain conscious.

Poor Angus was barking and jumping against the fence. How I wish I'd have let him back inside before answering the door. But would it have mattered? Would Charlie have simply killed us both?

He sat me down, letting me go and pulling a gun out of the waistband of his jeans as he did so. I hadn't realized tears were streaming down my face until he told me not to cry. He reached out a thumb and wiped a tear from my cheek.

"I'm not going to hurt you unless I have to." His voice was bizarrely gentle.

"All right. I'll do whatever you want me to."

"Good. Now let's go see Carrie."

I nodded. I knew I could've kept trying to stall or dissuade him from going to Carrie Monahan's home or to the hospital or to wherever she was, but I didn't want Ted to come into my house unaware of what was going on and get shot. I'd take my chances with Charlie.

With a firm grip on my elbow and the constant reminder of the gun at my side, Charlie walked me outside to his car. It was an older-model sports car. Orange. I wouldn't have taken Charlie for an orange-sports-car kinda guy.

He opened the passenger's-side door of the car and told me to scoot over to the driver's seat. "I can't have you doing anything stupid. You can drive a straight, can't you?"

"Sure." I slid over to the driver's seat.

Charlie folded into the passenger's seat. "Do what I tell you, and you'll come out of this fine."

"Okay. I will."

He instructed me to start the engine, back out of the driveway, and take a left.

"Are we going to the hospital to see Carrie?" I asked.

"No. We're going to her house."

"Have you ever been to her house?"

"Once. I went by there and helped her move some furniture one day. Why?"

"I just wondered. How did you know where I lived?"

"I looked it up. I'm not an *imbecile*, you know."

"Of course I know. Who said you were?"

"Sandra Vincent."

My blood got a little bit colder. "W-when? When did she call you that?"

"The first time I asked her to leave the hospital and take a job somewhere else. Watch where you're going."

"I-I am." I gripped the steering wheel.

"I don't want you to wreck us before we get to Carrie's house. This is important."

"Y-yeah. I know. Tell me more about Ms. Vincent. When did you ask her to leave?"

"Not long after Mom died. I told Ms. Vincent that she was smart and had a good background. She could go anywhere she wanted to get a job."

"Is that when she called you an imbecile?"

"Yeah. She said, *You imbecile! I've worked my way from the bottom to the top at this lousy hospital, and I'm not going anywhere!*"

"Why did you want her to leave?" I asked.

"I never thought she handled the organ-transplant list the way she should. And then I got to know Carrie, and I realized how much better Carrie would be for the job. Carrie cares about people. Ms. Vincent only cared about herself."

"I can imagine how mad it must've made you when Ms. Vincent insulted you like that."

"Yeah, it made me mad. That's why when I went to talk with her that Sunday, I took the knife with me. I thought if I scared her, she'd be sorry for calling me names and that she'd leave like I wanted her to."

"But it got out of hand," I suggested.

"Uh-huh. She laughed at me. The knife didn't scare her at all."

"She must've been crazy."

"She was!" His voice was filled with incredulity at her laughter even now. "I couldn't believe it. How could she just stand there laughing and telling me that I was not only going to be fired but that I'd spend the rest of my good years in prison while I was standing there holding a huge knife?"

"Well, I met the woman only once, but she must've been certifiably insane. I'm a reasonable person. I'm not arguing with you or laughing at you."

"Thank you, Marcy!" He sounded genuinely relieved. "If she hadn't been so stupid, I wouldn't have stabbed her. It was like I went into a rage."

"I can see it," I said. I would've told Charlie anything I had to in order to make him believe I was on his side at that moment. And what I'd said about Ms. Vincent must've been true. She had to have been insane to laugh at a man who was threatening her with a knife . . . *this* man especially. "Being underestimated sucks."

"It does, Marcy. It sure does. At first it was like I didn't even realize what I was doing, you know? And then I was like, *What have I done?* I had blood on me, and there was Ms. Vincent, bleeding out in that sleigh."

"Christmas is probably ruined for you forever."

"I don't know that I'd go that far," he said.

"Oh. Good." How long could I play Thelma to his

Louise? Bonnie to his Clyde? Here we were, two buddies driving to our doom.

"But I sprang into action. First I wiped all the fingerprints off that knife. Then I used the service elevator and went back to the locker room to change into a spare uniform. I put the bloody uniform in my duffel until my shift was over. Then I put it into a trash bag and put it in the infectious waste incinerator. And, last but not least, I ran back upstairs just in time to hear that Santa guy calling for help. Now, tell me: could an imbecile have done all that?"

"No indeed. You were thinking on your feet, all right. I doubt I'd have been able to keep my wits about me like that."

"Well, I am trained law enforcement."

"True," I said. "Does Carrie know we're coming?"

"Nope. It's going to be a surprise."

Chapter Twenty-nine

The longer I drove, the farther away from civilization we got. I'd been driving for only about twenty minutes, but it seemed like forever. And I was unfamiliar with where we were. Was going to Carrie Monahan's house a ruse? Was he taking me out into the woods to kill me?

"So, why are we going to Carrie's house? If you said, it's slipped my mind. The gun is making me nervous."

"I spoke with Carrie after she got off work today. I called her and told her about John coming in and scaring you like he did. She said she was going to stop by and see you."

"She did. And I told her I didn't want John Martin anywhere near me."

"Didn't you also tell her that you thought I'd misunderstood our friendship?"

I glanced at his face and then at the gun. My mind raced. *To lie or not to lie?* Had Carrie called Charlie after seeing me and told him what I'd said? Had she rebuffed him? Maybe a distraction was in order. "Charlie, I certainly think you're the better man for Carrie." *Yeah, sure, you killed Sandra Vincent. So what? We all have our little faults.* "I told her I thought you liked her—as in *liked* her—you know, in case she didn't realize it. Maybe she thought John was her only option."

"I figured you were trying to help. That's why we're going to see her. You can convince her that I'm the right guy for her—not John Martin."

I nodded. "So, she called you after she stopped by my shop?"

"Yeah. She told me I was making it obvious to everybody that I had a crush on her. A crush! What I feel for her is much more than a crush! She made me sound like some love-struck teenager."

I didn't know what to say that wouldn't make matters worse. After all, he was still pointing a gun at my head. And I liked my head. I'd have looked totally weird without it.

"Stop looking so nervous, Marcy. Everything will be okay."

"You promise?"

"Yeah. I promise." He pointed. "See that gravel road up there to your right? Turn onto it."

"O-okay." I didn't see a house in the distance, just trees. Was this where he was planning to kill me? I was debating whether to plead for my life or try to swerve the car to throw Charlie off balance when I turned onto the gravel road and saw a small ranch-style house up ahead.

"Carrie lives *here*?" I asked.

"Yep, she grew up here. Her parents gave her the place when they retired and moved to California."

"Isn't she afraid living out here alone? It's so remote."

"That was my concern, too, but she says she's used to it. Likes it here. Says it's peaceful."

At the moment, I felt it was anything but peaceful. I kept my opinion to myself.

There were two cars in the driveway: a small blue sedan and a brown pickup truck. I was guessing one of the vehicles belonged to John Martin. I pulled up behind the sedan.

"Put it in park and turn the engine off," Charlie said.

I did as I was told.

Charlie leaned forward and squinted at Carrie's living-room window. I could see what he was staring at. Carrie and John were playfully wrestling and kissing. I could tell they were playing because both were laughing. Apparently, Charlie saw an entirely different scenario.

"He's attacking her! I'll kill him!" he growled, throwing open the passenger's-side door.

Forgotten for the moment, I threw open the driver's-side door and ran as Charlie bounded up the steps to the log home. Too bad for me, there was nowhere to go. No neighbors, no convenience stores, no passing motorists to flag down.

Charlie had left the keys in the car, and I could've simply taken off in it. But I didn't feel right simply leaving Carrie and John without trying to defuse the situation somehow if I could.

Charlie crashed through Carrie's front door, and I scurried around to the back of the house. Maybe the back door was unlocked or there was a window I could get through and find a phone to call for help.

I heard yelling and screaming and then a gunshot. I froze. I was panting heavily and my heart was thudding against the wall of my chest. I heard only the single gunshot. Charlie couldn't have killed both of them with one shot. Or maybe John or Carrie had shot Charlie. Should I still try to get inside the house?

I crept closer to the back door. I could hear Carrie. She was sobbing and pleading. I had to get inside.

I reached out and turned the knob. Thank goodness, the door wasn't locked. I opened it slightly, peering inside. The door opened into the kitchen. I watched for a second to make sure no one was in the kitchen and that nothing indicated that anyone was heading my way. I widened the opening just enough to ease inside, and then I shut the door behind me.

I eased along the wall to the hallway, where I could see into the living room. Carrie was on her knees by John's side; he'd been shot in the torso and his shirt was soaked with blood. Getting help for John immediately was crucial to his survival. I glanced to my right and saw a bedroom. Hopefully, Carrie had a phone in there.

I slipped across the hall and into the room. I breathed a prayer of thanksgiving when I spotted the phone on the nightstand. I called 911 and whispered a plea for help.

Unfortunately, I somehow gave myself away.

"Who's there?" Charlie shouted. "Marcy, is that you?"

I didn't disconnect the call but dropped the phone behind the nightstand. The bed sat directly on the floor, so I couldn't hide underneath. I crouched behind the chest of drawers.

Charlie burst into the bedroom. "Where are you? Come out here." He moved into the bedroom. He spotted the phone and went to pick it up.

I eased past him and sprinted into the living room. I grabbed Carrie by the arm. "Come on!"

"No! I can't leave him!"

I heard Charlie telling the 911 operator that his little girl had called as a joke and that he was very sorry for the misunderstanding.

"She's . . . right," said John. "Go. It's our . . . only chance."

"We'll get help," I assured John. I looked at Carrie. *"Now!"*

She rose, and we raced out the door.

"Stop!" Charlie shouted. "Come back this instant, or I'll finish him off!"

This made Carrie falter, but I spurred her on. "He's lying." I didn't know whether or not Charlie *was* lying, but I knew I needed to get Carrie out of that house before she wound up being his next victim.

I slid behind the driver's seat of Charlie's sports car. As Carrie took one last look at the house, Charlie appeared in the doorway and raised his gun. She dove into the car and shut the door.

Charlie must've really liked his car, because he didn't fire at us. Instead he ran down the steps.

I put the car in reverse, placed my right hand at about the eight o'clock position on the steering wheel, and accelerated to around thirty miles per hour. I slammed the clutch and threw the wheel. The car spun around, and I popped the clutch back into first and sped away. In my rearview mirror, I could see Charlie climbing into the truck.

I quickly reached the end of Carrie's driveway, turned the hard left onto the main road, and drove as fast as I safely could. Still, we had a lot of road to cover before we got to civilization and could call for help.

I groaned as I heard the roar of a vehicle coming upon us really fast.

"Crap! It's him!" Carrie cried. "What're we gonna do?"

"Just stay calm."

I slowed slightly, allowing Charlie to edge closer to us. He pulled slightly to the right as if he were going to pass us on the wrong side of the road. I guessed he intended to either hit us or to appeal to Carrie in the passenger's seat to stop and talk with him.

I pulled the hand brake and spun around in the opposite direction. Charlie apparently forgot that he wasn't the one driving the sports car. When he swerved to miss us, the truck rolled onto its top.

I was speeding away from the truck when I heard sirens. "Help's on the way. We've got to go back and flag them down."

Again I spun the car around.

"Where did you learn to drive like this?" Carrie asked.

"Mom insisted on my taking a stunt-driving course when I was seventeen."

We approached the pickup truck as a police cruiser was pulling to the side of the road. I stopped the car, put it in park, and got out.

"Be careful!" I shouted. "The man inside that pickup truck has a gun!"

The officer instructed Charlie to toss the gun out the window. He did so, and the policeman radioed for an ambulance.

Carrie got out of the car and ran to the officer's side. "Please call for another ambulance. That man shot my boyfriend, and he's bleeding to death."

"Got it." The officer looked at me. "Is there anything else I can do?"

"Yes. Could you please get a message to Detective Ted Nash of the Tallulah Falls Police Department and tell him Marcy is okay?"

"Yes, ma'am. Could you get back into your vehicle and pull it off the road please? I'm going to need to question you both before I can let you go."

I walked back to the car on wobbly legs. I put the vehicle in gear and moved it over to the shoulder. Then I buried my face in my hands and sobbed.

Chapter Thirty

I was sitting on Carrie's sofa with a black and green granny-square afghan over my shoulders when Ted walked through the front door. I gasped and stood. He bridged the distance between us in two long strides and enfolded me into his arms. He kissed my mouth, my cheeks, my forehead, my mouth again.

"Are you all right?" His voice was strained.

"I'm better now that you're here." I clung to him with every ounce of strength I had.

"So am I. Let's get you out of here."

"Did Officer Franklin say I can go?"

Ted nodded. "He knows where to find us if he has any more follow-up questions."

"Good. I'm so ready to be home."

"Everybody is there waiting for you and are ready for you to be home, too," said Ted.

I frowned. "There are people at my house? Why?"

"When I got there and realized you were gone but that your Jeep was still in the driveway and Angus was in the backyard, I got concerned. Then I found your phone and became even more worried. I saw that the last number you'd called was Riley's, so I called her."

"Charlie Emerson confessed to killing Sandra Vincent," I said. "Not just to me, but to Carrie and to Officer Franklin, too. Captain Moe is in the clear."

"He'll be thrilled to hear that."

"I'm sorry. I didn't mean to interrupt. I'm just so happy that Captain Moe is off the hook. Charlie even admitted how he did it. He was proud of his cleverness. But what were you saying about Riley?"

"When I called her, she relayed your message to me. I was still afraid that John Martin had taken you, and I had police in five counties looking for him . . . and for Charlie Emerson, as well. Meanwhile, Riley came over. Captain Moe was with her at the time, so he came, too."

"Let me guess: Paul heard something over the scanner?"

Ted chuckled. "You got it. He and Vera are there, too. Probably half the town will be there when we get there."

He was right. By the time we got back to my house, Riley, Captain Moe, Paul, Vera, Sadie, Blake, Todd, Audrey, and Veronica were there. Sadie had brought food. Veronica had brought Clover, and the bunny and Angus were playing in the foyer when we arrived.

Veronica met us at the door and hugged me. "Thank heavens."

I got a hug from everyone else, and I was told what

food was waiting for Ted and me in the kitchen. I thanked Sadie, but didn't tell her that what I wanted most at the moment was a hot bath and to be alone with Ted. She insisted on going to the kitchen and getting Ted and me a plate of food. She told everyone else they could help themselves.

Sadie brought a tray of food into the living room and sat it on the coffee table in front of the sofa. "Are you sure you're all right, Marce? You look pale."

"I'm fine. Still a little shaken, I guess. I hope John Martin will be all right. Has anyone heard about his condition?"

"No." Ted took a sandwich from the tray. "Carrie has your number, so I'm sure she'll let you know something as soon as she can."

"I'd like to come by and talk with you tomorrow," said Paul. "I want Tallulah Falls to know what an important part you played in solving this murder and getting Captain Moe exonerated. But I know you need to recuperate tonight."

"Thank you," I said. "I'm going to wait till the morning to call Mom, too." I smiled. "She'll be delighted that my stunt-driving class finally came in handy."

Everyone looked at me as if I were joking. Instead of explaining, I selected a sandwich from the tray.

My cell phone rang. It was the default ring, so I knew it wasn't someone who called often. I picked up the phone and looked at the screen.

"It's Carrie." I answered the call.

"Hey, Marcy. I wanted to let you know that John

came through the surgery okay, and the surgeon thinks he'll make a full recovery."

"I'm so relieved."

"You saved our lives. Thank you."

"I'm glad I could help."

"John says come spring, he owes you a gazebo."

I laughed softly. "He doesn't owe me anything. I'm just glad he's going to be all right."

I ended the call and relayed the information that John Martin was going to be fine. Weariness set in, and my eyelids got heavy.

Ted took the sandwich from my limp hand and put it back onto the tray. "Why don't we get you upstairs?"

"No, that's okay. I'm fine."

"Ted's right," said Vera. "We all need to go so you can rest. We'll see you tomorrow, dear."

"I'm sorry," I said.

"You have nothing to be sorry for," said Captain Moe. "You're a heroine, Tink."

I let my head loll against Ted's shoulder.

When I woke up, the room was dark. I realized I was lying on my bed. I bolted upright.

"Hey, hey, hey. It's all right," Ted said soothingly. "I'm right here." He got up off the chair where he'd been sitting and moved to the side of my bed. "How're you feeling?"

"Groggy. I don't know why I got so tired. It can't be that late."

"It was the stress you were under this evening, babe. It exhausted you. Why don't I run you a bath?"

"That'd be great."

"Are you hungry?"

"Yeah." My stomach growled a confirmation.

Ted smiled. "While you're taking your bath, I'll go down and see what there is to eat. Mother wrapped up the food Sadie brought and put it in the refrigerator."

"That was sweet of her. And this is sweet of you. Thank you for taking such good care of me."

"Want me to bring a tray up, or do you want to come down?"

"I'll come down. I'm not an invalid."

"I know. While you eat, maybe you can tell me all about that stunt driving."

I smiled. "Maybe I will."

I lay back against the pillows and listened to the water filling the tub. Ted was wonderful. Captain Moe was a free man. Poor, banged-up Charlie Emerson was in jail, awaiting a psych evaluation. John Martin was going to be okay. And I had no intention of having that man build me a gazebo. I might've helped save his life, but he was still a jerk. Besides, I wasn't even sure I *wanted* a gazebo.

I luxuriated in my bath, and then I went downstairs to the kitchen. Ted had lit candles and put the food on the table.

"Where's Angus?" I asked.

"Had to go potty, so I let him out back." He pulled out my chair.

"Thank you." I sat down and noticed there was a beautiful little Christmas-tree ornament next to my plate. It was a hinged blue velvet box with a white bow. "How sweet! You got me a new ornament."

He held out his hand. "Let me show you something."

I handed him the ornament, and he stooped onto one knee beside my chair. He opened the box. Inside was a diamond ring. My jaw went slack.

"Marcy, I love you with all my heart. I was going to save this until Christmas, but after tonight, I just can't. Will you marry me?"

I blinked away the tears that were clouding my vision. "Yes!" I threw my arms around Ted's neck. "Yes, I'll marry you!"

He kissed me and then pulled back to place the ring on my finger. It was a perfect fit.

ACKNOWLEDGMENTS

A special thank you to Sophie Simpson for letting me mention her book, *Stitch the Halls*! You may visit Sophie's blog at whatdelilahdid.bigcartel.com.

I also want to give a shout-out to Joseph and Mary Moore, who play Santa and Mrs. Claus in Tennessee. (Do they have Christmas completely sewn up, or what?) Joe gave me the idea for the scene where Santa says he didn't recognize the child at first because he'd grown so much during the year. I saw him do that at a Christmas event in Kingsport, Tennessee, and I thought it was brilliant. What better way to explain how Santa knows everybody and delivers presents to their houses every year and yet doesn't know a child's name? Check out Santa Unplugged at facebook.com /santa.unplugged to see the best Santa ever! (Just don't tell Captain Moe I said that.)

If you love Amanda Lee's Embroidery Mysteries,
keep reading for an excerpt of the first book in
Gayle Leeson's new Down South Café series . . .

THE CALAMITY CAFÉ

Available wherever books are sold!

I took a deep breath, tightened my ponytail, and got out of my yellow Volkswagen Beetle. I knew from experience that the morning rush at Lou's Joint had passed and that the lunch crowd wouldn't be there yet. I put my letter of resignation in my purse and headed inside. Homer Pickens was seated at the counter with a cup of coffee. He was a regular . . . and when I say *regular*, I mean it. The man came to the café every morning at ten o'clock, lingered over a sausage biscuit and a cup of coffee, and left at ten forty. It was ten fifteen a.m.

"Good morning, Homer," I said. "Who's your hero today?"

"Shel Silverstein," he said.

"Good choice." I smiled and patted his shoulder. Homer was a retiree in his late sixties, and he chose a new hero every day.

You see, when Homer was a little boy, he noticed his daddy wasn't around like other kids' daddies. So he asked his mom about him. She told him that his dad had died but that he'd been a great baseball player, which is why she'd named him Homer. When Homer was a teenager, she'd finally leveled with him and said his father hadn't been a baseball player . . . that he'd basically been a bum . . . but that Homer didn't need a father to inspire him. Heroes were everywhere. Since then, Homer had chosen a new hero every day. It was like his inspiration. I looked forward to hearing Homer's answer to my question every day I worked. When I was off from work, he told me who his hero was the day I asked plus the day I'd missed.

I could sympathize with Homer's desire for a heroic father figure. My dad left Mom and me when I was four. I don't really remember him at all.

"That apple tree? The one he wrote about? I have one like it in my backyard," Homer said. "I cherish it. I'd never cut it down."

"I'm sure the rain we've had the past couple of days has helped it grow. You bring me some apples off that tree this fall, and I'll make you a pie," I told him.

My cousin Jackie came from the back with a washcloth and a spray bottle of cleaner. She and I had waitressed together at the café for over a year. Jackie had been there for two years, and in fact, it was she who'd helped me get the job.

My mind drifted to when I'd come back home to work for Lou Lou. I'd just finished up culinary school in Kentucky. Nana's health had been declining for the past two or three years, but it had picked up speed. As soon as I'd graduated, I'd come home and started working at Lou's Joint so I could be at Nana's house within ten minutes if I was needed. I was only biding my time at first, waiting for a chef's position to come open somewhere. But then Nana had died. And, although I knew I could've asked her for a loan to open a café at any time, I wouldn't have. I guess I got my streak of pride from my mother. But the money Nana had left me had made my dream a reality—I could open my café and stay right here at home.

"Morning, Amy!" said Jackie. "Guess what— Granny says she has a new Pinterest board. It's called *Things I'd Love to Eat but Won't Fix Because What's the Point Anyway Since I Don't Like to Cook Anymore.*"

I laughed. "I don't think they'd let her have a name that long."

"That's what I figured. It's probably called *Things I'd Love to Eat,* but she threw that last bit in there hoping we'll make some of this stuff for her."

"And we probably will."

Jackie's granny was my great-aunt Elizabeth, but Mom and I had always just called her "Aunt Bess." Aunt Bess was eighty-two and had recently discovered the wonders of the Internet. She had a number of Pinterest boards, had a Facebook page with a 1940s pinup for a profile pic, and trolled the dating sites whenever they offered a free weekend.

Lou Lou heard us talking and waddled to the window separating the kitchen from the dining room. She had a cigarette hanging from her bottom lip. She tucked it into the corner of her mouth while she spoke. "Thought I heard your voice, Amy. You ain't here for your paycheck, are you? Because that won't be ready until tomorrow, and you ain't picking it up until after your shift."

"That's not why I'm here," I said. "Could we talk privately, please?"

"Fine, but if you're just wanting to complain about me taking half the waitresses' tips again, you might as well not waste your breath. If it wasn't for me, y'all wouldn't have jobs here, so I deserve half of what you get."

Jackie rolled her eyes at me and then got to cleaning tables before Lou Lou bawled her out.

We deserved *all* of our tips and then some, especially since Lou Lou didn't pay minimum wage and gave us more grief than some of the waitresses could bear. That's why I was here. Lou Lou Holman was a bully, and I aimed to put her out of business.

Speaking of daddies, Lou Lou had been named after hers—hence the Lou Lou, rather than Lulu—and according to my late grandmother, she looked just like him. He'd kept his hair dyed jet-black until he was put into the Winter Garden Nursing Home, and afterward, he put shoe polish on his head. According to Nana, he ruined many a pillowcase before the staff found his stash of shoe polish and did away with it.

Lou Lou wore her black hair in a tall beehive with pin curls on either side of her large round face. Her eyes were blue, a fact that was overpowered by the cobalt eye shadow she wore. She shaved her eyebrows, drew thin black upside-down Vs where they should have been, and added false eyelashes to complete the look.

Today Lou Lou wore a floor-length blue and white floral-print muumuu, and she had a white plastic hibiscus in her hair just above the pin curl on the left. She shuffled into the office, let me go in ahead of her, and then closed the door. I could smell her perfume— a cloying jasmine—mixed with this morning's bacon and the cigarette, and I was more anxious than ever to get our business over with. She sat down behind her desk and looked at me.

I perched on the chair in front of the desk, reached into my purse, and took out the letter. As I handed it to her, I said, "I'm turning in my two-week notice."

"Well, I ain't surprised," she said, stubbing the cigarette into the ashtray. "I heard your granny left you some money when she passed last year. I reckon you've decided to take it easy."

"No. Actually, I'd like to buy your café."

Her eyes got so wide that her false eyelashes brushed against the tops of her inverted *V* eyebrows. "Is that a fact, Amy?"

"Yes, ma'am, it is." I lifted my chin. "I'm a good cook—better than good, as a matter of fact—and I want to put my skills . . . my passion . . . to work for me."

"If you think you can just waltz in here all high and mighty and take my daddy's business away from me, you've got another think coming," said Lou Lou.

"If you don't sell to me, I'm going to open up my own café. I just thought I should give you fair warning before I do."

Lou Lou scoffed. "You've got some nerve thinking

you can run me out of business. You bring on the competition, girlie! We'll see who comes out ahead."

"All right." I stood. "Thank you for your time. I'll be here tomorrow for my shift."

"Don't bother. I'll mail you your final check."

"I'll be here," I said. "I don't want any of the other waitresses to have to work a double on my account."

"Suit yourself. But don't be surprised if I take the cost of putting an ad in the paper for a new waitress out of your salary."

I simply turned and walked out of the office. I knew that legally Lou Lou couldn't take her ad cost out of my pay. But Lou Lou did a lot of things that weren't right. I figured whatever she did to me in retaliation for my leaving wasn't worth putting up a fight over . . . not now. I'd pick my battles.

I'd also pick my wallpaper, my curtains, my flooring, my chairs, stools, and tables, my logo . . . My lips curled into a smile before I'd even realized it.

"Bye, Homer! Bye, Jackie!" I called over my shoulder on the way out.

"Bye, Amy!" they called in unison.

I went to the parking lot and got into my car. I glanced up at the sign—LOU'S JOINT—as I backed out into the road. The sign was as sad and faded as everything else about this place. If I could convince Lou Lou to change her mind, I'd start with a brand-new sign . . . a big yellow sign with DOWN SOUTH CAFÉ in blue cursive letters. I wanted everybody to know what to expect when they walked into my café— Southern food and hospitality.

ABOUT THE AUTHOR

Amanda Lee is the national bestselling author of the Embroidery Mysteries, including *The Stitching Hour*, *Wicked Stitch*, and *Thread End*.